TIDING

TIDING

Siân Collins

HONNO MODERN FICTION

First published in Great Britain in 2023 by Honno Press
'Ailsa Craig', Heol y Cawl, Dinas Powys, Vale of Glamorgan,
Wales, CF64 4AH

1 2 3 4 5 6 7 8 9 10

A catalogue record for this book is available from the British Library.

Published with the financial support of the Books Council of Wales.

ISBN (paperback) 978-1-912905-70-6
ISBN (ebook) 978-1-912905-71-3
Cover design: Kari Brownlie
Text design: Elaine Sharples
Printed by: 4edge Ltd

For my sister and our children

'Nothing of him that doth fade,
But doth suffer a sea change
Into something rich and strange.'
('The Tempest' Act 1 scene ii)

Advent: CHAPTER 1

The bone house tunnels deep into the high bank, walled with mossy stones and ivy thick as seaweed. Ancient yew trees muster at the entrance, shadowed, conspiratorial; beyond the heavy wooden door, the space inside is hollow, lightless. It gives her the creeps.

A scrunch of paper—the map, Martin's list—snags in the shrivelled nettle stalks crowding the edge of the gravelled path. Dropped as they scarpered, the scaredy-cats. The clang of the iron kissing gate at the top of the steps, the boys' boots skittering on the gravel, Jan's blue cardigan dodging between the gravestones. Years later, Daphne will remember this, the casual treachery of friends.

With the heel of her wellington, she grinds the paper scrap deep into the nettles, turns and bends down for the box. The coal shovel, a black brute of a thing with a squat iron handle, is sticking out through the flaps. She opens them just a little and pushes it down, out of sight. A musty smell escapes: riverbank, old flower stems rotting in a vase. She holds her breath, slowly counts to three, breathes out. Closes the flaps and lifts the box with both hands, fingers scrabbling for a grip on the slippery cardboard.

It's late afternoon. The wintry light is dimming and a chill breeze stirs the fallen sycamore leaves around Rev. Josiah Owen's tombstone on the far side of the path. *Passed into the hands of Jesus 1776.* Away to the west a bank of cloud is slowly drifting in from the sea, inking the outline of the Moor. She follows the narrow path around the side of the church to where it joins the main avenue between the old graves lined with trees. The path is sprinkled with crimson yew berries; in ordinary times she likes to step on them, to hear that satisfying pop as each ripe fruit explodes, blood drops spattering the tarmac. But this is not an ordinary time.

1

The previous day, at morning break, the four of them huddled around Martin's desk, spellbound by their own daring. Smoke from Mr Duckford's playtime fag curled through the high window of the classroom. Martin's face was a frown of concentration, tongue lolling pinkly from the corner of his mouth as he drew the map of the graveyard: the lychgate, the wide, steep path up through the graveyard to the church porch, the narrow one forking around the building. Janice, leaning over his shoulder, giggled. 'Aw come off it, Marty, we all know where the bone house...' She clapped her hand to her mouth, the horror of naming the word. The classroom door banged open—Terry Dunn, come to collect his breaktime sandwich.

'What you lot doin'?'

Quick as a ferret, Martin folded the paper into neat squares and slipped it into his shorts pocket, away from those prying eyes.

'Mind your own blinkin' business, Terence.'

Manny Edwards kneels on the tarmac inside the lychgate. He is oiling the latch, swinging the heavy wooden gate back and forth to ease the joint. Hearing her footsteps behind him on the path, he gets to his feet and opens the gate wide for her to pass through. The soles of her boots sink into the mouldy drifts of confetti from last Saturday's wedding.

'Mind you don't drop that box, maid—looks heavy.'

Close up, the old man's face is puffed and blotchy; sweat beads in his wrinkles. Daphne likes Manny. He used to work in the quarry where they found the dinosaur bones and the remains of mammoths and hyenas. One time he called at the front door with two ammonites. Cleaned them specially for the girls, he told their father. 'No need to thank me, young ladies, I got plenty more at home.' Nestling her fossil in her palm, Daphne ran her finger over the tiny whorls and grooves, felt the stone weight of the creature's million years. It's still on a shelf in the toy cupboard with her other treasures. She has no idea what Sylvia did with hers; her sister is full of secrets.

Manny lifts his cloth cap and scratches at his wispy scalp. He comes up close, trying to look.

'Vicar sent you for that, did he?'

She shakes her head, hoisting up the box under her chin so he can't see. The smell from inside is really strong: the claggy stench of estuary mud, a whiff of something ancient, putrid. 'Lych' is an old word for a dead body, her mother explained; people used to leave the corpse inside the lychgate the day before the funeral to protect it from body snatchers. Which is what she and the others are, kind of.

'I won't tell on you, honest.' Manny grins, baring crooked teeth. 'Cross my heart and hope to die.'

She hurries past him out of the lychgate and turns left up Church Street, towards home.

'Right then, everybody, here's the list. We need a rope, a torch, the map, a whistle...'

'What for you need a whistle, Mart?'

'Case some nosy parker comes up the churchyard, obvious.'

'What, like her dad?'

Graham turned round then, gave her that look. Even Janice was smirking. She kept her head down, pretending to read Martin's list, tugging at her fringe, waiting for the barb—vicar's daughter, goody-two-shoes. But Martin didn't respond, there were more important things on his mind.

'A bag. We got to carry it.'

'How big is it then? You were closer in than me.'

Martin's hands splayed calloused, stubby fingers. Farmer's son. Graham's eyes were round as pebbles.

'Bloody hell, Mart. Could be a Neanderthal or a Bronze Age.'

Last term was ancient history; they knew everything there was to know.

'We better bring a box then.'

'And gloves, I'm not picking that thing up with my bare hands.'

'Don't be such a sissy. Alright then, one of you girls bring a shovel.'

The box bumps awkwardly against her thighs and its contents slide queasily into each other. It's not dark yet but some of the streetlamps have come on, casting shadows across doorways and windowsills, lighting up the bare stems of shrubs in front gardens. Somebody draws the curtains in the front room of one of the cottages opposite and she hears a child's brief cry. Inside the whitewashed milking parlour of Pentre Farm, the cows shift and stamp their hooves above the steady thrum of the machines. As she passes the forecourt of Jubilee Garage, Fred Davies in his oil-stained overalls is bending over the bonnet of a car, while Howie Clark his apprentice leans against the wall of the adjoining house, cups his hands to light a cigarette—the red burn as he takes the first long drag. From the open door of the office, Elvis crackles through the radio waves, *'You'll be so lonely you could die'*. She steps off the pavement onto the road to avoid Johnny Nebo in his long grey raincoat and fisherman's cap, shambling past with that funny lopsided gait of his. He's mumbling some kind of conversation with himself, shaking his head, and he doesn't notice her. A light snaps on in the Memorial Hall. She hears the scrape of chairs across the wooden floor, a toilet being flushed. Hetty Lewis the caretaker and her daughter Marge, getting the place ready for Friday's whist drive.

When Martin walked backwards out of the bone house with the shovel, she'd turned her head away, focused on the trees above the bank, the darkening sky. When he levered it into the cardboard box she still wouldn't look. Janice had draped the thing with the blue tea towel filched from her mother's kitchen. An act of courage.

Now it's Daphne's turn. She lowers the box carefully to the ground. Light from the nearby streetlamp spills inside. The tea towel has slipped off, exposing the smooth cranium the colour of rusty metal. There's a deep furrow running like a fault line across the slope of the forehead down to the left eye socket; her gaze takes

4

in the gaping hole of a nose, the rictus of stained, cracked teeth. She and her friends, they'd all seen dead things: fledgling house martins spilled from nests in the eaves and guttering; a pair of rabbits tied by their paws and left outside the back door; the grinning pig's head in the butcher's window; the chickens her father killed for Sunday lunch. Never a dead human being.

'What do you think it is then, Mart? It must be really, really old.'

Martin gathered up his drawing things and packed them away one by one in his metal geometry set. 'Roman, I expect. Or maybe pirate.'

Graham was decorating the margin of Martin's plan with a neat little skull-and-crossbones. He put his pencil down and stared, with his round pale eyes, into the beyond. 'Or maybe it's a Beaker man. Remember the skeleton they found up Raven Park when they were building the estate?'

Martin rolls his eyes. 'It wasn't a skeleton, stupid. Duckford said it was only a jawbone and a bit of pot with slimy stuff in. The archaeologists took them to the museum. If they'd found a Beaker man, they wouldn't have left him on a shelf in the bone house, would they?'

'Why you so sure it's a Beaker man?' Daphne said. 'It could be a Beaker woman, for all you know.'

Silence. Boys don't deal in contradiction.

'Don't be so daft, girl,' Graham snorted. 'Why would anyone bother to bury a woman?'

'What if there's a curse on it?' Janice's face had gone a bit pale, her lips wobbled. 'You know, like with Tutankhamun. People died after they moved his body; that could happen to us.'

Daphne stares at the Beaker woman's skull, imagines it covered in flesh, with long thick hair, maybe red like her own. Swiftly, she covers it with the tea towel and lifts the box once more. Voices from up the street, coming round the corner by Madras House. Two

5

women—Mrs John and her sister Joan, arm in arm in woollen headscarves and thick coats, walking fast against the cold. Remembering Manny's curiosity, she is suddenly afraid they will stop her and discover what it is she's carrying. Martin has made them all promise not to tell.

The women are only a few yards away. She steps off the pavement and crosses the road to the row of cottages. Turns down the cart track leading to the Morlas river which skirts the backyards and gardens of this side of town. The ground is uneven here: she stumbles over deep ruts made by tractor wheels and the muddy hoof prints of cows going back and forth for milking from Hollerton fields on the opposite bank. She can hear the familiar regular plashing of the water, the deeper gurgle where the Morlas rounds the bend from Quaker's Bridge. The track peters out at the ford and she turns left on to a narrow footpath above the river. A rusty outfall pipe juts from the bank into the water and there's a stale smell in the air—sewage, something rotting. The footpath skirts a low stone wall built to protect the riverside properties from flooding; there are gaps in places where the stones have fallen out and the gardens behind have mostly run wild, choked with weeds and bramble. Except for the one she is passing at this moment, which belongs to her piano teacher. Two neat vegetable beds, a narrow lawn edged with shrubs and a couple of ancient fruit trees, their branches bare now that winter has come.

Daphne's chest tightens. Ordinarily on a Friday afternoon she would be at her piano lesson. Her hands would be smarting from Miss O'Dowd's water torture: the bowl of melted ice in the kitchen sink, the scalding water poured straight from the kettle. 'For goodness sake, brace up girl, it's for your own good. Softens the finger joints, helps them stretch to the octave.'

Today is the first time she has mitched a piano lesson. Tomorrow there will be an envelope addressed to her parents, waiting on the bench outside the front door. The summons, on pale blue Basildon Bond notepaper.

Dear Rev and Mrs Morgan, your daughter did not arrive for her lesson yesterday. I trust she is not unwell. Since there was no advance notice of this absence, the usual payment is required.

Daphne knows this format; her sister was always skiving lessons. Unlike Sylvia, Daphne has no music in her, no dexterity in her fingers despite the ordeal of the water. Sylvia, who is afraid of nothing, would steal the clock from the mantlepiece when the teacher was out of the room and move the minute hand forward. Miss O'Dowd never leaves the room while Daphne has her lesson; she must be able to read her lying mind. Miss O'Dowd sits beside her on the hard music stool and notes every single mistake. 'Once again, please. Use your fingers as well as your thumbs this time.' And the old marble head in the corner, that dead composer her teacher worships, eyes her with cold white contempt.

There is no light in the back kitchen at the far end of the garden. Miss O'Dowd is probably in the front room composing her summons. Daphne halts and lowers the box onto the footpath. She rubs her cold, stiffening fingers, tries to get the circulation going. A thin moon slides out from behind the copse at the top of Hollerton fields; it catches the ripples on the far side of the river where the current moves faster. The water makes a strange, sucking noise around a heavy limb which has sheared off one of the alders on the field's edge and lies half submerged.

Flotsam clings to its branches, bobbing and stirring in the downflow: bits of plastic sheeting, barbed wire, a broken fencing post. A long skein of greyish wool drags in the current, like the hair of a drowned woman. Daphne shivers. The riverbank is her playground in daylight, but not now when the shadows are falling thick around her, not now when she is alone with the Beaker woman.

A sudden disturbance in the air above her head. Something passes, swift as a sigh: the thunk of a heavy object hitting the water upstream. Something else rustles in the undergrowth by the water's edge. There are rats living in holes in the bank, they eat dead animals and the filthy stuff people tip into the river. They're not fussy, Janice says. Daphne's heart is beating fast, she badly wants to get home. As she bends down to pick up the box some awful thing—grey, monstrous, flapping—leaps the garden wall and smacks right into her, sending the box and its contents flying and her tumbling off the path, down the bank and into the water.

CHAPTER 2

Eleanor O'Dowd closes her eyes and surrenders to the pulse of the 'Hammerklavier'. Her strong hands embrace the keyboard, their long deft fingers weaving the patterns of the notes, the tonal shifts and counterpoints, the driving fugue. Nothing matters outside this moment. This marvellous instrument, her capable fingers that infuse the dull little room with the majesty of Beethoven, transporting her to another place, a different time. The last thrilling chord lingering in the air, she allows her hands to rest a moment on the keyboard so she can listen to the dying echo, feel the ivory warm and pliant beneath her fingertips.

She sighs and reaches up to close the lid, briefly runs her fingers across the letters Steinway & Sons, picked out in gold against the polished ebony. The grand piano dominates her narrow-beamed parlour, leaving little space for her scant possessions: an easy chair upholstered in faded green velvet; a small oak bookcase where she keeps her music and poetry; and, in the corner by the window, the mahogany pedestal bearing the alabaster bust of Franz Liszt, the only man she has truly admired. In the house of her childhood, far from this place, he occupied an alcove in the lofty music room, a constant stony-faced reminder of her shortcomings, her fumblings at this same piano, when a wrong note earned a sharp rap over the knuckles from Frau Erdmann. Now she is sole mistress of the instrument, he the sole reminder of her many falls from grace.

The small clock on the mantlepiece trills the hour. She removes Sonata 29 from the music stand and replaces it with 'Easy Piano Pieces for Beginners'. Her next pupil is late: she always insists they arrive six minutes before the lesson in order to prepare. This one is hopeless, completely tone deaf. Such a shame the promise her sister showed has gone to waste, now she's in the grammar school distracted by boys and that thing they call 'pop' music. Eleanor O'Dowd lifts her gaze from the piano to the mantlepiece, to the sepia photograph in its tarnished silver frame. Two female figures seated together on a garden bench, the younger of the two clutching a small terrier which seems about to spring from her lap. The young woman's eager smile is directed at something beyond the camera. Her thick, rather wiry hair has come adrift from its pins and her long, patterned scarf spills over the edge of the seat. The ruination of a perfect moment.

Another headstrong girl who refused to listen, always so certain she knew best. Why do they squander their gifts? Reject the people who have sacrificed everything for them? 'How sharper than a serpent's tooth...' Eleanor O'Dowd knows all about that particular, permanent scarring of the heart. She pulls her cardigan closer around her thin shoulders and averts her gaze from the little photograph. Thankless children deserve no forgiveness.

She gets up from the piano stool and leaves the room, a lean, striking-looking woman dressed in her habitual old-fashioned skirt and cardigan, pale-eyed and high cheek-boned, her greying hair coiled neatly at the nape of her neck. In this low-slung cottage built for a smaller breed of Celt, her lofty Englishness, like her grand piano, seems out of place (for she is Oxford bred despite her surname). How she came to be living in this small township on the western edge of Wales is known only to her. She claims no near relations; her religion, nominal though it is for her, is alien to this Anglican and chapel-going community, the nearest unvisited Catholic church ten miles away in a forgotten corner of the county town. On the wooden draining board in the dank kitchen at the back of the house all is prepared: the washing bowl stands ready to be filled with icy water from the pump outside the back door; the kettle whistles on the stove. She opens the back door and stares out at the darkening garden, the wooded hillside rising beyond the Morlas. The late afternoon sky is leaden with clouds massing from the far west, beyond the Irish Sea. She pictures honey-coloured stone, graceful spires and domes, a wintry plume of swans drifting on the Isis, the clever conversation of serious people. She does not hear the front door open, the tread of footsteps on the parlour floor, the swish of curtains being drawn to hide the street. She sighs heavily, turns from the door and goes back through the hall, into the parlour.

'Ah,' she says, 'It's you.'

CHAPTER 3

Daphne stands thigh-deep in the freezing Morlas. Her boots are full of water, the bottom of her duffle coat is saturated and she cannot feel her legs. She's not a good swimmer yet, with only the sea to learn in and then only in summer. People have drowned in this river and further out in the treacherous currents of the estuary. Every child in Glanmorfa knows the perils of getting out of your depth.

The river is loud in her ears, she is losing her footing, weighed down by her sodden coat and the pull of the current. She will surely drown, like the Williams brothers, caught in the whirlpool out fishing below Cowyn Head. Johnny Nebo and his uncles only found the bodies a week later. She and her family were away on holiday, staying in a locum parish in Kent. Her father had to drive all the way home to take the funerals. If she drowns, it could be days before they find her, spat out by the river on some mudbank in the middle of the estuary.

The current keeps trying to pull her out into the deeper water and she has to use all her strength to turn back towards the bank. Her feet find traction on the stony riverbed. Slowly, she recovers her balance and drags herself out from the sucking mud. The riverbank is steep here. Her frozen fingers clutch the brittle spikes of reed and vicious bramble; they find the solid roots of a stubby alder and she hauls herself upwards, inch by inch, back onto the footpath.

She lies face down on the muddy track. It is very quiet, very still. Perhaps it is this absence of sound, the stopped air, that tells her she is not alone. She knows someone is standing close by, checking, perhaps, whether she is still alive. Her heart is loud in the silence and her hands throb from bramble stabs. She presses her face hard against the cold earth, inhales its damp, loamy smell. Closes her eyes and waits for something to happen.

A bird shrieks from the alders across the stream and she senses movement, a twig snapping, the sound of footsteps receding along the path. Normal river noises, breathing air. Daphne tugs off her wellingtons and upends them in a gush of dirty river water, puts them on again and gets slowly to her feet. Her heavy, sodden coat clings to her thighs. The shovel is lying a few yards away at the edge of the path. Midstream, the dusky remains of the cardboard box turn slowly in the current. For all she knows, the skull might still be inside or perhaps it's lying somewhere in the undergrowth. Darkness is falling and she's too frightened to stay to look for it. She grabs the shovel and hurries along the path. Near the junction with Morlas Lane, a sudden shadow moves in the hedge. Daphne stops and tightens her grip on the shovel, listens to the thump-thump of her heart. Up on Church Street, a sudden car makes a right turn out of the driveway by Maia House. Its headlights flood the length of Morlas Lane, sending into relief the long-defunct lamp post at the junction, the churned up muddy path and the straggling line of hedge. Nothing else.

Daphne sets off again, on surer ground now. The footpath skirts the backs of the grander houses up on George Street, their sprawling gardens concealed behind high walls and fences. It passes by empty barns and derelict coach houses, stacked with the carcasses of motor cars, their shredded leather seats colonised by mice and beetles. At last, she reaches the rickety wooden footbridge over the Morlas with the rope-swing hanging from the willow. The blessed garden gate. She shoulders it open and walks through the narrow passageway between the pigsty and the chicken house, into the garden. In the gathering dusk the path ahead is a gleam of cockleshells, winding past the orchard and the vegetable beds, up to the thick beech hedge that screens the top garden. The vicarage, a long, three-storeyed, grey-stuccoed house, fills the skyline, dwarfed on the left by the lofty wall of the Bevan House. Lights are on in some of the downstairs rooms: the kitchen and scullery on the right and the arched window of her father's study. There is a red glow behind the heavy velvet curtains of The Furthest Room. Only one light is on at the very top of the house. The outline of a figure standing at the window. Daphne keeps her head down.

Sylvia lifts the stiff latch and pushes hard at the window frame, swollen from all the autumn rain. With a bit more pressure it yields, and she leans far out over the roof. From up here, she has a grand twilit view of the dark hills on the far side of the valley and the roofs of the town clustering beneath the castle walls. Beyond them, a sliver of sea. The garden below is mostly in shadow now, the cockle path a chalk line reaching for the house.

The air is bitter, but she doesn't care; the colder it is the better she thinks, then she will catch a chill which will quickly become pneumonia and then she will fade, lingeringly, in her lovely bedroom, full of her favourite possessions. In the daytime she might languish downstairs on the sofa in the sitting room, pale and thinly interesting with her faithful spaniel at her feet like Elizabeth Barrett before Robert rescued her. And then Owen Howells will be sorry. She may forgive him before she dies.

Sylvia draws back inside and fastens the window latch; disappointingly, her chest and arms remain unchilled. Her glance sweeps the bedroom and, not for the first time, she admires her choice of decor: the crimson wallpaper above the bed with its black and red check coverlet; the white painted desk and matching chest of drawers, the little slatted chair with a red cushion to match the wall. The summer she turned thirteen, Sylvia moved out of the bedroom on the first floor she shared with Daphne and into the smaller of the two attic rooms on the floor above, once occupied by a live-in maid in grander clergy times. Opposite her bed she hung *The Piper of Dreams*—an elfin, sandy-haired boy squatting in the mossy bole of a beech tree, a gossamer drift of sprites about his head. This print belongs to both sisters; by agreement, in August it will be Daphne's turn to hang it in her bedroom.

A crumpled black and white photograph lies on the carpet: a tall dark-haired boy in running shorts and singlet embroidered with the school crest and motto, 'Onwards for the Goal'. Owen Howells is the athletic team's most handsome, most covetable member, but alas he is no longer Sylvia's. Her almost boyfriend: a chance encounter at the fair last month, a toffee apple and a ride on the Swirls where she fell against him and he put his arm briefly around her shoulder. And then went off with Susan Jones in form 4. Sylvia's eyes are full of ready tears, the weight of sorrow catches at her throat. She kicks the photograph under her bed next to *The Queen's Secret*, borrowed from the library on Gran's ticket. Treacherous Owen is no match for dashing Owen Tudor.

Three floors below, the telephone rings. Someone is banging at the front door; she hears the heavy iron knocker slam against the wood. She goes out of her bedroom to the landing and listens to the voices two floors down in the hall. They are too distant to catch the words, but something is clearly up. As she turns to go down the first flight of stairs, she catches sight of her own face reflected in the blank windows of the large walk-in cupboard she and Daphne call The Room of Doom. Her features are hollow, distorted as in a photograph negative. She is a stranger to herself, a woman abandoned.

Daphne enters the kitchen through the scullery. Light, warmth, the comfort of Friday fish pie. The table is laid for supper, on the wireless the posh tones of the weather forecast warn of plummeting temperatures in the north and west. She kicks off her sodden wellingtons and leaves them to dry beside the stove. Her socks are wringing wet and her feet leave damp prints on the floor tiles as she goes through into the living room where a meagre coal fire is struggling in the grate. The oldest part of the house is below street level; through the one window midway up the wall the disembodied heads of passers-by dip and bob their way along the lighted street. Steam rises from the wooden clothes horse in front of the fireplace, freighted with drying sheets and underwear. Daphne makes a space between a row of knickers, peels off her duffle coat and socks and drapes them over the bars. Her feet have a bluish tinge, they are

15

mottled like flounders. In his basket, Rusty, the cocker spaniel they've had since Sylvia was a baby, snores the deep sleep of old age.

The hallway is suddenly full of noise—someone at the front door, her father's brisk footsteps crossing the hallway, the violent crash of iron against wood. In older age, in another country, Daphne will close her eyes and re-enter this house of her childhood. She will steal through its many rooms, from cellar to attic, and she will recall each particular, intimate sound: the sitting room door opening, the echo on the upstairs landing, the loose floorboard in her bedroom. Now, she opens the living room door—hollow squeak of handle, brief resistance of the broken floor tile—and hovers at the bottom of the three steps leading to the hallway. Sees her father, a handsome stocky man with a shock of dark hair going grey at the temples, dog-collared and tweed-jacketed (for it is Friday evening and he is due at the Memorial Hall for the whist drive in an hour), talking to Mr Morris his churchwarden, a short thin man with round glasses and a bald head, trussed in heavy winter coat and navy muffler. Hubert Morris's voice is low and wheezy, and Daphne can't understand what he's saying; he and her father, Gwendraeth Valley boys, speak Welsh when they're together, comrades in arms in this sequestered township where only a few people speak the national language. Then her father crosses to the coat stand behind the door and, from one of its branches, unhitches his heavy black winter cloak. His eyebrows are a bristling line of worry, his expression is severe. Something is very wrong. As he pauses to fasten the cloak's metal clasp, he notices her at the bottom of the steps.

'Tell your mother I've gone out, not sure when I'll be back. There's been a nasty accident. Don't wait on supper.'

The front door slams behind the two men and the house is suddenly stilled. Upstairs on the first floor, beyond the country grandfather clock with the single hand—an heirloom from her mother's farming family—and beyond the tall window whose coloured panes spill the dying evening light across the carpet, she can hear her sister.

16

And this is how Daphne Morgan, years later, remembers that December afternoon when she was ten years old: the maybe Beaker woman, found and lost; the icy river's clutch; Sylvia sobbing on the stairs; and her piano teacher Miss O'Dowd, beaten savagely about the head and stabbed three times in the back and chest, a bloodied corpse at the foot of her Steinway Grand.

CHAPTER 4

'Poor dab, she had it coming to her if you ask me.'

Mrs Daley reaches across the table for the tin of Silvo, the stub end of her cigarette twitching at the side of her mouth. Daphne, sitting on the opposite side of the table, watches her tip the bottle and pour some of the pink stuff onto the cleaning rag. She picks up one of the large silver church candlesticks and begins to smear it all over with the oily liquid. Mrs Daley has magic powers: she can talk and polish and smoke at the same time. She's a thin, sallow-faced woman with cropped grey hair, always dressed in the same uniform—thick wrinkly stockings, men's black slip-ons and a navy overall which has a top pocket where she keeps her cigarettes.

'They're saying she had £300 quid under the bed. Should've put it in the bank, the silly woman, it'd be safer there. Don't you think so, missus?'

No response from the other side of the table where her mother is buffing the silver chalice for Sunday's communion table. She turns it round and round as she polishes, and the goblet catches fire in the morning light streaming through the garden window. Mrs Daley, belabouring the candlestick with her polishing cloth, gives a loud, theatrical huff and the cigarette wobbles dangerously.

'Well, that's what me and Elsie think any road.'

Elsie is her grown-up daughter; she cleans for some of the bigger houses upstreet. Mrs Morgan says not a word. Neither does Daphne. Mrs Daley lifts her empty teacup and slowly stubs out her fag in the saucer. She doesn't like to be ignored.

The kitchen table is spread with pages from last week's *Church Times* on which is heaped all the church brass and silverware for Saturday cleaning. Daphne's job is polishing the two collection plates—shallow copper dishes, no things of beauty. They are badly scratched and dimpled, with black grooves you can't get properly clean. Sylvia, as older sister, is assigned the more precious things to polish. This morning, however, she has pleaded a headache and her monthly stomach cramps, so she's excused from her chores, whereas Daphne, sleepless from guilt and aching bones, is badly in need of penance. Mrs Morgan gives her a sharp suspicious look when, instead of bunking off as soon as her plates are done, she offers to clean Sylvia's pieces too. Her mother selects the portable communion set and passes it across the table, which Daphne takes to be an early and hopeful sign of forgiveness. She picks up the little leather box with its delicate clasps, opens the lid. Inside is a miniature silver communion cup, a little paten embossed with a dainty cross and a small glass bottle with a silver lid. They are so beautiful, these tiny fairy objects; she doesn't like the thought of elderly sick people with no teeth slurping from them. She unscrews the glass bottle and sniffs the faint plummy smell of communion wine.

'You be careful you don't break that, maid,' Mrs Daley mutters. 'The vicar'll tan your hide if you do.'

Her mother looks up from her polishing and winks at Daphne. The vicar has a quick temper, everybody knows that, but he'd never raise a finger to his children.

When the polishing is done and her handiwork approved by Mrs Daley, Daphne puts the lovely treasures back in their leather container and takes it up to the study, a small room off the hallway. Her father is out—'seeing what is to be done about that poor woman,' says Mrs Daley. The study is their father's base camp unless he's on vicar duty, or at the bottom of the garden cleaning the pigsty and the chicken house. He's a country boy at heart, their mother says: animals are less trouble than parishioners. Enid Morgan seldom visits the study, its shabby disorder distresses her: papers strewn everywhere; a rickety metal cupboard where he keeps his stock of communion wine and boxes of wafers; two mothy armchairs with sagging brown covers; a dusty prie-dieu in front of the window overlooking the garden; and a large iron safe in the corner containing the few church valuables—an 18th-century silver salver and an Elizabethan chalice. The parish should sell them, Enid thinks, spend the money on doing up the vicarage, put in central heating like the modern vicarages. Her husband's vicar costume— cassock, surplice, embroidered stoles, a different colour for each season in the liturgical calendar—hang from pegs behind the door. The room smells of mothballs and the close stale odour of male clothing.

Daphne carefully puts the communion set in its usual place on top of the roll-top desk—a monster of mahogany dulled and scarred by a lifetime of vicars. The wood is pitted and gouged like someone has attacked it with a compass, and there are sprawling dark patches where the ink has spilled and soaked into the wood. Beside the communion set is a photograph of her parents in their wedding outfits, stiffly posing outside the west door of the cathedral. Her mother's red hair was long in those days and curly. Daphne thinks she looks very young and romantic in her embroidered veil and gown, holding a trailing bouquet of lilies and leaning towards her handsome, smiling husband in his dog collar and black cassock; his shoulders are lightly sprinkled with confetti, though it might be dandruff.

She undertakes a fruitless rummage in the deep drawers of the desk for her father's secret stash of Cadbury's Wholenut and finds instead a handful of communion wafers which have spilled from their box. A single wafer, she knows from past experience, tastes like one of those papery flying saucers but without the lovely fizzy sherbet inside; it can stick so hard to the roof of your mouth you have to prise it off with your fingers. A fistful of wafers, on the other hand, crammed into the mouth in one go, provides a satisfying experience—saltier, and with more of a crunch. Sylvia claims they taste better with a glug of communion wine. The wine helps her concentrate, which is why she passed the eleven-plus.

'Don't look so worried, Daph, it's only holy when dad does that wavy thing with his hands in front of the altar on Sundays. God won't punish you for swigging from the bottle, it's like drinking Ribena.'

Daphne pockets the wafers, closes the drawer, and goes over to the cupboard. She takes out a bottle of Ruby Red Altar Wine, unscrews the lid and has a mouthful. The liquid goes down sweet and warm, tasting of blackcurrant, but the colour makes her think of Miss O'Dowd drowning in her own blood, as described by Mrs Daley.

The sweet taste turns bitter as gall. The Beaker woman has vanished and now Daphne has no hope of putting things right. She pictures the skull turning in the Morlas current, roiling past the slaughter yard and the school playground, into the estuary towards the Irish Sea. The Beaker people came from Ireland, Mr Duckford said. She screws the cap on the wine bottle and shoves it back inside the cupboard. As she leaves the room, she glances at the large, framed photograph on the wall above her father's desk: a row of stern-faced clerics standing outside the entrance to a church. In the middle is a tall-mitred bishop wielding his crozier. Every eye is fixed on her.

Her mother is in the hallway loading the silverware into a basket to take up to church. She looks harassed, as she does every Saturday.

'Go up and check on Sylvia, would you? See if she wants a cup of tea or a biscuit.' She buttons up her coat and knots her flowered headscarf under her chin. 'Mrs Daley's finishing off in the kitchen, don't be getting in her way.'

It's a long trek up to the attic floor. The vicarage is a maze of gloomy corridors, with rooms on different levels leading off them: four steps down to one bedroom, two steps up to another, three steps down to the chilly, lino-floored bathroom and toilet. Like living on an ocean liner, Mrs Morgan complains, the kind that has seen better days. Leaking pipes, rotting floorboards, dank, grimy cellars. She misses the small, terraced curate's house in the county town where they lived before Hywel had his vicar promotion. In that house their sparse but good quality furniture fitted perfectly, the rooms were always warm.

Daphne reaches the attic landing and pauses outside The Room of Doom. A chill whisper of air, a ghostly shadow passing behind its blinded windows. Her throat is dried, her skin turned to ice. Cursed.

She turns away and enters Sylvia's bedroom. Her sister is sitting up in bed, wrapped in one of their mother's shawls and reading *Honey* magazine. The front cover has the slogan 'Young, Gay and Get Ahead' above a close-up of a smiling blonde woman with fleshy orange lips. Sylvia can't be that ill, Daphne observes, approaching the bed. Her fingernails are freshly painted with Cutex 'Pink Polish', pinched from the drawer in the bathroom chest where their mother keeps her make-up. Sylvia sees her looking and hides her hands under the eiderdown. Her face assumes a piteous expression.

'It's such hell, Daph, you've no idea. I couldn't eat a thing. All my insides are squeezed so tight I can hardly breathe.'

Daphne isn't really listening, being engrossed with the tangerine lipstick and the strapline beneath: 'luscious lips last longer'. Her class are learning about alliteration and she is wondering how she can incorporate this phrase into one of her homework sentences—'Sir Galahad leans graciously towards the fair Elaine and kisses her tenderly, murmuring "luscious lips last longer".' She can show off her command of punctuation and adverbs at the same time.

The magazine is snatched away. 'Just leave me alone, will you, I'm in agony.' Sylvia rummages inside the bed and fishes out a pink hot water bottle. 'Fill this up again will you? And don't take all day about it. One day you'll get the curse, then you might have more sympathy.'

If you only knew, Daphne thinks, taking the bottle, clammy as a damp fish. I am already cursed.

CHAPTER 5

On Sunday morning, the town's parishioners are gathered in tight little groups outside the church porch. Everyone has heard about the murder and there is much shaking of heads and solemn faces. Daphne avoids their eyes. She scurries past them up the side path and into the vestry; she does not look at the bone house door which is still ajar the way they left it on Friday. Dressed in her choir robe— blue tunic, white surplice—she slips into her usual seat in the front row of the choir stalls. Sylvia is already skulking in the back row on the opposite side, whispering with her friend Bron. Midway through the sermon, drowsy after a second night of broken sleep, Daphne feels a sharp prod in her lower back. Janice is squinting at her through the gap between the pews. She starts mouthing something, making an awful face. Daphne twists in her seat to hear better and Miss Bryer sitting beside her nudges her hard in the ribs.

'Stop fidgeting and listen to your father,' she hisses. 'Sit properly now, there's a good girl.' Silently seething, Daphne sticks out her tongue at Janice and turns to the front again. She hates this seat, wedged between Miss Bryer and Lorna Parrish, who always sits at the end nearest the congregation because she is the loudest soprano and can sing in tune, unlike the rest of them. This was all her mother's idea: 'Someone needs to keep an eye on you'. Miss Bryer was in charge of the Infants before she retired from teaching; her tweedy suit smells of cat pee and there are stiff little hairs sprouting from her chin. Every Sunday she makes Daphne follow the Bible readings with her, running her skinny finger underneath each word in the prayerbook as if she thinks Daphne is still in the Infants.

From his lofty pulpit overlooking the nave, the vicar draws his sermon to a close. In the posh Englishy accent he puts on for church services he intones, 'And now to God the Father, God the Son and

God the Holy Ghost.' It is the cue for the choir to get ready. Sounds of shuffling, slipping of sweet cigarette cards into pockets, stowing of nail files.

'Hymn number 34, Awake my soul. Choir only to sing the descant.'

They rise to their feet and Mr Williams at the organ strikes the opening chord. The choir has practised the descant several times before this service and Daphne is quite looking forward to singing the last verse. 'Give those Praise Hims the full whack,' Mr Williams has commanded. During the practices she hadn't really heard the words of the hymn; this morning they are utterly deafening.

Let all thy converse be sincere
Thy conscience as the noonday clear

In the tall, stained-glass window opposite, Jesus in his white robes levitates above a bright green hill and turns his solemn eyes upon her. He is sheltering beneath a silver umbrella held by two golden-haired angels. One has a sweet smiley face, the other looks sour and disapproving.

Think how all-seeing God thy ways
And all thy secret thoughts surveys.

Beneath Jesus's feet are small mounds, like multi-coloured molehills in the grass; they are the backs of the disciples, prostrated at their master's feet. No doubt every one of them has a clear conscience.

From the treble row someone coughs, then coughs again, loudly. Graham is trying to attract the girls' attention. He draws his hand slowly across his throat and mimes a scream. Beside him, Martin's face is white as his surplice. Daphne feels a bit breathless; her heart is thumping the way it did on the riverbank. She tries to empty her mind in case He—Jesus, not her father—is surveying her secret thoughts. Unlike His trusty disciples, her conscience is far from clear.

24

All the joy of whacking the Praise Hims evaporates and she mumbles through the descant until it's time for the prayers and she can kneel down out of sight on the hassock, one of several embroidered by Gran and her friends in the Mothers' Union. It's made of blue hessian and has a picture of a sheep waving a white flag with a red cross; the rough material prickles her bare knees. She puts her hands together as Miss Bryer insists and listens to her father praying for the soul of Miss Eleanor O'Dowd, which is a bit of a surprise because the dead woman was a Catholic and he holds no truck with the 'Romans'; his congregation are Church in Wales and therefore right about everything. When he asks God to comfort the deceased woman's family and friends, Miss Bryer fumbles in her suit pocket and brings out a pale violet handkerchief, unfolds it and dabs at her eyes. Daphne observes the drop of snot quivering at the end of her nose.

Her father concludes his petition. 'And may Almighty God bring to justice the perpetrator of this terrible crime.'

'Amen,' his congregation responds, fervently. Beyond the church walls the town is already loud with speculation.

Martin and Graham are hanging about outside the vestry, kicking stones and jumping on the grave slabs.

'You two don't half take a long time to change, everybody else went home ages ago,' Graham sulks.

Janice and Daphne are the last to leave only because Janice lost her collection money under the pews, so they had to scrabble about in the spidery dust looking for it and getting their white socks dirty and being told off by Mr Morris who wanted to lock up and get home. Her father has left straight after the service to give the sick communion, his vestments packed in his black bag alongside the little leather communion case with its sparkling contents. Janice slips her arm inside Daphne's and they set off at speed to avoid the boys, but Martin steps in front of them and holds out his arms so they can't get away. The yew trees rear darkly against the grey sky and the air is stinging cold, like a promise of snow. They are all of them bundled in thick coats and woolly hats and Martin is wearing a brown knitted balaclava that makes him look like a bank robber.

'What you done with it then?' His eyes are cold.

She pretends not to know what he's talking about. Janice shrugs, tosses her head. 'Go away Martin Evans, we're not speaking to you.'

Which is a bit rich, Daphne thinks. Last Friday Janice was quite happy to scarper with the others and leave her on her own. Martin's blue gaze is fixed on Daphne's face.

'You mustn't bring it into school tomorrow like we planned, you got to put it back in the bone house straight away. It's our fault she got murdered.'

Graham, who's been hovering in the background, steps forward. 'Yeh Daphne Morgan, Marty's right, you got to put it back in the bone house. There's a curse on it, we could be next.'

That's just superstitious rubbish, she wants to reply, but they're all thinking it now and she can't help a swift glance beyond them towards the bone house door where a skeletal hand is reaching round and pointing its shrivelled finger at her. She feels Janice tighten her grip. Martin is right, of course he is, but there's nothing she can do, the Beaker woman's skull is probably approaching the Irish coast by now, all battered and tossed about in the churning waves. The four of them were grave robbers and this particular curse would come upon them as surely as it had Lord Caernarfon and the Lady of Shalott and poor Miss O'Dowd who had £300 under her mattress instead of putting it in the bank like she should have.

'Alright', she squirms. 'I'll put it back.'

'When?' says Martin. 'Today?'

Janice pokes her tongue at him. 'Ask me no questions, Martin Evans, tell me no lies.' She beams at Daphne. 'You boys are just cowards, we're not afraid of curses, are we?'

Daphne does not reply; she knows Janice is putting on a brave face.

They leave the boys and race each other down the main path, skidding on the slimy yew berries as they round the corner by the bridge to the new graveyard. Janice gets to the lychgate first and waits for Daphne to catch up. She leans against the gate to catch her breath.

'Are you really going to put the skull back now, Daph? Couldn't you keep it for a bit? We could bring it into school later on, after they've caught the murderer.'

For a moment Daphne allows herself to imagine Mr Duckford's response when they produce their find. His eyes light up, the whole class is open-mouthed, agog with admiration. On the other hand, if he isn't pleased, they'll be for it, no question. He'll march them off to Mr Merchant's office for punishment—a caning for the boys, a stinging ruler slap across the hands for the girls. And then worst of all, the parents will be told.

'Let me think about it, Janice,' she says grandly.

Vicarage Sunday lunch is always best got through fast. It's a working day and nobody has time to talk, not even about the murder. The family are trained to eat quickly, heads down, blanking the noise of Gran's false teeth clacking through the roast chicken and apple charlotte.

Gran has been living with them for ever; she arrived when Daphne was four and their mother went back to teaching. She's short and round and she wears a rubbery pink corset underneath her clothes; when you hug her there's no give. Solid, like a boulder. In the daytime she lives in The Furthest Room off the hallway and at night she sleeps in The Furthest Bedroom at the end of the corridor on the first floor. On her way to bed she sometimes encounters the Lady in Grey. No-one else has seen her but Gran is sensitive to the spirit world, she says, unlike her son-in-law.

After the apple charlotte, Gran retires to her room for a nap, the vicar disappears to his study to prepare the evensong sermon, and his wife locks herself in the chilly sitting room with her cigarettes, a cup of tea and her brown leather bucket bag freighted with schoolbooks and lesson files. This austere room—high-ceilinged,

French windowed, damask-curtained—belongs to a more formal era. A place for reluctant piano practice, high days such as Easter and Christmas, and holy days when the plump little bishop comes for tea. It is Enid Morgan's refuge; she is not to be disturbed.

Down in the kitchen, Sylvia and Daphne stack the dirty plates and cutlery and carry them out to the scullery. They scrape the leftovers into Rusty's bowl and add some gravy for a treat. Sylvia washes, Daphne dries. Their weekly pocket money—sixpence for Daphne, a shilling for Sylvia—has no logic since Daphne does the putting away as well as the drying. Sylvia saves her money in a white porcelain pig on top of the bookshelf in her fancy bedroom. Daphne's pig smashed when she dropped it accidentally on purpose trying to winkle out some pennies with a kitchen knife. She now keeps her money under her bed, in an empty tin of pineapple rings. Though since the murder, she's having second thoughts—keeping money under your bed can have dangerous consequences.

'Some people are saying it was Johnny Nebo.' Sylvia unexpectedly breaks the silence; as a rule they don't talk during washing up, wanting to get the business over quickly. 'He was after her money, that's what Bron told me in church, but I don't think that's very fair. Just because he's a bit odd it doesn't mean he's a murderer.' She scrapes out the last of the dried bits of potato and carrots and plunges the pan into the soapy water. 'Get a move on with the drying Daph, we're going to be late.'

Sunday School after washing up. The children gather in the school hall and wait for Mr Morris, who is also the Superintendent of the Sunday School, to give them their tasks. The younger ones, including Daphne, are put in groups to do Bible quiz and colouring while Sylvia and the older ones go to another classroom to prepare for Confirmation, another mysterious thing that happens after you become a teenager. Today's quiz has a Christmas theme. It's only the beginning of December, the first Sunday of Advent. Perhaps Mr Morris has made a mistake and chosen the wrong leaflet. It has a picture on the front for colouring-in: Mary on a donkey crossing a stream. Inside are the questions: 'Where are Mary and Joseph going?' 'How do they know where to go?' 'What animal is Mary riding?' This is clearly intended for the youngest children in the group—Graham's four-year-old sister Bethan and her best friend Mikey whose nose is permanently crusted with snot and who may have nits, Daphne thinks, watching him scratching furiously at his scalp. 'What other animals are mentioned in the Christmas story?' She writes ox, ass, lamb and chicken, then adds dromedary to show off. This month's *Look and Learn* has a section on camelids. The crayons from the Sunday school crate are the thick sort, blunt at the ends and slippery on the page so Mary's blue cloak ends up ragged like the donkey's had a good chew.

When the hour is up, they all come together for a hymn and a prayer. This afternoon there is no hymn. Instead Mr Morris makes them stand in a semicircle and bow their heads while he prays that Miss O'Dowd's soul will rest in peace—even though she was Catholic—then they all say Amen. After that he orders them to go home in silence and no talking.

Daphne trails along behind Sylvia up the main street towards the vicarage, past Ainsworth's bus garage and the post office, the rows of tall Georgian houses with sagging porticos and peeling paint, the greengrocer's windows shuttered for Sunday. Inside Portland House the front room curtains are still open and they can see the flickering lights of Mr and Mrs James's posh new television. Daphne's secret wish is to open the vicarage sitting room door on Christmas morning and find their own brand-new TV underneath the tree; it will be housed in a polished walnut cabinet with little doors just like the one at Portland House. As instructed by Mr Morris, the sisters do not talk to each other on the way home. Daphne thinks about Miss O'Dowd, how sad to keep all that money under your bed and then not have the chance to spend any of it. Not even on a television.

Johnny Nebo is coming out of the Black Lion opposite. The pub's supposed to be closed on Sundays but everybody just uses the side door. Johnny can't hear or talk properly and he's got one leg shorter than the other because of the polio. Normally, Sylvia and Daphne will shout and wave at him, and he will usually gurn and grunt back at them. Today, Sylvia keeps her head down, increasing her stride, and Daphne hurries after her, not daring to look. Behind her she can hear the flip-flap of the man's wellingtons on the pavement as he limps down the street towards the side door of the Captain's Arms.

CHAPTER 6

'Enid, have you seen the shovel?'

From the bathroom upstairs where she is putting on her make-up her mother answers, 'No idea, try the cellar'.

Her father is in the boot room among the coal buckets and brooms; she hears him shout something back and then there's a lot of clattering and banging of the cupboard doors where Mrs Daley keeps the cleaning stuff. Daphne concentrates her attention on the newly opened box of Rice Krispies, shaking the bag to see if a plastic dog will come to the surface—the Collie, the Scottie or the Labrador, she doesn't mind which, though she'd prefer the little black terrier since she has the other two already. Her father's head appears round the kitchen door.

'You two seen the coal shovel?' he roars. His hair is sticking up all over the place and there's a brown smear of boot polish on his shirt sleeve.

'You could try the cellar,' Sylvia murmurs through a mouthful of toast and marmite. Daphne burrows deeper in the Krispies box to hide her burning face.

'Well, it's not where it should be, damn it!'

His head disappears. Moments later they hear him unlock the cellar door and then the fading sound of his footsteps as he goes down the stone steps. He will find no shovel there. Daphne knows exactly where it is—at the back of Rusty's shed where she tossed it on Friday evening before she went indoors. With so much else going on she has forgotten to retrieve it.

Sylvia sighs and licks up the last toast crumbs with her fingertips. Her nails have returned to their normal colour, polish is not allowed at grammar school. She leaves the table and picks up her satchel from behind the kitchen door; she has to be outside the Memorial

Hall by 8.15 or she'll miss the school bus and have to get a lift in with Mr Harries who teaches history, which is a fate worse than death, Sylvia says.

The Rice Krispies box has failed to deliver and there are no plastic animals inside. Daphne will ask her sister to write a letter of complaint, like the ones she does for English homework. They could use vicarage notepaper so the Krispies people will take notice.

Their mother comes into the kitchen, all of a rush and looking harassed.

'I've left Gran a note to tell your father the plumber's calling at eleven about the leak in the bathroom. Has he found the shovel yet?'

She comes over to Daphne and fusses with her plait, pulling and tweaking her hair until she yelps with the pain. 'For goodness sake, stop being such a baby,' she tells Daphne. The girls' grammar school where their mother teaches is in the town where they used to live; she has a lift share with Mrs Merchant, the headmaster's wife, who teaches biology. Classics is their mother's subject and is responsible for the girls' names. Sylvia loves hers because it means 'spirit of the woods'. Daphne wishes her mother had chosen Alice or Edith, characters from her current favourite book, *The Children of the New Forest*. Daphne is such an old-fashioned, dowdy name. 'Nonsense,' said her mother, 'it is Greek and means a laurel tree. You should be grateful I didn't call you Medusa.'

The front door bangs shut. There is no sound from the cellar depths; dad must still be hunting the shovel. No time to lose. The old dog lifts his head when she comes into the shed. These days he can't hear very well and his eyes are sort of filmy looking, but he knows her smell and thumps his stubby tail against the side of his basket when she bends down and pats his silky head. The air is heavy with the smell of dog farts and damp. The basket is surrounded by a thicket of garden tools: spades and hoes and iron rakes with long wooden handles, a rusted scythe. There are wooden crates full of crusting paint tins, an old metal tea tray, plywood shelves lined with empty bottles and lids for the elderflower cordial Gran makes every spring. Daphne spots the shovel on top of a pile of dusty theology books with mouldy covers which used to live on the study shelves until her father needed more space. She picks it up, gives Rusty a last pat. He closes his rheumy eyes and goes back to sleep. Inside the house all is quiet. The study door is closed, and she can hear her father talking on the telephone. She goes into the boot room and quietly places the shovel in the empty coal bucket, closes the door behind her and goes off to school.

For the first part of the morning, she tries to avoid the others. Her chest feels tight, like something heavy is sitting on it. Monday morning first thing is always mental arithmetic. Mr Duckford prowls up and down the rows to check no one is cheating. He stops by Terry Dunn's desk which is next to hers and peers down at his exercise book; wordlessly, he stabs a nicotined forefinger at a messy row of sums. Terry stares at the page, a bewildered look on his face. Mr Duckford tut tuts and shakes his head. Secondary Modern for you my lad if you're lucky, is what Mr Duckford thinks; sometimes he says it out loud if he believes it will make the boy or girl pull up their socks. He doesn't say anything to Terry. At break time, the pupils line up to collect their milk bottles from the crate on top of the classroom stove. Martin stands beside it holding the box of straws because he is straw monitor this week. When it's Daphne's turn, he leans across and whispers in her ear, 'Have you done it?' She carefully extracts a paper straw from his box and sort of wobbles her head.

'Good,' he says tersely, holding out the box to the next pupil in the queue.

She always goes home for lunch; the vicarage is only a few hundred yards from the school on George Street. Gran has boned the Sunday chicken and made soup from the carcass and some leftover veg. She ladles it into two bowls. Bits of sprout and carrot float greasily to the surface. They don't talk much. Gran's dentures are out so she's a bit dribbly. After lunch she goes back to The

Furthest Room to put her feet up and finish reading the *Western Mail*. Daphne heads back to school. The class is doing the Egyptians until the last week of term when it's Christmas decorations. This afternoon Mr Duckford has pinned to the blackboard a large diagram of the inside of a pyramid. They have to copy it into their exercise books and label the different parts: thin lines for the Air Shafts and the Grand Gallery, a square block for the Queen's Chamber and a bigger one in the middle for the King's Chamber. She enjoys drawing the zigzaggy steps at the base of the Pyramid leading down to the Dead-End Passage and the Subterranean Chamber. The vicarage has one of those, a black cobwebby room at the far end of the cellar. It has a coal chute leading down from the street. Once a month the coal lorry comes; the coal men wear leather aprons and leather caps and their faces are streaked with dust. When they were younger, she and Sylvia loved watching the avalanche of anthracite whoosh down the chute, great glistening chunks of coal ricocheting off the walls, choking dust everywhere. The trick was to race down the corridor to the top of the steps before the black cloud enveloped them. Daphne dips her pen nib in the ink well, gives it a shake. Ink the colour of coal spatters her drawing of the Great Pyramid of Giza.

'Put your pens down,' says Mr Duckford in his deep nasal voice. They do as they are told. Mr Duckford never needs to say things twice.

'Now, who can spell sarcophagus?'

The class is silent. She raises her arm.

'Hand down, Daphne Morgan, I know you can spell it. Let someone else have a turn.'

The others snigger and she feels her face grow hot. Spelling is her trump card, her guaranteed star turn; she has spelling tests with her father once a week with a follow-up if she gets any wrong. Susan Matthews has two goes and gives up. So does Harry Boyce. She's not surprised, they're useless spellers, so she sits there waiting for Mr Duckford to call her name. But he doesn't. Instead, the old meanie takes his chalk and writes SARCOPHAGUS in big letters on the board for everyone to copy down. Then he unpins the pyramid diagram and replaces it with two pictures of a pharaoh's coffin, an outside one and an inside one. The carved figure on the outside wears a golden robe with a fancy black and white striped headscarf. The other picture shows the dead person inside the coffin, shrunken and smothered in bandages, like Billy Two Gates in his Invisible Man carnival costume. There's a small gap in one of the pharaoh's bandages; you can see his dead white eye.

Graham is waving his arm about. 'Please sir, how can you stop a mummy's curse?'

Jimmy Richards at the back of the room shouts, 'You have to curse her back, that's what my dad does.'

The class starts laughing. Mr Duckford puts his hand up for quiet. He regards them from his great height.

'That's a good question, Graham. The easy answer is that the curse was made up to scare grave robbers from breaking into the tombs and stealing the treasure. But it is also true that an archaeologist once found an inscription on an ancient tomb which said, 'Cursed be he who moves my body; thereof cometh death, flood and pestilence.' So the real answer is that if you disrespect the dead, like all religions say you shouldn't, it's logical to expect trouble.'

The class is silent, pondering the weight of this statement. Janice's hand is up. 'Sir, do you think that's what happened to Tutankhamun? I mean to the people that moved his body?'

Mr Drakeford pauses. Tricky question. He strokes his chin, ponders an answer.

'Who knows, Janice, we're all in the dark.'

Daphne's chest tightens, she daren't look at Martin. Mr Duckford is writing a word on the blackboard.

'What is pestilence, boys and girls?'

'Nits!' someone shouts, and the class erupts.

Later that evening, she's in her bedroom trying to finish the practice test Mr Duckford has set for homework. She can't concentrate, her mind won't let go of the archaeologist story. Her eyes rove around the room she and her mother decorated last summer after Sylvia moved to the attic. The soft moss green carpet, the lovely wallpaper—knights on noble horses moving through a dappled glade, a lady with a falcon on her wrist, a keen-eyed hound. Sir Lancelot and the Fair Elaine. No death, no curses. If only real life were like that.

Early on the morning of the same day, Monday 15th December, as he returns home from checking his nets on the foreshore, John Parry, known locally as Johnny Nebo, later described in the court reports as 'a Deaf Mute by Visitation of God not Mute of Malice', is arrested on suspicion of murdering local piano teacher Miss Eleanor O'Dowd. Wearing his grey mackintosh, wellingtons and leather cap, he is handcuffed to Constable Ian Jenkins, bundled into Sergeant Phillips' grey Wolseley and driven to the county police station. In what will later be described by an eminent Member of Parliament as 'a flagrant infringement of his civil liberties', he is held for three days and then released without charge.

CHAPTER 7

Detective Inspector Ronald Blight returns to his seat after a hearty lunch at the Daffodil Bar. The last crossword clue completed, he folds his copy of the *Daily Mail* and lights up a Navy Cut. The smoke dissolves in the warm fug of the railway carriage. He takes out his watch, checks the time: 1.55 pm. Four hours since *The Red Dragon* express steamed out of Paddington Station, crossed the lovely plains of England, plunged into the Stygian depths of the Severn Tunnel and emerged into blighted, god-forsaken South Wales. The window is fogged. Taking a handkerchief from his coat pocket he rubs a circle in the smutty glass and peers out at the industrial landscape, dimly outlined against the steam from blast furnaces and engine smoke. Like a scene from hell, he thinks, this London man born of smog.

Inspector Blight has never crossed the border before this moment. Never been west of Swindon in fact, aside from a brief foray to Bristol cricket ground last summer to cheer on his home team against Gloucestershire: 325/3 as expected. The local ale and cod and chips at a tavern near the cricket ground were acceptable, the long drive in the Hillman back up the A4 to Palmers Green less so, resulting in several stops along the way to relieve a dodgy bladder—pesky bit of shrapnel from his war days with the Middlesex. A week ago, having just wrapped up a tricky murder case (London cabbie shot by an American in Notting Hill, complicated by diplomatic niceties), he had been enjoying a rare week off, pruning the last of the roses, battening down the garden hatches for the winter, when he got the call from the Boss. Elderly spinster, beaten and stabbed, chief and only suspect a deaf mute. No clear evidence, local bobbies clueless (both senses). Been on the case for days, getting nowhere fast. Between you and me, Blight, that South

Wales lot are a bunch of amateurs. Get down there, wrap it up before Christmas, there's a good chap.

The Red Dragon takes the long curve west out of Swansea station. Coal tips and cooling towers fade to hillsides stitched with wintry hedges, muddy sheep. It clanks across the Loughor swingbridge, under which the river's wide waters pour themselves into Carmarthen Bay. The light is clearer here, a limpid pearl. A flock of feeding geese, startled by the noise of the train, take off low across the water, pale wings catching the light. He couldn't place Carmarthenshire on a map. Not Pembrokeshire—the genteel Tenby of his sister Mabel's holiday snaps—or the grander-sounding Glamorganshire of county cricket fame. A place you pass through to get to somewhere else then.

Blight stubs out his cigarette and opens his briefcase. Extracts the manila folder containing the copious notes provided by David Phillips, the local sergeant in charge of the case. He gives a derisory sniff. Someone at this chap's training college should have taught him the value of brevity; his grasp of the English language is none too strong either. Blight takes out his silver fountain pen (a 40th birthday present from the lads in the Crime Office), unscrews it and, in his neat, precise handwriting, proceeds to make his own summary of the key points.

> *Suspect: John Parry, twenty-two years old, deaf mute. Next of kin: Ifor and Emrys Parry (uncles), Ferry House. Employment: odd job man, gardener, fisherman, ferryman. Poor communication skills. No previous police record. Parry seen in the vicinity of the victim's house before and approximately at the time of the murder. (See detailed witness accounts)*

An hour later, the train passes through the seaside village of Pentraeth, rattles along the east bank of the river Mynach, and arrives two minutes late at the station. Inspector Blight leaves his seat, smooths the strands of his dark oiled hair into place, picks up his leather briefcase and brown fedora (Lock & Co, St James's Street), and buttons his black double-breasted overcoat (Sheppards of London). He likes a good cloth, does Ronald Blight. Alighting from the train with his small valise—for he intends to have a brief, successful stay—he scans the busy platform. Short, thin-faced men in caps and grubby coats, bustling women carrying babies and shopping baskets, a porter pushing a trolley piled with boxes of butter and cheese. A solitary brown mongrel with a limp. He searches among the Welsh voices, loud and unintelligible, for an Anglo-Saxon word of recognition.

A tap on his shoulder.

'Inspector Blight, is it?' A plump florid man of middle age wearing a police uniform. 'Sergeant Phillips, West Wales Branch. The car's outside, sir.'

He takes the inspector's case and leads the way out of the station to the parking bay where the Wolseley is waiting. Constable Jenkins, whippet thin and barely out of school uniform from the look of him, stands to attention beside the open car door.

'Cold enough for you sir, is it?'

Inspector Blight does not answer. Insolent pup, he thinks, speaking before he's spoken to. Someone should have taught him police etiquette in the presence of a superior officer.

CHAPTER 8

'Do you think he stabbed her with one of those?' says Dilys, pointing to the bloody knife her father is cleaning with his butcher's rag. It is Saturday morning and Dilys and Daphne are in the old stable loft above the slaughter yard, dangling their legs over the edge and sharing a packet of Smith's crisps. Below them on the cobbles, upended on an iron trestle, its legs trussed together with bailer twine, a sheep is twitching its final breaths. Blood drips from the slashed throat into the brimming iron bucket beneath the trestle.

Daphne unwraps the blue paper twist from the packet and shakes the salt over the crisps. 'Mrs Daley says her head was bashed in as well, so the police are looking for two murder weapons.'

Walter Evans, who works with Dilys's dad and has the huge muscly arms of a wrestler, heaves the carcass off the trestle and wheelbarrows it away to the shed for skinning and butchering. In the pen next to the shed, a group of sheep are waiting their turn for the knife; they bunch together at the far end, with frightened, pitiful eyes.

'Dad's joining the search party after shop's shut, they're still looking for clues. Shall we go too?'

Daphne is silent. She's thinking about the policeman coming from London to take over the case. Sergeant Phillips isn't very happy about this, Sylvia says, he thinks he should be in charge not some bigwig from Scotland Yard. Sylvia knows this because Evan Phillips is in her class. Daphne thinks that perhaps this important policeman will discover the missing skull. Perhaps he will arrest the four of them for grave robbing and bringing the curse on Miss O'Dowd.

'Poor old Johnny Nebo,' Dilys sighs, emptying the last bits of crisp into her cupped hand. 'I expect he'll be hanged.'

She twists the ends of the crisp bag together, blows it into a balloon and makes it pop. She jumps to her feet.

'Come on, let's go and visit Granny Gloria.'

Granny Gloria is Dilys's mother's mother. She's very old and lives in her bed in the front room of the house adjoining the butcher's shop. The room has a huge bay window opposite the bed so the old lady can watch all the goings on up and down the street. People passing by sometimes give her a wave or press their faces against the window glass and mouth, 'How you doin', Granny G?' and she nods and smiles and waves back at them. She has wispy white hair which Dilys's mum brushes every day and weaves into a long thin plait which trails across her right shoulder. Granny Gloria always wears a crocheted matinee jacket over her nightie: sometimes it's the pale blue one, sometimes the pink. Dilys's grandmother has been in this bed for as long as Daphne can remember. She's like an ancient sleeping beauty, wrapped in her gauzy shawl and artfully arranged against the snowy pillows. The bed frame is made of dark oak and has delicate carvings of grapes and flowers across the headboard; when she and Dilys were small they had to stand on stools to see over the top, the mattress was so high. Granny Gloria is very deaf, so they tell her all their secrets, knowing she'll keep them safe. In the bottom drawer of the chest beside her bed, next to the bandages and cotton wool and tubes of ointment for her bedsores, are her stocks of dolly mixtures which Dilys's mum buys from the paper shop because they're soft for her gums. As a reward for visiting, Dilys and Daphne stuff themselves sick with delicious, sugar-coated jellies, liquorice wheels and—Daphne's favourite— little orange cylinders filled with soft white goo.

This morning, Dilys perches on the stool alongside the bed with Daphne beside her, mouth full of jellies, and regales her grandmother with the gory details of Miss O'Dowd's mangled corpse as she has imagined them. The old lady nods and smacks her lips. At some point in Dilys's saga Granny G closes her eyes and begins to snore, so they filch the last of the sweets from the packet and leave her to it.

Dilys disappears to the back of the house for her lunch and

Daphne wanders home along George Street, sucking on the last gobbets of jelly and imagining Miss O'Dowd's blood spurting from her wounds, her last frantic gasps for breath. Like that poor sheep. As she turns into the vicarage porch, a very tall man in a smart hat and overcoat is coming out of the front door, followed by her father. They shake hands.

'Thank you for your help padre, I'll be keeping in touch.' The man has an English accent, his voice is deep, like Handel Rogers who sings bass in the choir. She is sidling past them towards the front door when she feels a heavy hand on the back of her head.

'This your little girl?'

Her father nods, wearing his solemn Sunday face.

'Say hello to Detective Inspector Blight, Daphne,' he says in his Sunday voice.

The strange man bends towards her and doffs his hat as if she's a grown up. She shrinks away, not liking the look of him. He has a long narrow face with a fleshy nose and bruised looking skin under his eyes. She can see his mouth smiling but his eyes are staring right through her.

'Your father tells me you have a regular piano lesson on a Friday afternoon. You were at Miss O'Dowd's house that Friday, is that correct?'

She tries one of her silent wobbly head answers. This could be a trick question; perhaps he knows she wasn't there.

'Is that a yes or a no?'

The abrupt tone is a shock. She glances up at her father. Why isn't he saying anything? She badly needs to pee, which often happens when she gets into a panic, like in an arithmetic test when the numbers all jumble together on the page and her brain can't make sense of them. She concentrates hard on her feet in their scuffed Saturday daps, on the inspector's trouser turn-ups, on the pattern of red and black tiles on the porch floor. A shameful tear makes its salty trickle down her cheek.

At last, her father clears his throat and says in a firm voice, 'Better leave this with me, Inspector. Daphne's very upset about what happened to Miss O'Dowd; a terrible business, especially for those children she used to teach. We'll have a little chat later, won't we Daph? If there's anything you need to know, Inspector, I'll be in touch.'

Daphne is now watching the inspector's coat pocket, his large, rather hairy hand reaching inside it. Is he going to take out a pair of cuffs and snap them on her, like Sergeant Dixon on the television? He brings out a handkerchief and blows his nose vigorously, puts the handkerchief back in his pocket.

'I'll leave it with you then, padre.'

They watch him go out of the porch and across the road towards Madras House. It is spitting with rain and he turns up the collar of his overcoat. Bob the sheepdog leaps on to the orchard wall of Pantglas Farm opposite the vicarage, barking his head off as usual, but the inspector takes no notice. Dogs do not alarm him, only children.

She should thank her kind-hearted father who has seen her misery and not, she hopes, crossing her fingers, her guilt. But the need to pee is too great. She ducks past him into the house and runs upstairs to the first-floor landing, jumps the three steps down to the toilet and locks the door behind her. Afterwards she sits on the toilet seat for a while and studies the patterns on the linoleum floor. Like the tea leaves Gran swears will show you the future, the swirling lines and dots in the linoleum also have deep significance if you know how to interpret them. An animal shape, such as the blue cat or the dog which looks like a spaniel, means you'll have a happy day with no tellings-off; star patterns are good omens for maths tests. The witch's pointy hat and the bearded monster only appear if it's going to be a very bad day. Daphne concentrates hard, willing the lino to produce the happy cat shape, but the dots and squiggles refuse to co-operate. The witchy hat swims into focus and something new, which, depending on the angle of the wintry light streaming through the small window above the cistern, could either be a large potato or, horror of horrors, a skull.

Martin wants the skull returned before the curse strikes again. If she can find it then everything will be alright—not for poor Miss O'Dowd, of course, but maybe for Johnny Nebo, even if he does kill other things like fish and people's pigs and chickens. And sometimes kittens, like the ones Graham found in Johnny's bucket underneath Quaker's Bridge, all of them drowned. Her bottom is numb from sitting so long on the hard lavatory seat, but she is resolved. She will have to go back to the river and search for the skull. It could still be somewhere on the bank, perhaps caught in the brambles or hidden under some leaves. She will find a way of getting it back to the bone house and then everything will be as it was. More or less.

Ten minutes later, Daphne is hurrying down the garden path towards the pigsty. She is wearing her wellington boots and Sylvia's new blue raincoat which she has taken from the hall stand because it has a pocket large enough to hide her mother's string shopping bag, for carrying the skull. By the time she passes through the garden gate on to the back lane the rain is coming down fast, filling the holes in the tarmac. Daphne tugs the hood of Sylvia's raincoat over her head and starts to run.

She crosses the junction with Morlas Lane and follows the footpath behind the cottages. The ground here is all churned up as though a herd of animals has passed through; reeds and bramble are slashed about and trampled flat. There's a trail of footprints in the mud at the river's edge, disappearing around the bend towards Quaker's Bridge. She's alongside Miss O'Dowd's garden wall now, near the spot where she fell into the river. Or rather was knocked into the river. She can't recall the details, everything happened so quickly, but she hasn't forgotten the icy water and the terror she might drown. She hasn't forgotten the churning fear of knowing the murderer was standing over her on the footpath.

She should have brought Rusty. He's old but he still has his spaniel's instinct for digging up bits of bone and dead animals. Last summer he brought them a chicken in its last throes; it was from next door, not one of theirs, but they had it for Sunday lunch all the same. There are lights on inside Miss O'Dowd's cottage; the back door is wide open and she can see people moving about inside. In the garden, three men on their hands and knees, their backs to her, are searching through the wet grass and the sodden vegetable beds. Up near the house, others are turning over stones and plant pots, sifting through the heaps of dead leaves, peering into the thicker shrubs along the boundary fence.

One of the men straightens up, rubbing the base of his spine, and she recognises Manny Edwards. Has he seen her? He is beckoning to someone in a dark coat and hat who has just emerged from the house. Inspector Blight is striding down the garden path, heading straight for her.

She spins round and races as fast as she can, back along the muddy track, through the deepening puddles, blinded by rain and terror. All chances of putting things right have gone for ever. She daren't go back there again, not with that policeman around. In her haste she turns too sharp around the corner by the vicarage gate and there is a tearing sound. A rusted nail sticking out from the wall of next door's garden has ripped a huge tear at the bottom of Sylvia's new raincoat. The lino omens were right: this is not a good day.

CHAPTER 9

Out in the estuary below the Head, Emrys Parry stands on a sandbank watching the tide. One by one, the landmarks are disappearing beneath the encroaching sea. The iron marker pole is already up to its barnacled waist in water. On the horizon, the glistening ridge of Cefn y Morfil, the whale's back, graveyard of many a sailing brig and freighted coaler, is swallowing the black hulk of the *SS Merlin*, wrecked in 1893 on route for Waterford, its one remaining mast sticking out of the mud like a broken finger. Other landmarks—the sand dunes beyond the marshes, the grey stone watchtower at Hurst Point—are shrinking too. Out in the west, on the very edge of the sands, a line of white-topped breakers marks the start of the open sea, whipped into a frenzy by the freezing wind. Time to go.

Emrys shoulders his spade with one hand and with the other drags the heavy rope and anchor across the sand to the *Peggy*, named for their long-dead mother, and dumps them in the stern next to the fish buckets. The day's catch is fair for the time of year with the bad weather coming: mullet, a few bass—though a little on the small side—a heap of dabs flapping their last on the top of the pile.

'Any more?'

He leans across the wooden gunwale and lightly punches his nephew's shoulder to make him look up. He mouths the same question, pointing to the tangle of netting in the prow near the lad's feet. Johnny squints up at him from beneath his peaked cap and gives a wide grin through chipped teeth, spreading his arms wide. All done. He picks up the knife from his lap, leans over and takes a silvery mullet from the bucket, deftly slits the belly and scrapes the innards into the slops pail before reaching for the next fish.

Behind him Emrys's sandbank is shrinking rapidly. He unbuckles the heavy leather bag around his neck, upends it and leans into the boat to shake the contents into another bucket half full of seawater—a flurry of sand eels, crabs and maddies he's dug up for bait. Then he climbs into the boat and reaches for the wooden gaff. He points to Johnny, mimes the act of rowing. 'C'mon, time to go.'

Johnny drops the gutted fish into the first bucket with the bloody knife and empties the brimming bucket of entrails over the side. He reaches forward to take the oars while Emrys poles them off the sandbank with the gaffe. The boat moves out into the main channel of the Gwennol, the bigger of the two rivers of Glanmorfa that feed the estuary. Water slaps against the timber sides, the boat rocks violently as the incoming tide resists the river's seaward urge. This watery land is veined and runnelled like the oarsmen's hands and they know its treacheries from boyhood: the sudden shifts of sand, the sucking whirlpool at Cowyn's foot, the rocks that lie in wait beneath Black Scar. Seated in the stern beside the anchor and the coils of rope, Emrys leans back and watches his nephew at the oars, his steady hands working against the current and with the tide, the easy rhythm of the strokes. Behind the boat the headland grows smaller, fades.

Emrys trusts his nephew, the silent strength of him, his clear sightedness. Johnny's eyes are quicker than anyone's: the shimmer of an eel at the bottom of the river; the flash of a sparrow hawk before it takes the chick; the white flicker of tide on the turn. As a child he could spot the earliest primrose in the hedge, a nest of harvest mice, a spinning sixpence tossed from a bedroom window. One wintry evening when he did not appear for his tea, the brothers found him standing at the top of the field above the cliff path, with his hands full of snow and tears streaming down his cheeks. It was delight that had so moved him, not fear; they had to drag him home.

Now the tide begins to fill the estuary mouth. It rights the fishing smacks and the rowing boats beached amongst the reeds and sedge, prises the round glass fishing buoys from the clinging mud. As they approach the land, the buildings at the lower end of town appear: the cocklers' low-roofed cottages along Falmouth Row, the whitewashed Anchor Arms on the edge of the square, the shuttered cockle factory on the foreshore and the ivy-coated castle ruins. There are people out on the foreshore, locals going about their business, a dog chasing a stick, a child peeing into the Morlas, a tall man in dark coat and hat picking his way across the slippery rocks below the cliff path.

On homeward journeys such as this, Emrys will chat about the day's catch, the weather, the gossip from the Captain's, this and that. He's talked in this way to his nephew ever since the doctors confirmed he couldn't hear anything. Before that, when he was a small child, Emrys and Ifor used to shout the words, hoping their sounds would unlock the deafness, hoping that little Johnny might answer back, tell them to shut up. When they found he had no speech either, at least there was somebody else to blame—his mother, locked up in the mental hospital after she tried to kill herself the third time. An odd streak in that Beynon family, running like a fault line through the generations. Her older brother Delme was a halfwit, lumping around their farm in filthy overalls; no words with him either, though if he had any they'd only be in Welsh, none of that family were comfortable speaking English. Jack should have known better than go courting at Danyrallt farm. Still, for his sake, Emrys and Ifor were happy to take on the boy, teach him the basics, make up mimes to get him to understand what they wanted. Nobody thought to tell them there was a whole language of proper signs they could have learned.

Johnny backs an oar and turns the boat to face upriver in the direction of the Ferry House, the last dwelling place on the eastern edge of the town. The river becomes a narrower channel at this point, hugging the wooded shoreline as it flows into the wider estuary. On the hillside opposite, a sloping line of hedgerow marks the track down to Black Scar, a narrow spit of land where a small stone building houses the ferry bell for travellers to summon the

Parry brothers across the water. At very low tide it's possible to wade the river rather than take the ferry. The men are used to giving piggy backs to locals working on farms or visiting friends and family in the villages on the other side.

On this particular return journey, Emrys is unusually silent. No companionable chat, no gossip about the comings and goings of the town. He has nothing to say to his nephew. Three days they kept him in the cells, then sent him home without any explanation, no word of advice. But there is one, unutterable word which pulls at his heartstrings. Murderer.

They make the boat fast to the jetty and carry the slopping buckets along the walkway and up a flight of stone steps to the shed for sorting and packing. Emrys will load the best fish into the wooden trailer attached to his bicycle then cycle the four miles to the fishmonger in the next village. Johnny will take the rest of today's catch to his cousin Frances over in Falmouth Row for her to take round town in her wicker pannier and leather apron, pushing her little handcart with the bags of cockles dug at dawn that morning.

Ifor comes into the shed while they're sorting. He looks at Emrys and frowns. 'Best not send Johnny out, he's better off staying put.'

Johnny is laying out the fish in wooden boxes: the slim and silvery mullet, the freckled bass, the mossy dabs. His large strong hands are careful with the delicate flesh.

'Them kids been round again', Ifor says, watching his nephew. 'Mucking about up on the path, throwing stones. One of them just missed a window. Glad he can't hear the names they're calling him, the little shits. If I get hold of one of them, I'll beat the living daylights out of him.'

Emrys has started sluicing the empty buckets from the hose attached to a tap near the back door. 'What's going to happen to him now?'

Ifor shrugs. 'No idea. It's up to that copper from London, Phillips says. He's the one who decides. They've got no evidence Johnny did it; bloody police shouldn't have locked him up in the first place. Phillips says it doesn't mean he's innocent. They'll take him in again if they find something. We just got to keep Johnny at home. He can't do his jobs for people like he usually does. We'll have to go round the houses and tell them. They'll all know why.'

He runs a hand through his coarse black hair, shakes his head.

'Bloody nightmare this is. Better hope we can sell the fish, you know what people are like round here, they'll be calling us two murderers next.'

Ifor walks over to Johnny, still busy sorting fish at the back of the shed; he turns the boy round so he can look him straight in the eye. 'You stay nice and quiet by here, good boy.' He chucks him on the chin and mimes lighting up. 'I'll get you a packet of fags from the shop on my way home.' A broad grin spreads across Johnny's grimy face and he throws his arms around his uncle. 'Careful now, bachan, you'll knock me over!'

At the door of the shed Ifor pauses, casts an eye up at the northern sky. 'Weather's changing', he says.

CHAPTER 10

After Sunday School, the three of them—Daphne, Graham and Janice—mooch up Hangman Lane towards the cliff path, to look at the sea and find something to do. When they round the corner where there is usually a fine view, a thick sea mist is rolling across the estuary and soon the water and the sand and the sky become one indistinguishable grey. The mudflats and the rocks, the clumps of marram grass, have all dissolved; only the darker mass of the Head is visible beyond the murk.

'Where's Martin?' asks Dilys, who has appeared from nowhere and is tagging along without asking.

'P'raps he's sick,' answers Graham, curtly. 'He wasn't in choir this morning either.'

'Don't be daft,' says Janice. 'He was fine yesterday. I saw him in the butcher's with his mam.' She gives Daphne a sly look. 'Unless he's been cursed.'

They start picking up stones from the path and chucking them over the railings. It quickly becomes a throwing competition. Most of the stones land on the rocks below the path but a few make it further and strike the water.

'Johnny Nebo's been sent home,' Dilys announces.

'Why's he not in prison if he's a murderer?' asks Graham, cupping a heavy stone in one hand and weighing it like a professional shot-putter.

Dilys shrugs. 'It's 'cos they haven't got any evidence yet, my dad thinks. The police'll watch him, see if he digs up the murder weapons. They'll have the proof then won't they, so's they can hang him.'

'I bet his uncles know where he's hidden them,' says Janice. 'They've got to look out for him cos Johnny's like their child isn't he, even if he is a grown up.'

Graham lobs his stone over and they hear a loud crack. He shrugs it off; they are all getting bored with this game.

'Let's go and spy on the Ferry House,' says Dilys. She leads the way along the path, creeping low past the artist's studio, which is all boarded up for the winter when the visitors don't come, and on to the wooden gate in the wall above the Ferry House. It's not really a house but a crumbly stone cottage built into the side of the cliff which has seen better days, as Gran would say. To the left of the Ferry House is a small stony beach where the Parry brothers keep their fishing boat and nets. On the other side, a steep flight of steps cut into the cliff leads down to the landing stage where the ferry, a large shallow-bottomed boat with wooden slats for seats, is moored. The sea mist is denser now. They can hear the water slapping against the shingle beach and the timbers creaking as the ferry shifts in the tide. They hover beside the gate, waiting for something to happen. The harsh calls of snipe and curlew echo across the water.

After a while Graham stoops and picks up a stone. He takes aim and they hear it clatter on the slate roof of the Ferry House. They hold their breath and watch to see what will happen. The windows of the cottage face west, out across the estuary; the cliffside wall is blank stone apart from a small door on the right of the building. Graham bends down again and selects another stone. This time he throws it much harder, aiming for the door, but the throw goes wide and the stone strikes the tin roof of the little shed next to the house where the ferrymen keep their ropes and fishing gear. The door of the Ferry House bursts open and a stocky man with black hair and beard comes striding out. It's Ifor, the oldest and scariest brother. They watch him go over to the shed and stare up at the roof for a bit. Suddenly he spins round and glares up the cliff side like he knows they are there. Then he's leaping up the steep steps, two at a time.

Janice is off, belting like the devil down the cliff path, followed by Graham, then Dilys and Daphne. Janice is the best athlete in the school, there's nobody can beat her, which is why Ty Coch—Red

House—always win sports day. They only stop when they reach the top end of Hangman Lane and collapse against the wall of Lucknow House. Dilys is complaining of a bad stitch, Graham's face is on fire. Janice is a distant figure rounding the corner into George Street, breaking rank as always at the first sign of trouble. Daphne glances fearfully behind her but Ifor Parry does not materialise.

'Bloody hell,' Graham pants. 'He nearly got us.' He glances at the girls and shrugs his shoulders. 'The silly bugger, chasing us like that, it was only a stone.' He goes off down the road, trying to whistle.

There's a woman standing on the opposite side of the road, wearing a long winter coat and wide-brimmed hat. They have never seen her before.

'Can one of you help me?'

The woman crosses the road, comes right up to them. She's smiling.

'Are you two on the run from someone, you both look jolly hot!'

The girls exchange awkward glances.

'We're fine thanks,' answers Dilys quickly. 'Just been havin' a race. Daphne and me are practising for school sports, aren't we, Daph?' She gives her a meaningful look and Daphne blushes, acutely conscious of how improbable that sounds, given that it's December.

'I wanted to ask if you knew the way to the cliff path,' the woman says. 'Someone told me you could get a grand view of the estuary from there.' She indicates the camera she's carrying on a long leather strap across her shoulder. 'I'd like to take some snaps.'

Daphne regards the stranger. She's quite short for a grown up, only a few inches taller than she is in fact, and the coat she's wearing seems much too big for her. She seems quite friendly and has a nice smile.

'The cliff path's just round that corner.' Daphne indicates the bend in the road. 'Though I don't think you'll get much of a photograph today, the fog's so thick. Perhaps you should come back tomorrow. If you're staying here, I mean.'

'Thank you for that wise advice, I shall do just that.' Her voice is light and pleasant sounding, but her accent's English, like someone on the radio. Not from these parts. Dilys tugs at her arm. 'Come on, Daphne, I need to get back for tea, mam's going to kill me.'

'Interesting name,' the woman says to Daphne, ignoring Dilys. 'The girl Zeus turned into a laurel tree. Do you think he asked her permission first?'

Daphne is a bit thrown by the question. She knows the story of course: their mother made sure she and Sylvia knew their myths and legends. *Tales of the Greek Heroes* used to be her favourite book before she fell for King Arthur and his gang.

'I don't know,' she says slowly, thinking aloud. 'Perhaps Zeus thought he was doing the right thing, protecting her from danger.'

The woman shakes her head. 'Oh, but that's what they always say! Brave men saving damsels in distress. You seem like a clever girl, Daphne. Don't be taken in by those old tales, most of them were written by men who hadn't a clue about women.'

She turns to Dilys. 'And will you tell me your name before you drag your poor friend away?'

'It's Dilys, my granny's middle name. It means perfect in Welsh.'

'Such a pretty name! I do like the sound of your language, though I can't understand a word of it. My name's Vita, it means life. Which isn't necessarily perfect.'

She steps away from them. 'I mustn't keep you girls from your tea. I hope we'll meet again.'

'She seems a nice lady,' says Dilys as they turn the corner on to George Street. 'And she likes my name. She was a bit rude about yours though, Daph. Did you notice the way she kept staring at you?'

Daphne does not reply. As they reach the bottom of Hangman Lane, she glances over her shoulder. The woman has not moved position, she is still standing at the side of the road, watching them. Dilys was right, Daphne had noticed the stranger's—Vita's—interest in her. She'd called her a clever girl. Nobody had ever said that to her: it was a good feeling.

Her father is on his way to open the church for evensong. He's

54

wearing his Count Dracula cloak and the funny triangular hat made of black felt which he wears in cold weather to keep his ears warm and makes him look strange and holy. He stops by the porch gate and regards her solemnly.

'You weren't being entirely truthful with Inspector Blight, were you?'

She is silent, looking down at her feet. He sighs. 'We'll need to have that little chat when I get home.'

The gate clangs behind him and he sets off down the street towards the church, his sooty cloak taking wing behind him. Daphne shrugs off her duffle coat and goes to hang it on the peg next to Sylvia's raincoat. There are smears of mud all down the back of the coat and the jagged hole in the hem is clearly visible. In her haste to get away from Inspector Blight the day before she had forgotten all about it. She unhooks the coat and takes it upstairs to the bathroom, where she tries to clean off most of the mud with a flannel. The tear looks worse than she thought. Gran will know what to do.

Their grandmother is a whizz with a needle and thread. Since they were small, she has made all their clothes—skirts and dresses, winter coats, Easter jackets. Summer frocks are the worst: Gran makes them stand for hours in vest and knickers while she pins on sleeves and collars, tightens bodices, adjusts hems. The pins stab at their bare legs, prick the tops of their arms, the delicate skin covering the collarbones. Gran takes no notice of their squirming, smarting limbs, their squawks of pain. Her fingers work deftly and patiently, and she keeps up a muttered conversation with herself, even though her mouth is full of sewing pins. Remarkably, she has never swallowed a single pin. Sylvia says if Gran and Flora Lloyd, her sewing rival and fellow member of the Mothers' Union, held a competition who could carry the most pins in their mouths, her money (of which she has plenty on account of her unsmashed pig) would be on Gran.

The old lady is dozing in her chair beside the fire, a rug pulled over her short fat legs and a plate of buttered pikelets on the little embroidered stool beside her. *Family Favourites* is on the wireless, the usual Sunday afternoon sounds. Daphne hovers in the doorway for a bit, clutching the raincoat and eyeing the pikelets. Lunch seems a long time ago. Eventually, Gran stirs and reaches for a pikelet. She gives a little start when she sees Daphne and her book slides from her lap on to the floor. *To the Devil a Daughter* is one of her favourite Dennis Wheatley novels, she must have read it a hundred times. Judging by their lurid covers, Dennis Wheatley's books are all about Satan and ghosts and murders. This cover shows a red-headed woman with her arm being twisted by a man brandishing a large cross; green-faced monsters crowd around her, waving their long warty fingers. Gran loves any book about black magic or seances. Her daughter Enid does not approve, which Daphne thinks is quite hypocritical for someone who named her own daughter after a girl magicked into a laurel tree. Sometimes Sylvia takes Gran's books to the library for her; she exchanges them for the ones she prefers to read herself, historical romances by Georgette Heyer or Jean Plaidy. Gran goes hopping mad then. 'Never go giving me that old soppy stuff, Sylvia, I can't abide it.'

Daphne picks up *To the Devil a Daughter* from the floor and places it on the stool. She hands the raincoat to Gran—'Sylvia'll kill me if she sees what's happened to it'—who puts on her glasses and examines the tear, her tongue rummaging her loose teeth for crumbs. Her body's as round as her tub chair and she has thick silvery hair which she gets 'done' every Friday morning at the hairdressers on Perrott Street, after which she walks back to Flora's house for a cup of tea and a scone or three.

'What you been up to then, girl?'

'Oh, you know, this and that, Gran.' It's a necessary evasion.

Gran grasps the sides of her chair and levers herself up on to her little fat legs and puffs over to the sewing table on the other side of the room overlooking the garden. You can hardly see the surface, submerged under bolts of material, wool, lace, ostrich feathers, little boxes of sequins. There's an oval biscuit tin crammed with zips and thimbles and dressmaker's chalk, and a brimming button box with a bosomy lady in an evening gown on the lid. It's the season for mending costumes for the church nativity play. An old suitcase spilling with clothes lies open on the floor: cardboard crowns, tinsel angels' wings and stripy dishcloths, a camel mask, sundry sheep. Daphne follows her grandmother across the carpet, stepping carefully and wishing she'd kept her shoes on—Gran's fingers are buttery as pikelets and the carpet is littered with pins and needles lying in wait for Daphne's bare feet.

'You been playing down the river again.' It's a statement not a question. Gran scrapes at a gobbet of mud stuck to the raincoat lining. 'You missed that bit when you were trying to clean up.' She peers into one of her tins and brings up a reel of blue thread, holds it against the coat. 'This'll have to do.' Then she pulls out a chair and gets to work.

Watching her grandmother plunge her needle in and out of the stiff fabric, making tiny, neat stitches, Daphne thinks of the carnival costumes Gran made for them last year. She used that same blue thread for Sylvia's Alice dress and matching hairband. Condemned to be the Mock Turtle, Daphne had to make do with an old Omo box covered with stretchy grey vinyl.

Gran takes her scissors and snips the thread. She holds out the coat to Daphne. 'That's the best I can do, girl; better hang it up again before your sister sees. Worse still your mother, you'd be for it then.'

Daphne examines the hem. Gran's done a good job, the tear is barely visible, just the faintest line of stitching. At the doorway she pauses, for a question is nagging at her.

'Gran, do you think dead people can put a curse on you? I mean, if you took something from a grave by accident ... you know, like what happened with the pharaohs.'

Gran is now back in her tub chair with Dennis. 'I'm sure they can if they want to,' she says briskly. 'I reckon the lady in grey would be one for a curse if she set her mind to it.'

She is surely teasing. 'Come on Gran, I'm asking you a serious question.'

Gran lowers *To the Devil a Daughter* and pops a cold pikelet into her mouth. 'And here's my serious answer. It's a pity you weren't at your piano lesson on Friday, Daphne Morgan. I bet that poor woman's cursing you from up there, or the other place.'

CHAPTER 11

Detective Inspector Ronald Blight of Scotland Yard dons his grey flannel suit, overcoat and hat, and steps out of Madras Boarding House on to George Street. He sniffs the winter air. It is dank, sharp, with a fishy tang of sea and mud flat. Above the street, a thick mist is slowly descending; it folds itself across the roof tops and blurs the lofty first floor windows of the Georgian houses and the meaner attic casements above the shops. Tall, imperturbable, set of jaw and hungry of eye, the inspector sets off to investigate the ancient township. His polished city brogues rat-tat smartly along the pavement. He peers in through windows and shop doors, raises his brown fedora to the head-scarved women with their shopping baskets and fixes the young men idling against lamp posts with his grim pursed lips and immutable, glassy stare.

Detective Inspector Blight knocks at the dark green front door of Elvira House—in this odd little town, he has noted, all the houses have names not numbers. There is no response, no sound of approaching feet. He takes off his hat and rearranges the strands of thinning hair, Brylcreemed across his bony scalp. Waits. Still no response from inside the house. He unbuttons his coat, and from his waistcoat pocket takes out the handsome fob watch on its silver chain. He flips it open. *To RDS with gratitude 1956,* engraved in silver filigree on the lid. 9.30 am. Blight snaps the lid shut, tucks the watch back inside his waistcoat. He lifts the iron knocker and raps it hard against the door, once, twice. The green shutters of Elvira House remain firmly closed. Through the glass fanlight above the door, he can see a light bulb, suspended from a long cord attached to the ceiling rose. It swings slowly back and forth, stirred by the draught from an open window somewhere at the back of the house. His fingers drum a restless rhythm: he is impatient with the door's stubborn unyielding to his summons. He turns his back on it and reaches into his coat pocket, brings out a small leather-bound notebook with a gold-topped pencil attached by a piece of thin black ribbon. The page opens at a list of names and addresses. Inspector Blight runs his eye down the page; it alights on Thomas, Ivy. Elvira House. He licks the tip of his pencil and draws a neat cross in the margin. Ivy's is not the only name crossed out. The doors of more than half the houses along this street are firmly shut against the man from Scotland Yard. He is not welcome here.

The inspector thrusts the notebook back into his pocket, turns, and rat-tats his way towards the end of the street, past the silent watchful houses. Whose is that head so swiftly withdrawing from the first-floor window of Portland House? Whose hand is twitching the gauzy curtains of Alma Villa? Whose light footsteps, receding down the narrow passageway alongside the Moriah Chapel? More crosses appear in the margins of the notebook. A large gull, circling low above the butcher's shop to spy for offal, screeches and swoops at him. A second alights in a flurry of feathers on the weathervane above the whitewashed steeple of the Town Hall and sheds a single, white feather. It flutters down on to the paving stone beside his right shoe. From the bow window of the butcher's, the pig's head stares at him with slitty raisin eyes and a mocking grin.

Though Ronald Blight is making scant progress with his enquiries this morning, Sergeant Phillips and Constable Jenkins are zealous in their hunt for a wellington boot. Up and down the streets they go, in and out of the patrician houses, the workers' cottages, the hovels of the poor. They speak to the solicitor and the town clerk, the farm labourer, the council house tenant on the estate above the town, the surly cockleman, the vicar, though Constable Jenkins, who sings in the choir, blushes to the roots of his ginger moustache as he kneels in the hallway to take a print from Rev Morgan's size twelve wellington boot, still encrusted with mud from the potato patch. The doors of the township fling open for the sergeant and his young assistant: the two of them are well liked, locals born and bred, happy to share a pint and a throw of darts at the Black Lion on their off-duty night, turn the occasional blind eye to a poaching or a back-door home-brew fiddle, dress up in purple wigs and frilly garters for the rugby club float on carnival day. The townspeople in the main are content to have their boot and fingerprints taken by Constable Jenkins, their whereabouts on the evening of the murder noted down in Sergeant Phillips's black ledger. To assist the police in this enquiry is proof they have nothing to hide: their wellingtons are innocent.

Not so the muddy boot mark on the floor in Miss O'Dowd's front room. The thorough search of cottage and garden has found nothing of interest beyond this print. The murder weapons are still at large. Along the mud flats and the shell-strewn margins of the estuary, the stooping line of searchers moves slowly onwards, swollen by people from surrounding villages and farmsteads. They bend low amongst the spiky clumps of marram grass; peer into the muddy tidal pools, the little creeks and pills; stumble across the rocks of blood red sandstone and the treacherous mounds of stinking, slippery seaweed. The curlews and the oyster catchers stab their beaks deep into the muddy reaches while, perched upon a distant rock in the middle of the estuary, a stilted heron watches the tide, impassive as a statue.

The town clock strikes a loud midday. Inspector Blight has had quite enough. He turns into the Captain's Arms at the corner of Hangman Lane and enters the close, beery fug. Conversation dies around him as he approaches the bar and orders a pint of the local bitter and a packet of plain crisps. He pays the surly woman behind the bar and settles himself at a round wooden table in the corner by the window. The talk starts up again. Men in working clothes and caps call to each other across the room in unfamiliar accents and this language he cannot understand. Sniggering, a shared joke, heads turning with sly looks at him from faces hardened by weather and tough living. Whispers, nudges—they all know who he is.

From the left pocket of his coat Blight fishes out a packet of Navy

Cut and a small box of matches. Only his second smoke of the day so far, a good innings from a 40-a-day man. The loud convivial pubs of London are better suited to his temperament than this damp Welsh backwater, these scrawny, shuttered men. He has nothing in common with any of them. He makes a mental note never to cross the Severn again. He lights up his cigarette and takes a long drag. Slowly, he exhales the comforting blue-grey smoke across the room.

'Spare us one?'

The voice is rough, throaty. A young man is sitting at the neighbouring table. He has a lined, old man's face, tiny veins threading his cheeks, a livid scar running from the corner of his left eyebrow to the hairline. Blight takes a cigarette from his packet, lights it with his own, hands it to the man who draws it in deep, blows out a trembling smoke ring.

'Much obliged, sir. Better than Woodbines any day.'

He gets up, shuffles his chair alongside Blight's table.

'Found the knife then, have you?'

The inspector, practised listener that he is, says nothing. He opens the packet of crisps, proffers it to the young man. Calloused, grubby fingers reach inside, snaffle a quick handful.

'Ta very much.' He leans forward and, cocking a look back at the others by the bar, says loudly, 'You got the wrong man, inspector. Johnny Nebo's never hurt a fly, good as gold he is.'

The bar room has gone silent again; nobody moves. A man half turns on his stool, his frothing beer glass stilled at his lips in the action of drinking.

Blight leans back in his chair, lightly drums the sticky tabletop with his fingers. He takes another drag of his cigarette.

'You sure about that, lad?'

The man's jaw drops. His face reddens, a flush of colour spreading from throat to forehead. He gnaws at his thumbnail. Blight waits, fingers still beating out the rhythm. The lad starts to fidget in his chair, picks up a beer mat, turns it over and over.

'Yeh, well, we all knows Johnny means no harm.' He swivels

round to include the group of men by the bar. 'That right, boys?' One or two are nodding, but no-one speaks. The boy turns back to Blight.

'He's a child, Johnny is, see. Don't know no better. But he's good with his hands and a sharp knife, he can gut a fish in sec ...'

He breaks off, suddenly aware he's said the wrong thing. He pushes back his chair and gets to his feet, muttering to the silent audience at his back. 'I'm just saying, that's all.' Then he's out through the door. From the window Blight watches him hurry up the street—a thin, gangly lad, hunched against the cold, his ragged trousers flapping above his ankles. He takes out his notebook and pencil and writes, slowly, deliberately. The watching men shift uneasily on their stools; they tug at their caps, whisper to each other. 'Like the bloody Gestapo,' mutters one. Blight smiles to himself as he writes another line of gibberish. Works every time, this trick; won't be long before one of them snitches. As if by agreement, the customers down their pints, wipe their mouths with grubby hands and shuffle out of the pub. Only he is left now, and he is in no hurry. He lights another cigarette, ambles over to the bar and orders another pint of best.

Over his beer he watches the barmaid wash and dry the glasses, placing each one on the rack below the counter. She's a neat, small woman, unobtrusive in navy cardigan and skirt—not the kind of blowsy London barmaid he likes, with a ready smile and Jack-flash wit. This woman has a tired, drawn face, framed by a helmet of brown permed hair. Her hands are work-roughened, the skin chapped and sore-looking. Slowly, he taps the end of his cigarette into the ashtray.

'What's your opinion of John Parry? Bit of a child, is he?'

The woman puts the glass down, wipes her hands on her apron. She takes the ashtray and bends down to empty it into a bin beside her. He takes another drag, exhales and blows a smoke ring into the air.

'Good with a knife, I hear.'

63

That stops her in her tracks. She straightens up immediately and glares at him, dislike curling the corners of her mouth.

'You'd better be careful what you say about Johnny round here. The police shouldn't be arresting someone just because he happened to be by her house. Just because the poor dab can't speak properly, or hear what people are saying, that doesn't mean he's a criminal. Three days they had him up the police station and nobody come to help him the whole time he was there.'

For a long moment he says nothing, leaves her words hanging in the indignant air.

'You haven't answered my question.'

She hesitates. 'Well of course he's good with a knife, he's a fisherman, same as most people round here, or else they're butchers. Cows, sheep, fish, what else do you use to gut the things? You can ask anyone, they'll all say the same. Johnny's a good boy. People like you know nothing about goodness.'

She nods at the clock on the opposite wall.

'Closing time.'

Inspector Blight leaves the Captain's Arms and turns up Hangman Lane. The afternoon is greying, and he tightens his coat collar against the chill now rising from the sea end of the street. Outside the open doors of the bakery, he inhales the sweet, burnt smell of new bread and watches the baker place the long-handled iron paddle into the oven and bring out three small, perfectly risen loaves with crusty tops. One by one he slides them onto the wooden racks to cool. Red-faced, intent, he thrusts the paddle once more into the flames and chooses not to see the stranger at the door.

Ronald Blight walks on, takes the left-hand turn at the top of the street and makes his way along the cliffside walk. Beyond the rusted iron railings entwined with ivy tresses and cloudy old man's beard, the estuary in this grey light appears featureless, void of any sound or movement. He approaches the end of the walk before the woods begin and stops at the little gate above the Ferry House. A thin curl of smoke is rising from one of the chimneys. At the landing stage, the ferry boat, covered by a green tarpaulin, floats motionless upon the water. As he starts down the steep path towards the house, the gardener in him notes an unexpected blush of cyclamen nestling amongst the mossy stones, clutches of early snowdrops, the succulent leaves of sedum. Two cheerful pots of purple-yellow violas stand on either side of the front door.

He has to bend his head to enter the kitchen, a plain room furnished only with a scrubbed table and some rickety wooden chairs. The walls are mostly bare, the green distemper patched and peeling in the corners. On one wall a little black and white sketch— delicate birds flying against a wintry sky. Even from this distance he can appreciate the artistry, though the crudely fashioned wooden frame does it little justice. Elsewhere in the room, a grimy iron range, cookpots suspended above it from hooks hammered into the stone wall, one window looking seaward. The room smells of seaweed and the delicate scent of some white hyacinths growing in a chipped blue bowl on the sill.

The younger brother, Emrys, does most of the talking. The other one, Ifor, an ugly chap with grizzled hair and beard, sits opposite him at the table, glowering. Blight knows the type. Short answers, short fuse. Not someone to pick a fight with. Emrys's replies are defensive, as he would expect. His nephew Johnny's a good lad, never been in trouble. Does odd jobs round town, gardening, bit of fishing. Earns his keep and a bit over for baccy and comics. Never had a problem with understanding simple commands.

'What were his movements on the afternoon of the murder?'

Ifor pushes his chair back, leans across the table. Fury sparks in the eyes.

'Look Inspector, we've said this over and over. Phillips wrote it all down. If you want to see Johnny for yourself, he's down by there.'

He indicates the front door and mutters something in Welsh to Emrys, who takes Blight outside and leads him down a steep flight of steps towards the shoreline where a young man is at work scraping old paint off the sides of a wooden dinghy. He seems to sense their presence for he looks up and comes over to meet them. Wiping his hands first on the side of his overalls, he greets the inspector by taking his hand in both of his and giving it a vigorous shake, smiling and nodding his head. Average height, lean, muscular. Sandy hair. Eyes grey-green. Wide forehead, flattish nose (broken?) Open features, nothing remarkable. Missing two front teeth. Bruises on his right hand below the knuckles. A deep cut above his left eyebrow.

Blight has met all types in his criminal work—men and women, foreigners, every colour under the sun—but has never had dealings with a deaf and dumb person. He tries the usual pleasantries: introduces himself, explains the purpose of his visit. The young man stares blankly at him, then looks across to Emrys, shrugging his shoulders.

'You won't get nothing out of him, sir. He knows what happened to that poor lady, he does cry about it sometimes, shows he's sorry she's dead. He used to fetch her firewood you know, do a bit of gardening and digging for her. There's lots of widows round 'ere, see, from the Wars and all. Old women on their own, like, never got the chance of a husband living. They always need a bit of help.'

Emrys politely accompanies Blight back up the path to the cliff walk.

'What happened to his mother, your sister?'

'Sister-in-law. Mari died when he was four. Drowned herself out by the Head. Round the twist she was half the time, going off in the middle of the night, like, dragging the little boy with her. Poor dab didn't know whether he was coming or going. When she passed, her family didn't want to know him, did they, nobody wants a child with a handicap.'

He seems to anticipate Blight's next question. 'His dad was our oldest brother, Jack. Ship got torpedoed in '42. Mari was living with us by then, only right we kept the boy after she went. Fair play, he's been as good as gold all along.'

Near the gate Blight stops to smell the yellow flowers of a twiggy shrub bordering the path. 'Hamamelis mollis, witch hazel. Are you the gardener?'

Emrys gives a short laugh. 'Not me, Johnny's the one, loves his plants he does. Gets them from Miss Bowen up at Beacon House when he's been doing work for her, she gives him cuttings he can grow on, like. And his mam was fond of flowers, he probably gets it from her.'

'Why do the local people call him Nebo? It's not a real word, is it? I've never heard of it.'

Emrys says. 'He's had that nickname for years. Neb is the real word, means 'nobody' in Welsh. A bit cruel, I know, but then somebody added an 'o' on the end, for the ring of it, and the name stuck. His mother called him John after his dad. I suppose if you can't hear and you can't speak, people think you're a nobody, don't they?'

On his way back towards the town the inspector makes a detour, turning left and following a cobbled lane curving steeply down towards the shore. His brogues ring sharply on the cobblestones as he passes a pair of low-eaved cottages leaning against each other like gossiping neighbours. On the opposite side of the lane a high stone wall marks the boundary of the castle grounds.

The lane comes out on to the estuary foreshore, a long stretch of sand and shingle, blunted by clumps of purple rock. Blight walks out towards the sea, a silvery line on the horizon. The ground here is firm underfoot, matted with eel grass and the trailing roots of buckthorn and purslane. Near the strandline, clumps of bladder wrack trail salty fingers across the mud. The place reminds him of a different location, a different case: mid-winter, the lower reaches of the Thames near Gravesend, a woman drowned. A trainee detective with the Met, he found the body in a foot of water, wedged between a steep mud bank and the rotting timbers of an old fishing smack; the head was caved in and the ankles bound tightly together by a rusty chain. Now that was a bleak old place, mud and water as far as the eye could see, not a sound except the lonely cries of birds and the river a cold gun-metal grey running low between the flats. You half expected the convict Magwitch to rise from the mist brandishing his file.

The inspector halts, listens. This place, in contrast, is alive with sound: the mudbanks are groaning and gurgling like hungry stomachs, he can hear the clicking and bubbling of thousands of cockles below the surface of the sand, like air inside a soda bottle. A few feet away from where he's standing tiny wavelets are lapping the stones, starting to creep across the sand. The narrow channel of water on his right is brim full, beginning to spread across the mudflats, gobbling up the seaweed even as he watches. This tide is swift on the turn. It may appear to be a gentler landscape than the grim Essex marshes, more subtle in aspect, perhaps, but no less treacherous.

He quickly retraces his steps towards the safety of the foreshore, the ground spongy, less certain, beneath his feet. Above him, the castle ruins rise sheer from their wooded base, crumbling battlements curtained by thick ivy and stunted sycamore, with great gaps in the walls where windows might have been. Those castle builders knew where to choose their spots, he thinks, shading his eyes with a hand as he gazes at the ruins. From up there you could watch the smugglers' boats stealing in on the tide: bedraggled pilgrims crossing the Gwennol on the way to the shrine of St David in the far west (two pilgrimages worth one to Rome, according to the guidebook at Madras House), the glittering ambush of weapons massing on the opposite hillside. He's read the local history, absorbed the warning: never trust the Welsh. Those Parry brothers, so quick on the draw to protect the mute; they know he's guilty, he can see it in their faces, the way they look at him. And you don't get those bruises and a nasty cut on the forehead from fishing. There'll be a story behind it. Just a matter of time before the man cracks, he's seen that happen so many times.

He stops abruptly, policeman's hackles raised by the smack of a heavy stone hitting the rocks below the western tower. Rocking back on his heels, Blight scans the broken walls and battlements, the thin arrow slits. A rusted iron railing torn from its mounting dangles in mid-air from a flight of steps, a wall of thick ivy curtains a broken doorway. The inspector's sharp eyes detect a movement near the top of the tower, two small figures outlined against the darkening sky. Bloody Welshies, up to their tricks again. The tide is puddling at his feet and in the greying light he hears the hollow cries of wintering birds. A cold fish out of water, Blight shivers and turns up the collar of his overcoat. The first flakes of snow settle on the dark cloth.

Daphne wakes early. Snow light fills her bedroom with strangeness. In the wallpaper the proud lords on their dappled horses are stilled beneath the trees, the hooded falcon is frozen on the lady's wrist. A noble deer hound strains against his golden chain while beneath her feet the mossy carpet turns to silvery dust. All sound is muffled, spellbound. Even John Edgar, itinerant farm labourer, flapping past her bedroom window in his outsize wellington boots on his way to milking, does not disturb the magic of this moment.

Inspector Blight, wrapped tightly in his cashmere dressing gown (Harrods of London), draws aside the curtains of Mrs Price's best bedroom in Madras House. With his thumbnail, he scratches off the icy cobweb pattern on the inside of the glass and peers out at the silent, snowbound street. He had not expected this.

Granny Gloria, snug beneath her flannel sheets, woollen blankets and embroidered counterpane, opens her eyes and smiles up at her daughter Jean. Who puts her strong arms underneath her mother's little body and slides her up the bed, light as a bird, plumps her pillows, tucks a shawl around her and says, 'It's been snowing all night, mam, you've no idea!'

Johnny Nebo, standing tiptoe on the rocks below the Ferry House, opens his arms wide and embraces the whirling snow, the gulls and oystercatchers, the solitary heron on the mud spit. There is a woman, standing alone on a sandbank in the middle of the estuary. Her back is turned away from him for she is searching for the sea, hidden behind the silvery curves of Cefn y Morfil. The young man's eyes are full of tears.

And Miss Eleanor O'Dowd, shrouded and coffined in the county morgue, her lapsed, still Catholic hands folded across her bony chest, Sonata 29 tucked in close beside her, waits on for justice.

CHAPTER 12

'Take that thing off this minute, Alun Hughes. You're not in the Infants anymore.'

Alun, younger son of Mrs Hughes the paper shop, removes the antlers and his mother's black wig. He pulls a face. 'Just a bit of fun, sir.'

'And the rest.'

The boy sighs, unties the cotton wool beard, takes off the sunglasses and the tinsel. 'C'mon sir, it's Christmas.'

'Not for another week. Get out your Ridouts, page 35 comprehension, questions 1–10. Heads down, I'm timing you.'

Mr Duckford sits at his high desk, sniffling. He has a bad cold and his long hook nose is red and sore. It's too cold to go outside for a smoke and there are still ten days to go before the end of term. In the crate on top of the stove the ice is melting in the milk bottles; the children will have to stay in at breaktime today, no-one wants broken legs and arms before the end of term.

A hand is up at the back of the class.

'Yes, Christine.' Stuck on question 3 as usual: *In your own words explain the meaning of the following idioms.*

'Why's a pig bein' poked, sir?'

He shoots a glare at Jimmy Richards spluttering behind his hand. 'This is a test, Christine, I can't give you the answers. You won't get any help when it's the real eleven-plus.'

Christine huffs and tosses her pigtails, chews the end of her pencil, mutters ''s not fair'. Mr Duckford's seen it all before, many times. Girls like Christine Miller, no-hopers, what's the point of putting them through the exam every year when they'll end up having babies and picking cockles or, if they're lucky, behind the counter in Woolworths. Daphne is on the last question already, her favourite part of the comprehension. *Imagine you are one of the characters in the extract. Write a paragraph about what happens next.* Mr Duckford, now pacing between the rows of desks and dabbing at his sore nose, hovers above her shoulder. 'It's only a paragraph they want, Miss Morgan, not a novel.'

Outside in the playground, the snow is falling thickly now, great gobbets of it drifting down past the windows, catching on the ledges, settling in the gutters at the bottom of the classroom wall. The pupils fuss and fidget on their chairs, suck the ends of their pencils, pull faces, at each other, at their teacher when he isn't looking. The eleven-plus is a summer's lifetime away. Come on, sir, please. Let us out.

At half past two that afternoon, the classroom stove steaming with wet socks and gloves, Mr Duckford receives a message from the headmaster. Inspector Blight is in school, wants to ask the older pupils a few questions: nothing too complicated, won't take long. The children pause from glueing paper chains and fixing glitter stars to their Christmas calendars. They sit up straight and fold their arms as instructed. In his great black coat and hat glistening with melting snow, the inspector is taller than Mr Duckford and twice as scary. He removes his hat and leather gloves, places them on the teacher's desk beside the pile of *Better English Book 3*. A hush descends upon the classroom. Even Jimmy Richards is quiet, his face paler than usual, arms hugging his narrow chest. The inspector clears his throat and turns his cold attention to the faces in front of him. He is awkward with children of any age; he doesn't like them if truth be told, tricksy, wayward creatures. Give him a hardened criminal any day, know where you stand with one of them.

'Thank you, Mr Duck, for allowing me to interrupt your lesson for a minute or two.' Mr 'Duck' nods, sends a warning glare across the quietly sniggering room. The inspector eyes with distaste the cheerful chaos spilling over the desks. 'I see you are busy with your Christmas artwork. And very nice it is too.' Scrawny little beasts, he thinks, some of them need a good wash behind the ears. No evidence of the dentist either, judging by the state of their teeth.

'As you all know, boys and girls, the police are investigating a murder. Lots of adults in this town—your parents, your aunties, uncles—are assisting us in our enquiries and that is very helpful. But I believe...' He makes a pause here for maximum effect. 'In fact, I am strongly convinced, you children can be even more helpful to us than the grownups.' His wintry eyes, roving across the silenced classroom, alight on the red-haired girl in the corner next to the window, the vicar's daughter, who he suspects knows more than she's telling. Her head is down, she's trying to hide behind the boy sitting in front of her, a telltale sign. His policeman's instinct knows she is not an innocent.

'Now, boys and girls, let's suppose you and your friends see a stranger hanging around Glanmorfa, looking a bit suspicious. You'd tell your parents about him, wouldn't you?' A few heads nod, look round at each other to check, return their scared eyes to his face. He smiles. 'Of course you would. Now, suppose you, or perhaps one of your friends, happened to be playing in Church Street the Friday before last, around teatime, and you saw a stranger going into Miss O'Dowd's house, or coming out of it, you'd tell someone about that, wouldn't you?' A few more nods and a pig-tailed little girl in the back row looks nicely terrified.

Now, the inspector becomes more friendly. He perches on the end of Mr Duckford's desk and looks benevolently down upon them, especially at the red-haired girl in the corner.

'Well done, boys and girls, that's exactly the kind of good behaviour I would expect from you. Now I want you to think hard. What if that person you or your friend saw going into—or coming out of—Miss O'Dowd's house wasn't a stranger at all, but someone you all knew well, someone who has always lived in Glanmorfa. Would you tell your parents about him?' One or two of the children start to nod, then stop, realising it's the wrong answer. The inspector leans forward.

73

'No, of course you wouldn't tell them. He's not a stranger. However, let's imagine that there's something odd about the way that well-known person is behaving. Perhaps he's in a bit of a rush, perhaps his clothes are a bit dirty, a bit bloody even. What should you do then, boys and girls?'

Silence. Lots of upturned, anxious faces, chewing fingernails, wiping snot. Except for the vicar's daughter, still keeping her head down. The question could have been better phrased but he's running out of time, and patience. 'I'll tell you what you would do. You would inform your parents immediately about what you'd seen and then they would go straight to the police and report it to them.'

From the back of the classroom a boy half raises his hand, wavers, puts it down. Blight is on to him. 'You, lad with the striped jumper, what do you want to say?'

The boy stumbles to his feet. Beneath the patched grey flannel shorts his legs are trembling.

'Please sir, are you talking about Johnny Nebo, sir? Is he the murderer?'

Inspector Blight gives him a long, hard look and Jimmy goes red in the face and sits down. The man gets up from Mr Duckford's desk, pulls on his gloves. He addresses the class once more.

'I am not naming any names, yet. My message to all of you is simple. If you know something about this case, if you have seen something or someone out of the ordinary or if you hear your parents or members of your family talking about it, then it is your duty to tell me or the headmaster immediately. Do you all understand? This is very very serious. Thank you for your time, Mr...er... Duck.'

The children exchange fearful, wondering glances. Inspector Blight takes up his hat, claps it on his head. A brief nod to Mr Duckford and he's gone.

Outside, the snow has stopped but the high-ceilinged classroom feels chilly, ice light; Christmas cutting and sticking have lost their appeal. Grim-faced Mr Duckford, pressing a reddened nose into his damp handkerchief, instructs the class to tidy the room in silence. The bin fills up with tinsel shreds, gluey scraps of card and cotton wool, soggy blotting paper. Down in the Infants at the bottom of the playground, Miss Tucker is ringing the bell for home time; they can hear the distant screams and chatter of the little ones milling at the school gate. Dilys and Christine, monitors this week, collect the pens and pencils, the empty inkwells for washing at the sink. The pupils stack their chairs on top of their desks and line up in pairs for dismissal. Janice shoves past the girl in front and joins Daphne. Behind them Graham whispers, 'He was looking at you the whole time, Daph, do you think he knows what we done?'

Mr Duckford stops them at the classroom door with a parcel wrapped in brown paper. 'Could you lot take these practice tests up to Martin, his mother's asking? She wants him to keep up with the rest of the class.'

'Isn't he coming back to school then?' Graham asks. Mr Duckford shakes his head. 'Poor lad's not well enough, they're not sure what's wrong with him but his mother doesn't want him out in this weather.'

They take the parcel of books and set off along the street towards the church, doing skids on the slushy pavement, showering their clothes with snow from the vicarage hedge as they pass and trying to snowball the cats outside the Memorial Hall. Martin lives out of town, at the top of Church Lane. They take the short cut through the graveyard and chase each other up the slippery path, leaving a trail of slushy footprints across the lumpy gravemounds and tombstones. Melting snow slops from the branches of the yew trees. Somewhere in the undergrowth a lone bird calls. Janice, running ahead, has stopped in front of the bone house. When the others catch up with her, they see the iron door is now padlocked. Janice turns to Daphne and smiles.

'You put it back then.'

Daphne does not answer. They file through the kissing gate at the top of the steps out on to Church Lane. Martin's house is up on the right, set back from the road behind a thick hawthorn hedge. His mother answers the door and leads them into the kitchen where Martin is sitting in a chair by the fire with a copy of *The Beano* on his lap. He seems pleased to see them though they are shocked he looks so wan and bleary eyed, not at all like the Martin they know, full of plans and restless energy.

When his mother's out of the room, Janice whispers, 'You'll be better soon, you know. Daphne's put it back.'

Martin looks at her, a bit puzzled, rubbing his sore eyes, and suddenly doubles up, seized by a racking cough which shakes his thin frame. His mother rushes in with a glass of water.

'I think you'd better go,' she says to them. 'Be sure to thank Mr Duckford for the papers, won't you. I'll see Marty does them when he's feeling up to it.'

They trail disconsolately down Church Lane. The light is fading and there's a cold mist coming in from the sea, wreathing the spectral trees and hedgerows. They take the longer route this time, avoiding the graveyard. None of them wants an encounter with Captain Arthur Bevan, late of the Bevan House next door to the vicarage, whose drowned body was washed up on Glanmorfa sands in 1884 and buried in the mariners' plot by the west door of the church. Gran swears she saw him once on her way home from the Mothers' Union festival. She was on her own because Flora Lloyd was away visiting her daughter in Milford. Captain Bevan's wraith was hovering by the church path, she said; it was dressed in his naval uniform, white breeches and a blue frock coat.

'Do you think Marty's going to die?' Graham asks.

Janice says to Daphne, 'You'd better ask your dad to do a special prayer, just in case the curse has got him.'

Ronald Blight leaves the Juniors entrance and turns left along George Street. He is hopeful that his message has left its imprint. He remembers that's how they caught the Hackney strangler in '42—school kiddie grassed on his uncle after the class had a talking to from the chaps on the case. Had him banged up the day after. Four days he's been in Glanmorfa, the case should be in the bag by now, given his track record. Despite the police searches, the careful combing through foreshore and marsh, the witness interviews, the measuring of boot soles, he still has no concrete evidence for an arrest.

'Wrap it up before Christmas, Blight.' Behind the Chief's instructions lies a host of promises: the expected promotion to detective superintendent; headlines in *The Times*—'London sleuth triumphs again in murder case'; a further chapter in his forthcoming memoirs *Tales from the Great Detective*. During the long evenings after tea, ensconced in one of the wing-backed armchairs in Mrs Price's chilly front room with the one bar heater, he goes over the details of the case as reported by Sergeant Phillips and his team.

Parry's fingerprints are all over the dead woman's kitchen and the fireplace, but then so are they evident in most of the houses in this town—he chops wood, carries coal, makes up fires, runs errands for all the old ladies, and by God there are a surprising number of them: war widows, spinsters, older women whose husbands are too frail for physical labour of any kind. In all probability Parry is guilty, but the town has other suspects. That surly crew in the pub, for instance, with their suspicious eyes and hard labourers' fists—any one of them could have done her in. He's heard the common gossip, she had money hidden in the house. That young man with the scarred face who begged the smoke off him, he was just that bit too keen to appear to be defending Parry. And what about the uncles? The softer one, Emrys, perhaps not, too protective of the nephew, but the other one? You wouldn't want to tangle with him on a dark night. There are other lines still to pursue: getting this wrong could harm Ronald Blight's reputation.

A post van speeding up Perrot Street takes the corner too tight and an icy slush drenches the polished brogues and neatly tailored turn-ups of the inspector's trousers. The day's snow is melting fast, replaced by a chilly sea fog spreading inland across the tidal pools, up along the lanes and alleyways and into the town. Must be something to do with the location, Blight speculates, all these old houses crouched in this damp hollow between hillside and sea where snow lasts no longer than a day. No wonder that teacher and half the population seem to have a cold; he can feel the beginnings of one himself. He must finish the case as soon as possible, so he can leave this benighted country and get home to the comforts of Palmers Green.

At the foot of the narrow flight of steps leading to the front door of Madras House, Ronald Blight halts. He stays very still, staring at the worn stone, his fingers lightly drumming the iron handrail. What if something has been missed, that clinching piece of evidence so often hiding in plain sight at the scene of a crime? The inspector turns away from the steps and continues along George Street, around the corner into Church Street. He passes the forecourt of Jubilee Garage, dark and shuttered in the freezing fog, the locked Memorial Hall and the now silent milking parlour of Pentre Farm. He crosses the road to the row of cottages. Stops outside the middle one and from his pocket takes out the key to number 3, where for weeks there has been neither cheerful light nor echoes of the 'Hammerklavier'.

CHAPTER 13

At four thirty that afternoon Sylvia is walking up George Street from the bus stop, her satchel with its heavy load of books dragging at her shoulders. As she opens the gate of the vicarage porch she is pushed aside by her grandmother, muffled in thick navy overcoat and hat and carrying a small suitcase. From inside the house, she hears her mother scream, 'And don't come back!' Over her shoulder Gran retorts, 'No I won't, you cruel witch.' She bangs the gate shut and loudly huffs and puffs her way up the street so all the neighbours will hear. Sylvia rolls her eyes and goes inside.

Down in the kitchen, Daphne is painting a nativity scene at the table. Her paintbox has the perfect blue for Mary's cloak, cerulean, which matches the tips of the angels' wings. She dips the brush into the jampot of water and watches the blue swirls cloud the glass. She hears the porch gate clang and looks up to see the top of Gran's navy felt hat with the jaunty peacock feather bobbing past the window. Off to Flora's again. The sisters are unperturbed: their mother and their grandmother have been working up to this for weeks, following the usual pattern. First, the Snide Remarks: 'Mrs Daley says there's no point cleaning The Furthest Room, your clutter keeps jamming the hoover'; 'the Mothers' Union are asking why the vicar's wife missed the meeting again last week'; 'Hywel says he couldn't eat your sausage pie, mother, it was disgustingly undercooked'; 'that shade of red really doesn't suit you, Enid'. Next, the Mannered Silence, each keeping to their own part of the house for days, looking the other way if they pass in a corridor. After that, the inevitable Explosion.

Sylvia comes into the room, throws her satchel on the floor and flops into a chair beside the fire. From the scullery beyond the kitchen comes the sound of breaking glass, a plate smashing on the floor. Silence. A few minutes later their mother enters, marches past them to the boot room. She returns with the dustpan and brush and goes back out to the scullery without a word to either of them. Sylvia fishes out a copy of *Seventeen* from her satchel. Daphne dips her clean brush into the paintbox and selects vermilion. With extreme care she colours in the lining of the Virgin's cloak—red for blood of martyred babies, poisonous yew berries, the splintered skulls of Beaker women and piano teachers. In an hour Gran will be back from Flora's, replete with sympathy and tea cake, and they will have shepherd's pie for supper because it's Wednesday. The debris of their battlefield is cleared; wordlessly, Enid and her mother have agreed a truce.

Their father joins them for supper. He looks harassed as he always does this time of year. He doesn't ask the girls about their day or tease Sylvia about her latest boyfriend, Darren Gough, who sings in the choir. Even Rusty, lying cravenly beside his chair hopeful of scraps, gets short shrift. No point asking him to pray for poor Martin, Daphne thinks. Rev Morgan ploughs on through the gristly shepherd's pie and then goes back to the study, shutting the door firmly behind him. His mind is clogged with Christmas lists: sermons to prepare, readers to organise, the nativity play to oversee. How many home communions, how many visits to the sick and dying? Besides St Mary's he has two other rural parishes to tend; many of his parishioners live outside the town, in farms and cottages, down rutted lanes and muddy tracks. They all need visiting at Christmas. Enid's always going on about it. You need a curate, she tells him, ask the Bishop next time he visits. Fat chance, he thinks, the diocese has barely enough money to pay its vicars, let alone provide them with an assistant. Down in the kitchen the sisters help their mother clear the table then Sylvia goes up to her room to do her homework and Daphne returns to painting the stable donkey. On the radio the weather forecast is warning of an arctic front heading in from the Atlantic.

Ronald Blight stands in the gloom of Eleanor O'Dowd's narrow hallway. So far as he knows, nobody has entered her cottage since the forensic search. The place smells clammy with the fustiness of absence. Emptied of human habitation—the warmth of a coal fire, the whistling kettle—it's already reverting to its riverine origins. From the ground beneath the worn flagstones the damp is rising. Blight opens the door of the room on his right. His eyes are immediately drawn to the ugly gap in the floor where the flagstone bearing the imprint of the boot has been removed. He snaps on the light; in the centre of this small room the single bulb in its glass shade casts a bleak light across the walls. Inspector Blight stands at the threshold of the room, his sharp eyes noting everything. He listens. Crime scenes often yield their secrets in the quiet aftermath of violence; their echoes can be better heard in the gap of time.

The heavy curtains are still drawn across the window which faces the street. An old-maidish damask print—pale hydrangea heads against a purple background—their sagging hems and bunched pleats suggest a remnant from a grander, wider window. The same flowered material covers the long piano stool and the cushion on the green armchair. He notes the turkey rug in front of the fireplace, worn and faded, but the quality unusually fine. Along the yellowing limewashed walls is a range of hunting prints in gilt frames—hard-faced men on sturdy horses, the vivid fox cornered by hounds.

There are patches of damp below the window, cobwebs looping the beams. He runs his finger lightly across the top of one of the picture frames and it comes away coated with a viscous mix of soot and dust. Evidently not so house proud, the deceased. That old plantstand in the corner's not seen polish for a good while.

The Steinway piano, on the other hand, is definitely no stranger to beeswax. Ronnie Blight of Palmers Green, only son of Robert Blight, carpenter and French polisher, knows craftsmanship when he sees it. From the doorway he admires its graceful lines, the way the light teases out the deeper gleam of ebony, the rosewood panels' satiny sheen, the gilded lettering. This glorious piece is in the wrong place, it seems to him: it requires a gracious room, hung about with rich fabrics and oil paintings. There should be space around it and a hushed attentive air. Reverence, that's the word which comes to mind. Inspector Blight approaches the Steinway and carefully raises its shining black lid. He strokes the surface of an ivory key. Depresses it. Hears the true bass G deep in the belly of the instrument.

Alas, he never had the opportunity to learn to play the piano, though there was money enough for his father's beer and weekly flutter at the bookies, his only solace after the bad war injury he never talked about, which kept him out of work for the rest of his life. His mother's cleaning jobs brought in just enough to feed the three of them and pay the rent. It was she who instilled in him and his sister the hard graft which got them both into college.

Blight gently closes the piano lid and surveys the room once more. Notices a photograph on the mantlepiece beside the little ormolu clock. The silver frame is tarnished from age and the absence of polish. He picks it up and studies the picture: two women sitting side by side on a garden bench, one of them holding the lead of a little wire-haired terrier whose attention has been caught by something beyond the camera. The other woman stares into the lens with a wide-eyed seriousness. Thin and elegant, in the low waisted dress and long cardigan of an earlier fashion, she rests a languid arm across the back of the bench, her thin fingers holding the stem of a drooping rose. The other dark-haired woman is younger, her round features still unformed, her posture less controlled, as though at any moment she might leap from the bench and run away. Mother and daughter, perhaps, though there is no family resemblance he can detect. Distant relatives then, or close friends, there are no other clues. The suggestion of an arched construction behind them, a rose arbour perhaps and, in the far distance, the fuzzy outline of some buildings. He senses this is an urban rather than a rural scene. But then again this could simply be the photographer's studio, one of those backdrops artfully constructed for effect. Even the rose may be a fake. Carefully, he undoes the little metal clasps at the back of the frame and prises the photograph from the card backing. A date, a place, written in fine pencil on the reverse side: E and A, Oxford, June 1938. Which is which, he wonders, studying the faces again. He has scant details of the murdered woman, Eleanor O'Dowd: her age, born at the beginning of the century; profession, teacher of piano; place of birth, St Alban's, Herts. Only child, parents deceased, no living relatives. No recent photograph either, leaving out the gruesome forensics—the jagged splinters of bone at the back of the skull, a dark patch of blooded hair, the three knife wounds, two to the sternum, one in the lower back. The chalky outline of the body, still visible on the stone floor, indicates a taller than average female. St Alban's. Oxford. What in God's name would bring such a woman to this backwater?

Blight replaces the photograph in its frame and returns it to its place. Runs his gaze along the mantelpiece, down to the iron grate, heaped with coal ash and bits of wood long grown cold. He gets down on his knees, takes the brass poker from the fire set and stirs the pile of ash. He reaches forward and extracts a charred cigarette end. Rolls it in his fingers, sniffs. Woodbines. Odd that, he wouldn't have put her down as a smoker. He brings out a handkerchief from his trouser pocket, wraps the stub inside it, places it back in his pocket. Still on his knees, he glances over at the little oak bookcase beside the fireplace. Music books mainly. Poetry lover too, judging by some of the titles. He selects one with a brightly decorated cover, *Idylls of the King*, quickly flicks through it. Tucked inside the back of the book is a little clutch of pencil drawings, each one separately folded. People, buildings, landscapes. He recognises the row of cottages on Church Street, the estuary drawn from somewhere up on the cliff, a solitary heron perched on a rock. They are all rather good. The last sketch is a young woman in profile; she has fine delicate features and her long hair is woven into a thick plait that reaches down to her waist. In her right hand she carries a bunch of flowers—large blooms, lilac probably, he knows his plants. They are clasped tightly to her heart.

CHAPTER 14

Johnny Nebo stands in the middle of the estuary. It is low tide and he has been out spearing flatfish since before dawn. His feet and legs are bare, blue veined with the cold. He moves slowly along the edge of the mudflat, feeling with his toes for the smooth, rubbery give of a flounder, the sharp pinch of its spine. Across his shoulders is slung the canvas fishing bag. In his right hand he carries the fishing spear, a sharp-edged blade attached to a slim wooden pole. The black surface of the mudflat shifts and slides, sucks at his feet. A small flock of oystercatchers flies in from upriver and alights at the edge of Black Scar. The birds start to feed in the shallows, picking amongst the stones with their scarlet beaks, and he pauses to watch them, though he cannot hear their busy chat. She is there; he knew she would turn up on such a fine, clear morning. Her hair is loose, tendrils blow about her face and her feet are bare. He wishes she would turn so he could see her face properly. She would smile and he would be content with that.

Westwards over Cowyn Head comes a shrieking arrow of barnacle geese, aiming for the Scar. The oystercatchers take off, a flurry of black and white and red. And the woman, too, is gone with them. She would never stay for geese, or for him. He senses a slithering beneath his feet. His blade flashes, strikes the water, and the flounder—white bellied, mottle-backed and neatly speared—joins its fellows inside the canvas bag.

He straightens up then and looks back towards the shore; uncle Ifor is on the jetty below the Ferry House, waving to him. Standing behind him he can see Sergeant Phillips in his uniform and cap. Johnny hoists the fish bag higher and starts to wade back to the land, sure footed in the squelch and ooze, across the ribbon of the Gwennol; at low tide the water only comes up to his knees. The two men watch his approach from the jetty.

'Don't see why you got to take him in again, Dai. You lot never got nothin' from him last time.' Ifor's strong hands are tightly clenched at his sides, the sinews of his arms taut as rope.

The sergeant gives an awkward laugh. 'Duw, no need to tell me that, Ifor boy. It's Inspector Blight what's called him in this time, not the local police.'

Ifor gives a contemptuous snort. 'Blight, that's a good name for 'im an' all. He is a bloody blight, that man, stickin' his nose into people's business. Doreen said he was round the Captain's the other day buying pints, asking questions about Johnny.' His gaze shifts seawards to his nephew wading the river. 'Look at him out there, he's an innocent. Happy as Larry on his own with the birds and the dabs.'

Sergeant Phillips studies Johnny slip-slapping across the last stretch of mud towards the end of the jetty. 'He don' look too happy to me, Ifor, the poor sod's freezing to death, look at the colour of his legs. Get some warm clothes on him quick. The inspector's waiting up at the car. I'll see Johnny gets something to eat at the station.'

Up on the cliff walk, in the passenger seat of the Wolseley, Blight is observing John Parry's progress across the bay through Sergeant Phillips's binoculars, handily stowed in the glove compartment. He watches the stooped, intent young man, in his cloth cap and heavy jersey, trousers rolled up to the knees, wading slowly across the river. He notes the way he hoists the heavy fishing bag across his shoulders as if it weighed nothing. He has noted, too, the steady swing of the fish gaffe out on the mud flat, the flash of the killing steel. Johnny Parry knows his business. Blight watches Emrys step down from the jetty and walk to the edge of the water. He leans forward and grasps his nephew's hand, gently pulls him up on to the rocky shore. He puts an arm around his shoulders and together they go up the steps to the Ferry House and disappear from view. Sergeant Phillips, following behind them, looks up the cliff, at the stationary car and its sole occupant. He raises his right arm, the fingers splayed. Five minutes.

85

Inspector Blight pulls out his pocket watch. It is 8.15 am. In an hour the three of them will be sitting in the interview room in the central police station. Inside the black leather briefcase in the well of the car are the records of the investigation to date: a street map; detailed witness interviews from the night of the murder; police photographs of the deceased, her cottage and garden; a trace result which shows a match for the smear of green distemper on a raincoat sleeve and the wall colour of Miss O'Dowd's hallway. The inspector lights up a Navy Cut, winds down the seaward window and breathes a puff of smoke into the clouded air. The echoing cries of gull and cormorant, of sandpiper and curlew, heron and plover, criss-cross the wide expanse of estuary and wooded cliffside.

Inspector Blight hears only the questions forming in his head. Last night, after he returned to Madras House from his visit to the murder scene, a telegram was waiting on the hall table. 'Sort the case smartish. Double murder Tooting. Capstick unavailable. You start Monday.'

A thin smile twists the corners of his mouth. The famous Inspector Capstick of the Yard is unavailable; this is his chance to grab the limelight. He has two days left down here. If he charges Parry before Friday noon, he can be on the afternoon Great Western straight back to London.

Ronald Blight has bigger fish to fry.

Christmas: CHAPTER 15

'Budge up, can't you, I've got no room.'

Janice, late as usual, is shoving and squeezing herself into the end of the pew. The other girls mutter to each other—'Why do we always have to move for her, can't she sit with the boys?'—but because it's Janice and they're a bit afraid of her they obediently shuffle along the seat, squidged up against each other like fish fingers. Daphne, at the far end of the row, wedged between Christine Miller and the lumpy stone wall, can hardly breathe. The mask isn't helping either. Gran has covered the cardboard in brown sticky back plastic and the holes for the nose and mouth are too small. To make matters worse the tight elastic strap holding the mask in place is now giving her a headache. In the pew in front of her, Dilys is sucking the end of her plait; it is tied with ribbon to match her velvet cloak, of pale insipid blue not cerulean, which is of some comfort to Daphne who would like, just once in her life, to have been picked to be the Virgin Mary instead of a weird cross between a camel and next door's old brown mongrel. Too bad vicar's children don't get special treatment in this town. Two rows further up and below the transept, Sylvia is whispering with her friends and exchanging glances with the older boys in the pews on the opposite side of the aisle. She is still wearing her school uniform because this year, at last, she is old enough to be a reader and doesn't have to dress up in a silly costume and embarrass herself in front of the likes of Darren Gough.

Mr Hubert Morris is directing the dress rehearsal. He stands at the top of the steps overlooking the nave and issues long-winded instructions in a boring monotone. Mr Morris is not nearly so stern and scary as Mr Duckford—he's only the Sunday School teacher and therefore not a real teacher—so there's a lot of giggling and whispering and passing of sweets along the pews. Christine nudges Daphne and presses a warm, gluey wine gum into her hand. Tricky eating if you are wearing a mongrel/camel mask with a too small mouth hole. Janice in her angel costume leans across Christine.

'Martin's not coming', she whispers, too loudly. 'They still don't know what's wrong with him, his mother's proper worried.' She lowers her voice—Christine, stolid winegum-chewer, might be listening. 'Should we tell someone, Daph? About the you-know-what?'

Daphne does not respond. For once she's glad to be inside the camel mask so Janice can't see her fear.

The volume of chat increases. In the end Mr Morris has to summon Miss Bryer from the vestry where she is sorting out props. She marches in and stands foursquare in her tweeds glaring down at the lot of them. Immediately, silence descends. All the children in this town have at one time or another been under the skinny thumb—and more often the wooden ruler—of Miss Bryer. In that reedy, high-pitched voice they quake to hear, she orders each row in turn to get up 'in silence' and process 'in pairs' out to the church porch for the start of the rehearsal. In that freezing, dimly lit space three members of the Girls Friendly Society, the GFS, shush and prod and hand out props. They hear the muffled notes of the organ start up 'Once in Royal David's City'.

The organ plays on into the second verse and, prompted by the GFS girls, the performers shuffle forward two by two into the light. Daphne is near the end of the queue, paired with Alun Hughes draped in a sheepskin, his mouth working away at a gob of chewing gum. As they wait their turn to move, she pushes back the stuffy mask and silently reads the inscription carved in stone on the opposite wall.

Behold the place where I do lie
As you are now so once was I
As I am now so shall you be
Cut off by Death and follow me

She knows the words off by heart of course; they are a *memento mori*, her mother explained, the Latin for 'remember you will die'. In the bottom corner of the stone tablet, she sees something she hasn't noticed before; it's a tiny skull, etched into the stone, and its dead eyes are looking straight at her.

Down in Glanmorfa, an icy wind is slicing through the streets, sweeping the last leaves of autumn from the paths, whipping the slates from off the roofs. Perhaps it is a foretaste of what is to come.

Sergeant David Phillips leans back in his chair and runs a hand through his close-cropped hair. His stomach is rumbling, he hasn't eaten a thing since the sandwiches he ordered for the three of them when they got back to the police station that morning. It's now 3.20 pm, according to the clock on the wall of the interview room. Evan will be getting on the school bus now and he'd promised his wife, on late shift at the hospital, that he'd be home by four to give their boy his tea. And still they sit, no further on in this second round of questioning the poor bugger than he and Ian Jenkins were weeks ago.

He steals a glance at the inspector seated next to him, still scribbling away in that notebook of his. Odd chap, he thinks. Doesn't make much effort with the chat like you'd expect from a fellow copper. And not a word of thanks for getting in the cheese and chutney sandwiches double quick. His gaze moves across the table to Johnny. Starving he was, *y boi bach*, wolfed them down. *Chwarae teg*, he'd been out in that freezing water since dawn. The lad's all hunched up in the chair, turning that old cap of his round and round in his hands, staring at the floor, muttering away. What in hell's name is he talking about? Has he any clue what will happen if a jury finds him guilty? The news they've taken him in again will be all over the place by now; people won't be so keen to stick up for him a second time.

Scattered across the plain wooden table are the drawings, produced by the inspector out of his smart briefcase. Who taught Johnny Parry to draw like that? Bloody marvellous they are. There's the Ferry House with the fishing boat and the old ferry tied up at the jetty. And the castle rising from the foreshore, half hidden by the trees and ivy. That old cockle woman, Fanny the Fish, walking down Hangman Lane with her basket; got her likeness down to a T he has. Even Hubert Morris with his bald head chatting to Effie Hughes the paper shop. Some of these are better than photos. The inspector has removed three drawings from the pile, placed them in the centre of the table facing Parry. One shows the cottages in Church Street. The knife in the second drawing is meticulous, the hasp and blade perfectly aligned and in proportion. Something familiar about the woman in the third sketch, but he can't put a name to her.

'Got to hand it to you, Inspector, this is one hell of a clever way to persuade a deaf mute to confess.'

If you can call this a confession, thinks Ronald Blight, as he finishes writing up his notes. Parry has given them nothing throughout the hours-long interview. Whenever they mouth or gesture a question, he simply stares at them uncomprehendingly. He hasn't even mimed an action that could be interpreted as murderous. That boyish face with its mild eyes has a gentle expression, trusting like a child's. Just as they described him, those wily chancers in the pub. Mind you, that knife he drew in the picture, it's the kind you'd use to gut a fish or slit a pig's throat. Or stab a spinster in the back.

Not enough to charge him with murder, yet. Such flimsy evidence wouldn't stand up in court, it would make Blight a laughing stock and put the kybosh on promotion. He'd have to take out that chapter from *Tales from the Great Detective*. There has to be more.

'That's as far as we can get today, Sergeant.' He collects up the papers, the sketches and his notebook, drops them into the black briefcase. Phillips is hovering by the table.

'I'll take him home then, shall I? Tell his uncles we'll bring him in again tomorrow.'

'No, he stays here tonight; I want to see him again first thing in the morning.'

He pauses at the doorway.

'And find someone who knows how to talk deaf and dumb. Pronto.'

It is a long evening. Blight sits hunkered at the small writing table in his room, the only warmth the single bar electric heater he brought up from Mrs Price's front room and propped on a stool; now and then it fizzes, a faulty switch in the wall, perhaps. Still fully clothed, he has pulled on his plaid dressing gown for extra insulation and wound around his head a red woollen scarf—a long ago present from Mabel—to keep the draught from the window at bay. The several floors of Madras House are silent: no creaking doors or floorboards, no sound at all of the other lodgers long gone to their beds. Mrs Price is shut away in her quarters at the back of the house beyond the kitchen. Behind the faded net curtains covering his window, the fitful streetlamp trembles in a sudden blast of winter and goes out, leaving the only illumination from the angle-poise lamp beside him. The light falls across the little table and the heaped papers and the photographs, Johnny's drawings, and a metal ashtray spilling with pencil shavings, cigarette ends and spent matchsticks.

Blight has the full report of the investigation in front of him; he has read it many times. Tonight, he reads again the witness report made by Sergeant Phillips.

3pm JR (the suspect) seen in Church St by Morgan Parry, Curlew House, coming out of the home of Miss Beatty Bryer, retired schoolteacher. Parry said JR delivered firewood to her twice a week and did odd jobs around the house.

3.15pm approx. JR waved to Mrs Mary Evans as she walked past him in C St. Ted Perkins, Bay Cottage passed him. JR showed him his torch was out of batteries.

3.30pm Fred Davies said JR called at Jubilee Garage to replace batteries.

3.45 pm Seen by Miss Gertie Lewis walking by her house on C St. Said he called with her around 10 that morning to fix a broken drainpipe at the back of her house.

4.00 pm approx Bryn Watkins, Pentre Farm saw JR passing the front door.

4.05 pm JR called at Morlas Stores for a pkt of cigarettes and a bag of crisps. Purchases put on tic by Mr Mervyn Jones Stores. One of the uncles comes in every Saturday to pay.

4.45pm JR left C St. Stopped outside Portland House on George Street and asked Jack Evans for a light for his cigarette.

4.50pm Seen smoking outside the door of The Captain's Arms, corner of George St and Hangman Lane. Gerry Black, Perrott Street, offered to buy him a pint and Johnny shook his head, no.

5.15 JR passed by the bakery on Hangman Lane on his way home—waved to Mrs Davies inside.

5.25 Called at Beacon House to collect half a dozen eggs from Ethel Roderick the housekeeper on his way home to Ferry House. Does this regular every Friday.

5.30 Came home for tea. Did not go out again. Witness: Ifor and Emrys Parry, uncles.

Additional Notes

Around 5pm a farm labourer, John Edgar Evans, was walking past Jubilee Garage when he noticed a light on in the front window of Miss Eleanor O'Dowd's house. Assumed she had a music lesson as usual, but he didn't hear the piano. He walked a bit further then heard a woman screaming inside Miss O'D's house. Tried to get inside the house but the door was locked. Shouted through the lock, 'Leave her alone!' and she cried out a name. When asked by Sergeant Phillips if the name was Johnny, Evans replied, 'I'm not going to say that it wasn't Johnny, but it could have been. Or maybe something like Larry. Or could have been Peter.'

Approximately 5.15 Oliver Price, Bolton House, next door to Jubilee Garage, heard his dog barking and growling in the front garden. Opened the door and saw someone running along the footpath at the back of the cottages. He called out to him but there was no reply. The person kept running, he was pulling up the collar of his coat. It was a long grey colour. He thought the man was bare headed but by then it was dark so he couldn't be certain about that. Price said he would have recognised Johnny because he had been doing odd jobs around his house and the Garage for over 10 years.

All the witnesses assert that the suspect has never shown any signs of violence or aggression. 'A good tempered, simple child in a man's body.'

Inspector Blight closes the report. Unwinds the scarf, scratches his head for a bit. Tips the overflowing ashtray into the wastepaper bin underneath the table. He lights another cigarette and selects one of the sketches from the pile. The way Parry has drawn the cottages means he must have been standing on the other side of the road with his back to Pentre Farm. To give him his due, the mute has quite a talent for someone with no education and precious little encouragement at home. The pencil strokes, the shading, the particular details of each building are unerringly accurate. There's a man in a cloth cap passing by on the road, trailed by a small dog, two children playing in the doorway of the cottage at the end of the row, a woman looking out of the upstairs window of number 3, probably the victim herself, though the face isn't clear, some of the lines are smudged, maybe Parry was too heavy with the rubber. Or maybe he was trying to rub her out altogether. Interesting.

He rummages through the pile of photographs and finds the close-up taken by the police. Eleanor O'Dowd had a long, fine-boned face with a strong jawline. Her eyes were a pale colour, though in the photograph the left eye is partly closed by the ugly gash running in a jagged line from her crown to below her left temple. An older, harder version of the serious woman in that

93

photograph on the mantlepiece. Life had not been kind to Miss O'Dowd, Blight concludes, despite the consolations of her music.

He brushes off the moment's twinge of sympathy and leans back in his chair, chafing his cold fingers. His breath steams in the frozen air of the room. The mute has not confessed yet, but he will twist the screws tomorrow. As he has written in Chapter Two of his memoir-in-progress, a good detective always has an extra trick up his sleeve.

CHAPTER 16

Johnny Nebo wakes from a restless night on the hard wooden bench in the holding cell of the police station. He remembers the place from the time before and is grateful for the pillow and the two thick woollen blankets the sergeant fetched for him from home.

'You can't leave the poor man to freeze in there, David. Give him these.' Sergeant Phillips's wife, Betty, is a Glanmorfa girl, she remembers Johnny from primary school—as simple now as he was then, always tagging along after the other children, never fighting back when they poked him in the ribs and called him rude names he couldn't hear. Hardly ever at school, she recalls, poor dab couldn't learn anything. Spent most of the time wandering round the streets or up to his knees in the sticky mud picking cockles or crabbing. She heaps the pillow and the blankets into her husband's arms. 'He's a good lad, it makes no sense he would do such a terrible thing.'

At seven in the morning, duty constable Rees arrives at the station. He unlocks the door of the holding cell and brings Johnny a mug of strong tea with two heaped spoons of sugar and two thick slices of bread and jam. At 8.00 am sharp, Constable Jenkins is outside Madras House. He opens the rear door for Inspector Blight and they drive in silence the twenty-three minutes from Glanmorfa to the police station. The inspector does not stir, he appears to be deep in thought.

When Blight enters the interview room, Sergeant Phillips rises to his feet and introduces him to a dumpy, middle-aged woman in a grey suit. She could be anyone's granny were it not for her spectacles; the speckled tortoiseshell frames are elongated, narrowing to a point at each end, like the eyes of a cat.

'Mrs Edina Evans, sir.'

The woman remains seated, extends a grey-gloved hand.

95

'Mrs Evans works at the magistrate's court: she translates the deaf and dumb language. Lucky we are she could come here at such short notice.'

Blight gives a polite nod and takes his seat on the opposite side of the table, alongside Phillips who as usual is taking notes. At 8.35 am, Parry is brought into the interview room.

8.35 am Friday 19th December. Interview with suspect (John Parry) carried out by Inspector R Blight. Mrs Edina Evans, deaf and dumb translator for Swansea Magistrate's Court, was also present. Parry was shown the photographs of the deceased taken on the night of the murder. Parry looked a long time at each photograph but did not respond. Mrs Evans used sign language to ask him if he knew the deceased. Parry did not appear to understand her. Inspector Blight produced the drawing Parry had made of the row of cottages and pointed to the people in the picture. Mrs Evans again used sign language and gestures, to no effect. Parry became agitated, shaking his head, banging the table with his fists. He indicated he wanted to draw something. Paper and pencil were provided. He drew a woman's body lying on the ground and made a number of stabbing actions with his arm and mimed throwing something away. After that he buried his head in his arms and cried for a long time. Mrs Evans tried to communicate with him but to no avail. The interview concluded at 9.45 am and Parry was taken back to the holding cell by Police Constable Rees.

Blight reaches for another cigarette, his fourth of the morning. Phillips lifts his eyes from the report book where he has been checking his notes. He shakes his head.

'Not enough to convict him yet is there, sir? He could have just been showing us he was sad she was dead. He knows how she was murdered, everyone in the town does, the details are common knowledge. You still think he killed her?'

The inspector does not reply. He takes a long drag of the

cigarette, inhales the smoke and blows it out into the small room. He stares impassively at the wall opposite; his eyes are red-rimmed, restless fingers drumming the surface of the table. David Phillips's hazel eyes are also stinging; he's never been a smoker, can't stand the smell of the wretched things. He glances at the station clock above the door. 10.45 am. Time he sent Mrs Evans home; she's been sitting out in the waiting room for ages. He pushes his chair back and stands up.

'Shall I be releasing Parry now, sir?'

Inspector Blight does not shift his gaze, just gives the faintest of nods. Phillips leaves the room and goes down the corridor to the holding cell. A few moments later he enters with Parry in tow. The young man's face is grey with fatigue, his body hunched, hands hanging loose at his sides. Rees goes round the back of the station to fetch the car.

Blight gets up from the desk and reaches inside the pocket of his coat, brings out his pack of Navy Cut and offers one to Parry, who wrinkles his nose in disgust, shaking his head. Sergeant Phillips, watching, gives a short dry laugh.

'I could have told you that, sir. Johnny's very particular what he smokes.'

Without a word, Blight reaches into his other pocket and takes out a different pack of cigarettes. He proffers one to Johnny. Without hesitation Johnny takes the cigarette, lights it from the inspector's match and a smile of pure delight spreads across his face.

'Always been a Woodbine man, Johnny. You've made his day, sir.'

Blight discards the packet on the table. He motions to the man to sit down again, then he turns to the sergeant.

'Get the charge sheet ready, Phillips. He's as good as confessed in my book. And bring Mrs Evans back in pronto. She can have a go at spelling out the charges to him in her way, just make sure he puts his mark on the document. If she can't make him understand, then at least it's on the record that we followed correct procedure.'

CHAPTER 17

'Into position and not another word from any of you or else I'll set the vicar on you.'

Some of the children turn round and nudge each other, looking in Daphne's direction. She stares at the ground, no need to be reminded whose daughter she is. Mr Morris is standing by the open vestry door while Miss Bryer, muffled in a heavy coat with a green velvet collar, is outside with her clipboard, checking them off one by one as they file past her into the frosty evening. The straggling, shoving troupe makes its way along the slippery path between the gravestones towards the church porch: virgin, Joseph, donkey, shepherds, angels, innkeeper and his wife squabbling who goes first, two wise men because Terry Dunn's not turned up, a sheep in a rug and something that resembles a very short camel. The actors in the vanguard come to a halt inside the porch, clustering together and whispering in the shadows, while scary Mrs Morgan, the vicar's wife, and the GFS girls fuss with tea towels and tinsel circlets and posh Mrs Edwina Crowe, who was born in India and knows about these things, re-drapes Dilys/Mary's blue silk saree correctly then hands grumpy Graham the wooden cigar box plus the china jar painted with gold butterflies because he's got to give the myrrh and the frankincense to the baby Jesus now, thanks to that mitching bugger Terry Dunn. Outside in the graveyard the bit parts, bare-limbed and goose-pimpled, wait their turn, hopping to keep warm. Like the innkeeper says, there's no room for them inside.

Through the eye slits in her mask, Daphne peers up at the stained-glass figures in the windows, their jewel colours aglow in the candlelight. Then the church doors open wide and there is complete silence; people are waiting for something to happen. She hears a familiar voice. A bit croaky at first, but by the time Martin

98

gets to '*Where a mother laid her baby*' the notes are coming out pure and sweet. Her heart lifts. Graham turns round, beaming. He gives her the thumbs up. Maybe they'll all be ok now.

The performers in front of her shuffle forward and then she too walks into the light and the church is a warm Aladdin's cave of flickering candles and tinsel and colours and everyone is singing and Mr Williams is soaring the organ notes high into the chancel roof. And there's Gran sitting near the front with Flora Lloyd and giving her a huge wink as she goes past, and Mr and Mrs Merchant with Mrs Price Madras and even Mrs Daley two rows behind them in a navy coat and hat instead of her overall, and in the front row of the nave sits the portreeve wearing his chain of golden cockle shells.

The performers form a semicircle at the top of the chancel steps facing the audience as they have practised and there's a moment of silence. Martin has gone to sit with his mother in one of the pews; she has bundled him into a thick coat and her arm is around his shoulders. His body sags against her and his face is really pale; it's obvious he's still very poorly. Daphne's heart sinks, they are not out of the woods then. There's a bit of a kerfuffle at the back of the line and everyone starts shuffling sideways to let the vicar through to the front to welcome the audience. Daphne finds herself facing the front right-hand pew, which is full of people she knows, apart from the person sitting next to Mr Jones Stores, the woman called Vita. Under her mask Daphne's face is burning. Why couldn't she be dressed as Mary, or an angel, or a shepherd even? Any costume would be better than this stupid camel outfit.

Mr Morris turns off the lights in the nave and the vicar takes his seat on the other side of the aisle where the portreeve's sitting. Sylvia emerges from behind the pulpit. She is First Narrator and is wearing the outfit she bought in town when she went on the bus with her best friend Bron to do their Christmas shopping: it's a red tartan miniskirt with matching waistcoat and jaunty little peaked cap. She's curled her hair specially and may even be wearing lipstick, though Daphne's gaze is too blinkered by her mask to be sure. Trust Sylvia to steal the limelight. Some of the older boys sitting in the choir stalls are smirking and nudging Darren whose face has gone bright red. Sylvia comes to the end of her reading then she steps back and the play gets underway, smoothly and seamlessly as if they'd all been practising for months except that it's always the same play with the same costumes and everybody knows exactly what to do even if they've been given a different part this year.

The little ones, the lambs and seraphs, tag along quite happily trailing their wands and shedding bits of costume down the aisle. There's always the lovely moment near the end when Lorna Parrish walks in, barefoot and draped in a paisley shawl because she's meant to be a poor penniless orphan even though she's 23 and works in the hardware section of Owen & Wilkins in the county town. Mr Morris switches off all the lights so it's only the candles quivering and Lorna sings 'What can I give Him, poor as I am; if I were a shepherd, I would bring a lamb/ If I were a wise man, I would do my part/ yet what I can I give him, give my heart.' And it's as though everyone is holding their breath and feeling sad and joyful at the same time. At the end of the play all the children and the teachers and the helpers come out in front and bow and the audience claps and then her father says a short prayer. And after that Mr Williams plays his favourite Bach fugue as the people start to file out of the church chatting and laughing and paying no attention to the music, the same as every year. Daphne pulls off her mask and shakes her hair loose, her scalp is hot and itching from the fabric.

'Bravo, Daphne.' Vita is standing in the aisle smiling up at her. 'Better a camel than a laurel tree, don't you think?'

Daphne blushes, returns the smile; she likes this private, shared joke.

'Such glorious hair, you are lucky,' the woman continues. 'Flame, the colour of Athena. I bet you resemble her in other ways too— strong- minded, very wise, good at keeping secrets. Am I right?'

'I don't know, I don't think so,' Daphne stammers, perplexed by

100

the question. Is she being teased? Or is it the way grown-ups talk if they're not from round here?

'Don't underestimate your strengths, Daphne, I know what I'm talking about.' Vita gives her a little wave and walks off down the aisle to join Mr Jones who is waiting for her at the door.

'Come on Daph, Miss Bryer wants your costume.' Janice has already changed back into her own clothes, she sounds impatient. 'The others are waiting outside, hurry up.'

The four of them gather outside the vestry door. Frost glisters on the tarmac and yew berries.

'Wasn't Marty great!' cries Janice, losing her balance on the slippery path and making a grab for Dilys. She's still wearing the pink ballet pumps from her angel costume, silly girl. 'His voice was a bit wobbly to start with, wasn't it, but then he got proper going. Like an angel in the heavenly host.'

Graham isn't smiling. 'Heavenly ghost more like, I thought he was going to throw up. Now the skull's back in the bone house he's supposed to be getting better, isn't he?' Graham's looking at Daphne when he says this.

'Johnny Nebo's in the police station again,' announces Dilys. 'This time they've really got something on him, dad says.'

'Howard Darke told my dad he saw Johnny jumping over the wall at the back of Miss O'Dowd's and running away,' adds Janice, not wanting to be outdone by Dilys and hopping on one leg while she scrapes a splodge of berry off the side of one of her pumps. New footsteps crunch along the path. Mr Morris, looming blackly over them.

'Why are you lot still hanging around by here? Get on home now quick, before you catch your deaths in this cold. No messing around, mind, I'll be watching you.'

And so he does, waiting by the lychgate until they are halfway up Church Street before he shuts the gate. How exactly do you catch your death, Daphne wonders, trudging along behind the others? Is it a bit like tag, death grabbing you with his chilly fingers and freezing you to the spot? Or like the icy river creeping into your bones? Somebody wanted death to catch Miss O'Dowd that afternoon and it wasn't Johnny Nebo. A shred of memory is stirring. Whoever knocked her into the river was smaller than Johnny, now she thinks of it, lighter on their feet; she remembers that now, the too-big coat flapping like wings. Whoever stood over her on the path was still as death, made no sound. She would have known if it was Johnny Nebo: he's never quiet like that. The police have made a terrible mistake, she should tell someone.

She's in the vicarage porch, pushing open the front door and crossing the hall, hurrying down the steps towards the kitchen door. From inside she can hear the murmur of family voices. She stops. Telling someone means having to come clean about everything: mitching the piano lesson, stealing the skull, awakening the curse. The evidence of her crime is already clear: Miss O'Dowd's murdered, Martin's terribly ill. She will be in deep trouble and so will Graham and the others. They believe the skull is back in the bone house so what will they do when they find out she's been lying? And it's nearly Christmas. Better leave things as they are, say nothing.

At 7.35 on the following morning, grey river mist rising with the boiler steam, in a scream of metal and piston and brake, *The Red Dragon* gives one last blast from its whistle and moves slowly out of the station. Gathering pace and rhythm, the train follows the long curve of the river Mynach, past fields and scattered homesteads, heading eastwards beside the waters of the bay. Seated at the window in the third carriage, in his well-cut black coat and fine red woollen scarf tightly knotted against the morning chill, Inspector Blight bids a relieved farewell to this strange, unsettling, watery domain: first casualty of empire, plundered by Roman, Saxon, Plantagenet; last bastion of an ancient Celtic language. And further back, the bones of Beaker folk, and a dark cave of raptors, hyena, mammoth, brown bear. The train turns eastward, still hugging the shore and behind it the headland plunges back into the steely sky and the saltmarsh and sandbanks of the estuary submerge, dissolve, swallowing with them castle ruins, several public houses, a Norman church, a Steinway grand piano, a Ferry House. And a lone, silent man out on the tide, fishing for dabs.

Blight opens his leather notebook and turns to the fledgling chapter notes: his observations on the town's quaint architecture; choice snippets from its maritime history; some witty portraits of the natives; the Parry case. He takes his pen and jots down the title that has just come to him. 'Drownings and Depravity'. The alliteration is very pleasing.

CHAPTER 18

They are gathered at the graveside when the first flakes of the afternoon start to fall. Slowly at first, then more thickly until the grey skies above the churchyard are a swirling vortex of white and the dark-clad mourners are quickly spattered and daubed with snow. Only a handful of local people have come to pay their respects to a woman not greatly loved in the town. She was not a joiner, poor Miss O'Dowd, nor even a secret drinker or gambler which would have endeared her to many. Piano lessons were only for the upstreet dwellers, the children of professionals, the teachers and doctors, the vicar. Only the manner of her death has given her notoriety and not everyone—including Mr Morris the churchwarden—is happy to have a Catholic's last resting place in an Anglican graveyard. But the vicar has agreed it with Father Michael, the parish priest of St Benedict's in the county town: best to do it quietly, given the time of year and the necessity to get the business done with the minimum of fuss or unwelcome attention from the press. Besides, the woman was not 'practising' and St Mary's graveyard is full of misfits of doubtful faith: drowned sailors, unnamed infants, a few decidedly unAnglican artistic types, a Belgian swindler with an unpronounceable name. She will be in good company.

The six school children selected to attend as former pupils of the deceased seem to have forgotten why they are there. Alun and Janice have dutifully laid the wreath of holly and chrysanthemums Mr Duckford handed to them at the graveside. Now they are nudging each other and giggling, opening their mouths wide to suck in the ice crystals which dissolve so quickly on the tongue. You cannot call this a solemn occasion for all its murderous origin. Snow, three days before Christmas Eve, is always a cause for rejoicing. The coffin is lowered, the bearers pull up the ropes and leave it to settle at the bottom of the claggy, snow filling hole. It could be interesting for the pupils, this business of death and burial, were it not for the greater excitement of the snow.

Caught up in the thrill of it, Daphne does not hear her father at the graveside intoning the last rites in his solemn vicar voice, nor the hollow thud as the first clods of earth land upon the sealed lid of Miss Eleanor O'Dowd's simple wooden coffin, hastily constructed by Sid Davies the local joiner. Nor does she notice the quiet presence of a woman standing on the periphery of the group, her red-gloved hand resting on the marble angel watching over Martha Llewellyn, beloved wife of Raymond and devoted mother of Sandra, Theresa and Edwin. It is only later, after her father has concluded the prayers and is walking down to the lychgate in his black cloak and biretta, accompanied by the undertaker and his men, and the pupils are being herded together by Mr Duckford ready for the walk back to school, that Daphne looks back through the whirl of snow and sees Vita approaching the graveside. Her dark fur coat and hat seem too big for her small frame and the bright posy of flowers she's carrying startle against the wintry background. Vita comes right up to the edge of the grave, bends down and drops the flowers into the hole.

Manny Edwards, halfway through infilling from the mound of soil alongside the grave, has his back turned to scoop another shovelful and he does not notice the woman's action. He only gives her a brief nod as he offloads the shovelful into the grave and then returns to his mound. Daphne hesitates, wondering whether she should wave, show she has recognised her, but Vita is already walking briskly back up the path towards the little gate in the wall at the top of the graveyard. In the deep snow-filled silence, Daphne hears the gate lock click shut.

'Stop dawdling, Daphne, keep up please.'

Mr Duckford, his long nose blotched and blue with cold, tightens the scarf around his neck and frogmarches his pupils across the bridge to the old graveyard. Daphne stands in the graveyard, questions whirling like snowflakes. How does this mysterious woman know Miss O'Dowd? Why did she only arrive after the service was over? What's she doing in Glanmorfa?

Janice comes running back across the bridge, calling to her. 'C'mon, Daph, what you hangin' around for? Mr Duckford's hoppin' mad!'

When they get back to school the classroom is a warm fug of steaming gloves, hats and scarves drying on the stove. Today is the last day of term, the decorations have to be dismantled and stored in the back of the cupboard for another year, the paper chains and lanterns and calendars allocated for taking home at the end of the afternoon. The snow has stopped for the moment, the heavy clouds have dispersed and the sky is now a bright icicle blue. Soon the playground surfaces will be glassy and perfect for sliding.

But first there are desks to clear, inkwells to empty and clean, stiff nuggets of blotting paper to flick with rulers when sir's not looking. Jimmy Richards opens the lid of his desk to dodge the bullets and knocks over the bowl of water he was using to scrub off last week's splodges of ink and paint. He'll be staying behind after school to clear it up if he's not careful, end of term or not. Rummaging inside her own desk amongst the paper scraps, broken crayons, sweet wrappers and desiccated apple cores, Daphne finds a crumpled red jotter, *Tales of Mystery* by D Morgan written in clumsy blue ink on the cover. Inside there is only one rather disappointing tale, 'Fair Elaine and the Pale Rider'. A year ago, Elaine was her favourite name, after the maid of Astolat who broke her heart for love of Sir Lancelot and floated down the river on a barge with her long hair loose, a white lily trailing from her hand. No wonder she caught her death, patiently waiting for her on the icy strand of Camelot. She should have worn a coat. There's a little pencil drawing after THE END—the barge is a reasonable effort, but fair Elaine is just a lot of hair and a large pair of feet.

She stuffs the jotter into her bag with the Christmas card to the Rev and Mrs Morgan from Mr Merchant the headmaster reminding them to see that Daphne completes all her exam practice over the holiday. Mr Duckford hands out copies of *11 Plus Practice Papers* to take home, though he's pretty sure some of the pupils, the ones doomed to failure and the secondary modern, won't even open the book.

And so, at the final bell ring of the term, chairs neatly stacked on tidy desks, floor swept clean of rubbish, out they troop, the top class, staggering under the burden of Christmas crafts, coats, book bags. They whoop and slide and shove each other down the playground slope and cannon into the Infants who are pressing at the gates with frosty breath and reddened faces, waiting for John Edgar to drive his afternoon milkers along the lane and turn them into the farmyard opposite the school. The last cow past, the gate is opened and the children head off in little groups, dodging the steaming dung pats and stamping their boots in the roadside gutters where the snow has drifted a little and begun to freeze.

Back in the classroom, the teachers gather for the last meeting of term, the festive variant. Miss Tucker totters up the slippery playground from the Infants classroom with a plate of mince pies and a bottle of sherry covered in a tea towel just in case. From inside the teacher's desk Mr Duckford produces a half bottle of Johnnie Walker and two cups, and Mary Evans, who also helps in the Infants, arrives with a packet of Cadbury's mixed chocolate biscuits from her mother. Mr Merchant, who has not brought anything because he is the headmaster, accepts a generous cup from his deputy Mr Duckford. They gather around the stove on which the mince pies gently steam and toast the departure of the term, the holiday to come. Outside, the sky has shifted to a bitter violet. Mr Merchant takes another swig from his cup. Glancing out of the window at the retreating afternoon, he says, 'It'll all be gone by tomorrow, mark my words. Check the pipes will you, Duckford, before you go home.'

In the far frozen north, Boreas, god of snow and ice, is flexing his arctic wings.

CHAPTER 19

'Now watch how easy this is, you two. You go like this.' Dilys starts moving her hips, swaying her body from side to side, her feet firmly planted on the attic floorboards. Janice shrieks and claps her hands over her mouth, 'God, Dil, you're like one of them belly dancers.' Dilys's face is flushed; she is concentrating hard, building her rhythm. Her hands clasp the yellow plastic hoop around her middle. She gives a little twist and the hoop starts to spin, faster and faster, skimming her waist and her narrow hips. Her whole body is swaying in step with the hula and she lifts her arms, floats them wide, eyes bright with triumph. 'See, I told you it was easy; you just need to learn the technique.'

Daphne and Janice are sitting together on the bare floor, sharing a box of Black Magic. They are tired of admiring the hula hoop routine. Daphne leans forward, whispers to Janice. 'Don't know how she managed to get one of those for Christmas, they're not in the shops in town, not even in Swansea.'

'Her uncle give it her, brought it all the way from America. He's got a job on one of them cruise ships. She's such a show-off.'

Daphne sighs. A Troll Doll and this year's *Girls Crystal Annual* are no match for a hula hoop. Even the longed-for television set has not materialised in the vicarage sitting room on Christmas morning. Instead, a poor substitute, a square black box called Black Box is waiting under the tree. Sylvia is delighted because next to it, wrapped in festive paper with her name on, are three much coveted single records: 'Love me Do', 'Surfin' Safari' and Pat Boone's 'Speedy Gonzales'. These are all they will hear that day and throughout Boxing Day, even though the record player is meant to be a family present and Hywel Morgan is longing for a bit of Bach.

'Johnny Nebo's been let out again,' says Janice. 'He's on prole, my dad says. That means his uncles have to keep him locked up until the trial 'cos he's a danger, but I don't think he is, he's just a bit simple.' She rummages in the Black Magic box for another toffee. Daphne thinks about Johnny Nebo, locked up in the Ferry House, not allowed to go fishing and walking around the streets like he usually does. Being hanged for something he didn't do.

'Did you know, there's a woman living in Miss O'Dowd's house?' Janice mumbles, jaws working the toffee. 'Everyone's talking about it.'

'Her name's Miss Vita Robinson,' puffs Dilys, hips gyrating. 'She's been here for ages. We met her, didn't we Daph? She said she liked my name.'

She drops the hoop on the floor. It's impossible to hula and impart important gossip at the same time. 'She come in the butcher's for a couple of chops and half a pound of sausages. Told dad she was an old friend of Miss O'Dowd.'

'Lucky she wasn't staying when the murderer arrived, she could have been killed too,' sniffs Janice. 'I wonder how long she's going to stay, can't be very nice living in a place where there's been a death.'

Dilys gives one of her superior looks. 'I expect she's cleaned all the blood off by now and given the house a good tidy up. We should go and call on her, be friendly like. I could show her my hula hoop. What you think?' She picks up the hoop, starts another round of twisting and spinning.

Daphne ignores the question, concentrates on peeling off the red ribbon from the chocolate box. Much as she would like to see Vita Robinson again, she cannot imagine arriving at the door with Dilys and her hula hoop in tow—it would be too embarrassing.

'Hey Daph, what's your favourite number, one to twenty?'

Janice has gone over to the painted wooden wheel propped on its tall stand in a corner of the attic, next to the lucky dip barrel and the wooden tea chests full of crockery, jugs and teapots belonging to the parish council, and stored in the vicarage for church fetes, whist drives and the annual carnival.

'Fifteen.'

Janice stands on tiptoe and spins the arrow. It stops on three. 'Bad luck. What's your favourite colour then?'

'Green.' The arrow does two revolutions and slows to a stop plumb on the line between green and red.

The hula hoop clatters to the floor. Dilys has realised her audience has deserted her. 'I'm starving, hard work this is, any more of those chocolates left?'

The Black Magic box is almost empty, only a liquid cherry and two yucky orange creams that none of them like.

'You could always have an apple, Dil,' says Janice, winking at Daphne. Last year's apples are laid out on loose sheets of Gran's *Western Mail* in a part of the attic where the floorboards aren't so rotten. They look like shrunken heads, the skins all shrivelled and leathery, and the fruit has a sour taste—goodness knows why Daphne's mother does this ritual every autumn, there's only so much apple crumble you can eat on a Sunday. The vicarage pig gets most of the apples in the end, mixed in with the slop.

Dilys wrinkles her nose. 'How much money we got in the jar?'

Janice fetches a large vinegar jar from inside one of the tea chests, unscrews the lid and empties the money onto the dusty floor.

'Three shillings and ninepence halfpenny. That's nearly a bridle with a plaited browband.'

'What if we just took out sixpence, enough for a big bag of sweets?'

Dilys has no scruples about raiding their savings, even though it was her idea they should buy a pony and call it Rushing Wind, which is a silly name for any animal. Janice purses her lips and puts the money back in the jar, screws the lid tight. No words are needed.

'Well in that case I'm going home before I starve to death.'

Dilys picks up the hula hoop and stalks out of the room. But she doesn't go downstairs and they can see she's hovering on the landing.

Daphne calls out, winking at Janice. 'If you like we can look for the ghost.'

Sylvia thinks there really is a ghost inside The Room of Doom. She can hear it sometimes, she says, scrabbling in the wall or tapping on the door, wanting to get out. Now she's moved into the room next door, she's got used to it; it doesn't bother her like it did when she was younger. It's probably a friendly ghost, she says; living in a vicarage it knows how to behave. Once, when Daphne was about six, Sylvia pushed her into The Room and wedged the door so she couldn't get out. It was completely dark inside and deathly cold; a smell of ancient dust and the acrid reek of rat pee. Something scuttled in a corner and Daphne screamed. Suddenly the door opened and the light from the long window on the floor below flooded in. Sylvia was on the landing, laughing at her foolishness. They never talked about what happened in there.

'Can you see the ghost?'

Her friend's voice is trembly in the thick darkness. Dilys, who can watch unmoved the stricken sheep pump out its lifeblood in the slaughter yard, who wrings a chicken's neck without a moment's thought, is deeply unnerved.

'If you're very quiet,' Daphne whispers, 'you might hear it.'

With her free arm she feels in the darkness for the wall on her left. As she runs her hand along it damp flakes of plaster cling to her skin; she recognises the familiar smell of mould and old limewash. Her fingers find the small trapdoor in the wall. She makes Dilys kneel down beside her, lifts the wooden latch and slowly the door swings inwards. There is a sudden rush of cold air. Dilys screams and Daphne smiles in the secret darkness; there is such power in these subtle terrors. Beyond the little door is a long crawlspace between the rafters and at the far end of it there is another trapdoor which opens into the attics of the Bevan House. There really are spirits living in the Bevan House, everyone in Glanmorfa knows about them.

'Perhaps,' Daphne whispers in Dilys's ear, 'today they will pay a visit to The Room of Doom.'

Dilys shrieks, and backs away on her hands and knees, blindly fumbling for the exit she cannot see, the walls she cannot touch, the icy fingers she knows are reaching out to her. The door flings open and there is Janice, stolid in her sensible skirt and Fair Isle jumper, holding the hula hoop and munching one of Mrs Morgan's decomposing apples.

'You look terrible,' she says to Dilys. 'I'm hungry now, let's go home for tea.'

Daphne stands a moment on the threshold of the haunted room, listening to her friends clattering down the stairs and the front door banging shut. She feels a bit giddy, like a deep-sea diver breasting the surface of the water. Her hands are trembling slightly, her skin is prickly with goose bumps. For she has sensed something in there, in her bones—a reek of river mud, of burial chamber, charnel pit. The bloody corpse of Miss O'Dowd rising up and winding its bony fingers in her hair.

Epiphany: CHAPTER 20

And then the real snow comes. In Glanmorfa it arrives on the morning of Dydd Calan, New Year's Day, whilst groups of children are traipsing up and down the streets of the town, calling at doors and rapping at windows, to sing in the new year and extort calennig, the new year money, from the hapless occupants. On the hall table of the vicarage, as in other upstreet houses, the little bags of new pennies, collected from the bank the day before, lie ready to be given out.

Sylvia sits on the hard wooden chair in the cold hallway, shivering in her purple patterned tights and velvet mini skirt. Her father is out visiting the sick and dying, her mother and Daphne are visiting the bored and lonely. Sylvia is hoping Darren Gough might be one of the calennig callers, though more likely he'll be hovering in the street outside the porch, shuffling in embarrassment, while his little sister and her friends do the singing and begging bit. The knocker thuds against the wood and she gets up to open the door. A blast of arctic wind blows in snow and two little ones from downstreet. Beneath their knitted hats their faces are red and chapped. They hold each other's mittened hands and rattle through the song, tunelessly and out of breath.

Blwyddyn Newydd dda i chi,
Ac i bawb sydd yn y tŷ,
Dyna yw'n dymuniad ni,
Ar ddechrau'r flwyddyn hon.

They falter a little at the last line, unsure of the words even though Miss Tucker made them go over and over the song on the last day of term. Welsh is a bit of a foreign language in Glanmorfa.

They hold out their hands, palms up, ready for the money. Sylvia drops one bag into the palm of the taller infant, as instructed by her father: 'only one between two, you have to be fair to everyone'. The two children grump and gawp for a bit, trying to peer around her for a glimpse of mysterious vicarage life—the grand staircase with the grandfather clock, the lofty hallway, the holy sanctum of the vicar's study, all those spooky corridors. Sylvia shoos them away and shuts the door. Far too cold to be hanging about like that, letting in the draught. She goes back to her chair, longing for midday, the official end of calennig calls. She eyes the dwindling mound of money bags still waiting for dispersal. Vicars' children are not allowed to sing for their suppers, or dress up to blackmail the neighbours at Halloween, or hold ropes across the road on wedding days to ambush the bride and groom and collect sixpences from their guests. These customs set the wrong example, lead to greater crimes. She glances at her wristwatch—still an hour to go—tugs at her skirt, which has ridden up her thighs as she sat down and wishes she'd worn trousers instead, Darren or no Darren.

Daphne, too, is watching the time. Or rather, to be precise, the exotic painted face of an elaborate mantel clock above the fireplace in Mrs Humphrey's shabby drawing room. A preening bird of paradise, blue tailfeathers brushing the XII, clusters of fruit—plums, apricots, grapes—at each corner and, in the oval frame above the clockface, a lady in a red satin dress, with a little white dog on her lap. She and her mother have been sitting in this room for forty-five minutes already and in that time Mrs Humphrey has barely drawn breath, the usual stuff about the old days and the war. Do these old ladies have nothing else to talk about, is there nothing in the present that interests them? The pale green horsehair sofa is hard and unforgiving; whenever she shifts position the sharp end of a broken spring pricks her left buttock. Enid Morgan swallows the dregs of cold tea and puts her empty cup back on its saucer. There are brown tea stains on the inside of the china and the rim is chipped. She leans forward to pick up her handbag from the floor, the sign it is time for them to leave. Daphne is on her feet immediately, reaching for her coat from the chair nearest the window.

'Won't you have another cup of tea, Mrs Morgan? There's still some in the pot.' The old lady doesn't want them to go. Daphne sees this, but outside is the magic of the whirling snow and perhaps a leftover bag of calennig money waiting on the vicarage hall table.

'I'm afraid we can't stop any longer, Mrs Humphrey. I'll call again next week. Thank you for the tea. And a happy new year to you.'

'And the same to you, Mrs Morgan, though these days every year feels exactly like the last one. Do bring your little girl with you next time, so nice to see a young face for a change. Perhaps you'd like to borrow a book, Daphne. Goodness knows it's high time the library had some use, it's been shut up for months.'

As they are in the hallway putting on their coats and hats Mrs Humphrey puts her hand on Enid's arm. Her face is creased with anxiety.

'I can't stop thinking about that poor fellow Parry, cooped up in the Ferry House like a prisoner. Some people are condemning him when the trial hasn't even started. Such a gentle soul, he's not capable of such brutality. And always so helpful, I'd never manage to keep this huge garden in check without his help. You mark my words, Mrs Morgan, the real murderer is still out there, I'm sure of it. They've arrested the wrong man.'

Daphne stares at the pattern in the hallway rug, biting her fingernails. Christmas is over, she should confess now. Time is running out for Johnny Nebo.

'Stop biting your nails, Daphne, say goodbye to Mrs Humphrey.'

The front door closes behind them. They are standing in a landscape without bearings. Mrs Humphrey's old house is at the top of a little rise. It has a lovely view of the town hall and the castle with the wide expanse of estuary stretching behind it. But this morning you would not know that. Daphne and Enid are walking in a blizzard, through a shrouded wilderness, a whiteout so complete they are blinded. They cannot breathe properly, cannot hear any sound beyond this deep silence. The snow has obliterated the short driveway and its shrubby borders; the orchard trees are unrecognisable, ghostly shapes. Daphne can barely keep up with her mother striding ahead. The familiar brown coat and scarf, so solid and reassuring, are vanishing into the whiteness. This doesn't feel like that playground shower at the end of term nor the tongue-tingling excitement of that brief graveyard flurry. This is a different kind of snow, brutal and implacable; it is removing all the landmarks, cancelling the safe passage home.

Her mother has stopped at the end of the driveway, waiting for Daphne to catch up. She takes her arm and tucks it inside her own. Bound together like this, they turn on to the lane leading into town. The roads and pavements are deserted, even the calennig children have given up early and gone home. Although it is only the middle of the day, the brooding snow clouds plunge the town into an early evening. Slowly, the two of them pick their way along George Street, huddled into each other, eyes fixed on the ground in front. The snow is already ankle deep. This sudden, ferocious assault is unlike anything Enid has experienced, not even the terrible winter of '47 when, a newly qualified Classics teacher in her first post at the grammar school, she fell in love with Hywel Morgan on a frozen pond one moonlit evening and skated away with him into matrimony and parish life.

They reach the vicarage gate, furred like an ermine tippet. Inside, the hall's dull grey light offers little warmth, though the smell of burning wood and coal from the kitchen means someone has thought to light a fire, early though it is. Little does anyone know that in only a matter of weeks, a coal fire will seem a luxury.

In the kitchen of the Ferry House, Johnny Nebo takes another log from the dwindling heap and thrusts it into the fire. The wood flames immediately, spitting sparks into the freezing room. He must fetch more wood. He remembers Emrys jabbing his finger at the grate, mind you don't let the fire go out. Johnny pulls on his boots by the door and steps out into the wilderness. He feels the hush—

land and water in a white smother. The sky is shedding snow; fat soft flakes brush his upturned face, dissolve like sherbet in his open mouth. His bones ache from the long, pent-up days and he feels the urge to run—up the cliff path, into town, buy himself a pint at the Captain's and those fags he likes. He closes the front door, starts walking. Stops. He's seeing Ifor's worry face, the warning fist. Stay home. Johnny drops to his knees in the snow. He lies full stretch, arms spread wide, watching the stars fall out of the sky.

CHAPTER 21

Over the coming days a freeze sets in. Thin sunshine sparkles on the mounded roofs and gateposts of the town; hedges and walls are sculpted into new and puzzling shapes and leafy garden shrubs transmute into the frozen creatures of Narnia. At the bottom of the vicarage garden the outbuildings assume the twisted, crenelated shapes of spellbound castles and ice palaces. Sylvia and her friend Bron drag the rusting metal tea tray from the shed, dig out the path almost to its frozen cockleshell bottom and take turns to luge an alpine run from the kitchen door to the orchard, finessing a shoulder lean into the sharp bend by the vegetable beds. The slopes of Hollerton are full of shrieking sledgers and sliders; a few terrified bullocks cower in a corner of the field.

The clouds mass from the north and east, and once again it snows. Pipes freeze, the toilet doesn't flush, milk stays frozen in the bottles. Watching her mother melt snow for making tea, Daphne thinks of Miss O'Dowd's kitchen: the lumps of ice dissolving in the scalding water and the roughness of the cotton towel to dry her hands. She remembers her awkward fumbling at the keyboard, the teacher's impatient sighs. She imagines splintering bone and blood.

In the old churchyard, the ancient tombs are fathoms deep in snow, humped like frozen billows in an arctic sea, the petrified, blackened limbs of withered shrubs thrusting from the ground. Twice a week Rev Morgan and Mr Morris make the treacherous journey along Church Street to the lychgate, between hillocks of frozen snow heaped from shovelled pathways. They pass the silent houses, shuttered against the cold, the empty petrol pumps in the forecourt of Jubilee Garage. Behind the frosted window of Miss O'Dowd's cottage, there's a flicker of candlelight.

'Miss what's-her-name's still there then.' Hubert Morris shakes his head. 'Duw, that old place must be cold as the grave, I thought she would have gone back to England by now.'

'Miss Robinson won't have the choice much longer,' says Hywel, wrapping the folds of his cloak about him. 'They say it's very bad over there already. I called round the other day to see how she was managing. She likes to be independent, she said, plenty to do sorting the house. She was emphatic about not wanting any help. Seemed quite a nice woman, though, very polite.'

Outside the church they check the pipes and gutters, search inside the building for leakage, tell-tale cracks in the plaster and broken windowpanes. Their breath smokes in the cavernous nave. Their hobnailed boots ring on the tower's spiral stairs as they climb towards the little door opening on to the roof. The wood has splintered under the weight of snow. They clear the guttering and gargoyle spouts, check the leads, patch the door as best they can. Down in the nave, a starving jackdaw is fluttering wildly back and forth between the rafters; bits of feather and plaster float down and settle on the faded carpet of the aisle.

'Gad iddo fod, Ficer, bydd e'n marw'n fuan.' Indeed, thinks Hywel, watching the bird's frenzy above their heads, that poor thing will soon be dead, like the rest of us will be if things don't improve.

By the middle of January, Glanmorfa is snowlocked, icebound. Nobody can get out or in. The steep hills which bind the township to the sea—ancient protectors from assault and ambuscade, custodians of dialect and tradition, harbourers of petty criminals and fugitives—have become barriers to relief, the delivery of vital goods and services. People huddle inside their homes, protect their elderly relatives, eke out their meagre food rations. Over at the slaughterhouse, Walter Evans whistles as he picks up his knife to begin butchering the last of the sheep, the pigs and bullocks, and a couple of cows from Pentre Farm whose milk has dried up. The blade is sharp as hell. He chops and fillets, slices gristle from bone, carves up haunches and hocks, slings carcasses from hooks in the cold store, no need for extra ice in this weather. Blood pools and freezes in the gutters.

Johnny Nebo sits at the kitchen table and draws: roofless farm buildings in the snow; smoke curling from the cigarette of a hard-faced man in a Fedora hat; a woman with long flowing hair, a young child in her arms.

Down in the vicarage cellar, Hywel Morgan eyes the dwindling heap of coal. He casts around for other stuff to burn: a couple of broken chairs, old tea chests, some rotting timbers from the lean-to where he dispatches the hens past laying age. There's a pile of cedar logs hewn from the tree in the churchyard which came down during last October's storm; they need another year to season but needs must. Gran abandons the freezing Furthest Room and moves her tub chair, sewing things and copies of *Readers Digest* to a corner of the living room. Enid puts on extra layers, woollen mittens, double socks, and retreats to the chilly sitting room with Virgil, a packet of cigarettes and next term's lesson preparation. The silver candlesticks and brass trays, the copper warming pans and the christening mugs continue to shine brightly, for Mrs Daley will not allow weather to become her master. Twice a week she braves the slippery channels of beaten snow in boots and thick winter stockings, fag slotted between her blistered lips, along the treacherous pavements from downstreet to vicarage door. 'She needs the money,' Enid says to her husband. 'The welfare's not nearly enough to feed a family.' The sisters share the bedtime sprint along the ghostly freezing corridors. They thrust the scalding hot water bottles under bedsheets and eiderdowns and close the heavy curtains which keep the ice at bay. Outside, the street is dark and silent, Bob the sheepdog has long given up his wall patrol and the county has turned off the streetlamps to preserve the electricity supply. Everybody lives by snowlight.

CHAPTER 22

Without a headstone there is no landmark, though Vita Robinson knows exactly where the grave is; she can see fragments of the wreath the children brought scattered across the spot. Elsewhere in the graveyard, slabs of dark granite, marble obelisks and crosses pierce the snow-crust like the skeletons of ancient ships marooned in ice. At her feet she notes the delicate traces of birds and the pawprints of some small questing animal. No human has visited in weeks. Hers are the only footprints, though she is careful not to walk too close to the grave. Unwise to set tongues wagging. Who in their right mind would be visiting this particular grave and in such appalling weather? And indeed, in her right mind she would not have left the cottage this early in the morning and struggled all the way up the church path to the graveyard, just to make sure. It had been a bad dream, nothing more. Eleanor O'Dowd is still safely six foot under in the icy earth and has not burst her cerements and come howling for revenge, as if she were the innocent victim.

Vita thrusts her gloved hands deep inside the pockets of her fur coat. Remembers another graveyard scene, snow-filled like this one. The same sombre memorials. High stone walls, dark lines of yew under a bitter sky. Family generations, all together in the same plot. She would have been about ten years old, the same age as that girl Daphne. Leah, her beloved Oma, would be well over a hundred now if she were still alive. But that was nonsense of course; back then she'd have died anyway, along with all the others of her kind.

After Oma's funeral rites were over, she walked behind her parents along the icy path to the gates of the Weißensee. An elderly man in a kippah was standing outside the grand entrance to the cemetery. He was wearing a torn and shabby overcoat and he was playing a violin, badly. The instrument was in poor condition and she remembers covering her ears with her hands and her father pulling them away—'Hör auf damit, sei nicht so unhöflich!' The first time anyone had reprimanded her for being rude, perhaps that's why she remembers it so well.

On the ground at the violinist's feet was a scuffed tin bowl with a few coins inside. Without warning, two young men dressed in uniform, passing by on the opposite pavement, crossed the road towards them. One of them shouted something to the other, then he snatched the violin from the old man's hands, threw it on the ground and viciously kicked over the bowl. The old man cried out and fell to his knees, scrabbling in the snow to collect the scattered Reichsmarks. Her mother was tugging at her hand, trying to pull her away. 'Komm nun, Avital, gehen wir.' But Vita resisted, she wanted to stay. To watch her father, on his hands and knees—in his best winter coat and hat—helping the old man gather up the rest of the coins and the remains of the broken violin. She saw him take out his wallet and press some money into the musician's trembling hand. When her father turned away, she noticed that his face was wet with tears.

All this while, the two young men were standing only a few yards away. Their arms were folded across their chests and they were laughing, like they were watching a street comedy. As her father passed them, the man who had attacked the violinist, cleared his throat loudly and spat. The gobbet landed on the collar of her father's smart funeral coat. He paid no attention to this insult, simply took her mother's arm in his and the three of them walked away.

Across the years, she can still hear those two men shouting after them. 'Tiere, animals!' Still feel the trembling of Mutti's hand in hers and her own burning anger. Why did her father not react? 'Always show respect for others, Avital, no matter how much you are provoked.' That sentiment made no sense to her; she would have struck that man.

They were her father's last words to her, before the train left the city and her new life among strangers began. Vita Robinson stares across the snow at the blank space, the final resting place of Eleanor O'Dowd. Respect, forgiveness. Such empty words. She closes her eyes and prays to a God she does not believe in, may there be no eternal rest for that woman.

CHAPTER 23

The older boys have built a snow ramp in the middle of Hollerton field. They line up at the top of the run by the boundary hedge and take turns to board. Face forward, kick off, gathering momentum towards the ramp. The sled soars, ethereal, above the sloping field, then drops, with a bone-breaking thud and shudder of gritty snow and iceballs. Winded, the boy lies on the ground for a moment to catch his breath. Shouts from the top of the field, 'Get out the way!' He staggers to his feet, gathers the ropes, and hauls his sled out of the path of the next boy in the queue.

Sylvia and her friends disdain the ramp, for they have discovered the hidden talent of the tea tray, dubbed Waltzing Matilda. It lives up to its name, a fast and giddy roundabout that spins down the slope until it hits a ridge of hard ground and spills the rider headfirst into the snow. Everybody wants a go.

Someone yells from the top of the field. A small figure in a blue bobble hat sits astride the sled, preparing to take the ramp. Daphne, standing midway up the field with Dilys and Christine Miller, watches Janice tighten her hold on the sled ropes and lean forward. Alun Hughes gives her a shove. The field is stilled, everyone watching. The sled gathers speed, hits the edge of the ramp and takes off; it travels some feet in the air then tilts to one side and slams hard into the packed snow.

From every corner of the field people are running, slipping and skidding on the frozen ground, towards the spot where Janice lies spreadeagled. Her sled is a jumble of broken struts and tangled rope. Her face is very white, and there's blood trickling from a small cut on her chin. She stares up at them, but her eyes don't seem to be focusing properly.

'You alright, Jan?'

Alun is bending over her, red-faced and panting from his sprint down the field. He goes to take her hand to pull her up and she screams, 'Don't touch me!' Alun shouts, 'Someone get help, quick.' Jason Dunn is off at once, legging it across the field towards the road. Janice is breathing hard; she tries to stand, sinks back down, clutching her arm.

'Put your head between your knees, Jan,' someone suggests. 'Seen it on the telly, stops you fainting.'

Instead, Janice turns her head sideways and sicks up her breakfast over Dilys kneeling beside her.

Jason comes back with Howie Clark and Mr Davies from the garage. Mr Davies seems to know what he's doing. He crouches down beside Janice and asks her what happened, which bits of her are hurting. His voice is very gentle, he calls her 'the queen of speed' which makes her smile in a wan sort of way. Then Mr Davies and Howie knit their hands together to make a seat. On a count of three they lift Janice up and carry her back across the field to the lane. After that, nobody feels much like sledging; they drift off in pairs and small groups, carrying their sleds, pieces of sacking, empty plastic bags of animal feed.

'Trust Janice to be sick,' Dilys sniffs. The two of them are taking the short cut across the field towards Quaker's Bridge. 'She could have waited a bit longer before she threw up. Can you smell it on me?'

Daphne does not respond. She is feeling a bit sick herself. First Martin, now Janice—she could be next.

When they get to the stile at the end of the field, they see a man on the bridge. He's peering into the water. Dilys stops dead.

'Look who's there!' she hisses. 'It's Johnny Nebo, he must have escaped from the Ferry House. We can't go past him.'

'Why not?'

Dilys rolls her eyes. 'Because he's a murderer, stupid.' She starts gnawing at her fingers.

'Why you doing that?'

'Cos I'm scared, that's why. He's not s'posed to be out on his own, my dad says, in case he murders somebody else.'

She backs away, dragging Daphne after her. 'Let's go home the long lanes, it's safer.'

They turn round and start walking back across the field. Dilys strides ahead, stumbling over the frozen lumps of churned-up snow. Daphne takes a look over her shoulder, in case Johnny Nebo is following them, but he's still on the bridge. He's not alone though; the scary uncle with the beard has joined him. They're standing side by side looking over the parapet, like they've seen something in the water. Johnny is rubbing his eyes with his fists, like he could be crying. The scary uncle puts his arm around Johnny's shoulders and steers him away from the bridge, back up the lane towards Church Street.

CHAPTER 24

In another country, some two hundred and fifty miles east of Glanmorfa, Ronald Blight rests his shovel against the back door of his semi, Number 17 Priory Road, and surveys the ghost of his precious garden. The fragile plants, his prized rose bushes, the camellia planted in memory of his late mother, all are dungeoned beneath three feet of snow. Even the privet hedge has withered, wracked to death by the freezing temperatures. Priory Road itself is barely passable and nothing seems to be moving on Palmers Green High Street: no buses or taxis, not even one of those manky stray cats he hates. All the bins are frozen solid, serves the buggers right.

He turns from the beleaguered garden and enters the house, leaving his boots to dry out on the sheets of newspaper by the back door. He draws the heavy baize curtain across it to keep the cold at bay. The kitchen is the warmest place in the house, but he keeps his coat and scarf on and the woollen mittens his father used to wear in the workshop after his arthritis set in. They are a size too small for his large hands; young Ronnie did not inherit Robert Blight's slight frame, nor his craftsman's slim fingers. Mabel was always the skinny, arty one. There's a photograph of the two of them on the mantelpiece: he in his smart new constable's uniform straight out of Police College and Mabel, two years older, about to start her first teaching post. They've done well, the Blight kids, pulled themselves right up the ladder, Robert and Ada would have been dead proud.

He switches on the wireless for the latest from Australia, pours a cup of lukewarm tea from the pot and settles himself in the wooden armchair next to the stove. Something is niggling him. Is it the disaster unfolding in Melbourne, Dexter's bowlers about to throw away the 3rd Test? Or that he's down to his last two cigarettes? He's been stuck in this blessed house for over a week now and the pubs are shut, maybe that's all it is, what they call a touch of cabin fever.

He glances over at the little sideboard, one of several pieces of furniture his father made for his mother when they were newly-weds and short of cash. The oak veneer is still in good nick from all that meticulous polishing. From its place between last summer's postcard of Tenby and the little porcelain goldfinch he bought his mother for her eightieth, Mrs Price's spangled Christmas card winks at him. A frosted church atop a hill, a couple in furred Victorian costume holding hands with a small child. Seasons greetings from Madras House, she's written inside in lilac ink.

Unfinished business, that is what's gnawing at him. The date for the Parry trial is still on hold, everybody's waiting for the weather to improve. Ronald Blight stares long at Mrs Price's card, his fingers drumming the chair arm. A sooty fag end, a handful of sketches, a hasty document. To be honest, these are thin scrapings for any conviction. No spoken confession. No murder weapon.

CHAPTER 25

'Mr Merchant's just telephoned.'

It is Friday afternoon, three days before the start of term. Their father has left his study, warmed by the only two bar electric heater in the house, and come into the kitchen to announce the news.

'He's closed the school until further notice. Teachers can't get in. I'll put the word round.'

He shuts the kitchen door. Two seconds later he's back again, the hint of a smile at the corners of his mouth.

'I forgot to tell you, Daphne, Mr Merchant wants the exam group at his house on Monday morning, nine o'clock sharp. It's lessons as usual for you lot.'

An eternity of piano lessons would be preferable to this. Assuming, of course, Miss O'Dowd were still alive, though in this weather she'd have hacked lumps of ice out of the river for her pupils' hands, the old meany. Daphne leans against the window of the headmaster's front room and with the sleeve of her jumper rubs a clear patch in the frosted pane. Like every other garden in the town, this one has lost all shape and colour, it's just a flat and frozen waste. Even the solitary robin grubbing for vanished seeds at the bottom of a laurel bush has lost its red breast.

'Do I take it you've finished, Daphne?' Mr Merchant is flicking his pencil between his fingers, over and over. 'You have another five minutes before the end of the test. Remember what I said: use the time wisely; don't waste it.'

She turns back to the page in front of her.

My best friend is tall and dark. I am ten and he is eleven. He is one of these four boys below. Read the following sentences and write down my best friend's name. Harry is younger than me. He is short and dark. Dick is eleven. He is a tall boy with fair hair. Tom has dark hair. He is older than me and is a tall boy. Frank is a tall boy with dark hair. He is ten.

She will be eleven in August and she will fail the eleven-plus on account of these pointless questions. Not in a million years would she choose somebody called Frank or Dick to be her best friend. The silly sentences wobble and fade in front of her eyes, they make no sense at all. The robin is at the window now, pecking forlornly at the wooden frame, hoping for grubs. Martin's sitting opposite her on the sofa. He still looks thin and a bit ghostly and he coughs a lot; his lungs are bad, he says. Janice is sitting in the stiff wing chair with her left arm plastered up to the elbow. She looks miserable too. The six of them—she, Dilys, Martin, Graham, Alun and Janice—are the chosen ones, imprisoned with their test papers in the headmaster's front room. The no-hopers haven't been invited to these extra lessons, the lucky beasts. Or if they have been, they've chosen not to turn up. They're all off sledging and skating and building the ice tunnel at the bottom of the town with the other liberated children.

At 10.30 they are allowed a break, to keep up the pretence this is the same as real school. Mrs Merchant brings in lemonade and a plate of Garibaldi biscuits. She places a little table beside Janice's chair, with two biscuits on a little china plate decorated with roses. Daphne slides an extra biscuit into her pocket, for the robin. They like raisins. Three weeks they have been stuck in this room from nine in the morning until the town clock strikes noon, after which Mr Merchant releases them into the chilly brightness and the distant voices of their schoolmates having fun.

Martin catches up with her at the bottom of the Merchants' driveway. He's bundled up in a heavy duffle coat, wellies and a bright green balaclava. His mother is taking no chances with the weather. 'Which way you goin' home?' he wheezes.

'I'm going to try the river. Sylvia did it yesterday, she said the ice was pretty thick even in the middle.'

'I'll come with you then, we can use this if we fall in.' He's carrying a walking stick with a carved top in the shape of a fox's head. 'Used to be my dad's. Mum said I had to take it with me in case there's an avalanche.'

The Morlas has frozen all the way from Quaker's Bridge to the estuary. At supper yesterday Sylvia announced she saw a heron in the lane on their side of the river. 'They never come this far inland, it must be starving, poor thing. And John Edgar was round the Hughes's back yard all day Saturday, slaughtering their pigs, you could hear them screaming. Glad dad didn't get a pig this year.'

Martin and Daphne walk along the road towards the river and slide down the bank by the children's playground. The frozen river is glassy at the edges, a glaze of weeds and stones trapped beneath the ice. Further out, the surface is opaque, pocked with frozen twigs, small stones and globs of duck poo. Daphne grips the bottom end of Martin's walking stick for safety and takes a first step out on to the ice. It gives a little, but she knows the river isn't deep here, she'll be ok even if her foot goes through. She ventures a little further. The ice feels solid under her feet, it can take her weight. She is now standing mid river and the Morlas is a strange white road winding between the trees, full of mystery. She takes a deep breath and draws the air's sharpness into her throat. She wants to hold this moment for ever.

'C'mon Daph, stop standing there like an idiot, it's my turn. Don't let go the stick.' Martin is gingerly edging across the ice towards her, clutching the fox-head end. His thin face beneath the green balaclava is pinched with concentration. He looks scared stiff.

'It's fine, Mart, honest. Look!' She stamps her feet hard. 'See? No cracks.'

It feels so peculiar to walk on a river, not in it. Daphne goes in front, navigating between branches splintered under the weight of snow and shards of broken metal and plastic stuck fast in the ice's grip. They peer into snow-filled gardens and the unfamiliar backs of houses and spy on Mr James, Portland House, shovelling the path to his outside toilet. Emboldened, their steps become slides, become skids, they forget the water is only inches below their feet. If only they had proper skates. On the opposite bank belonging to The Gables, Miss Vaughan's elderly black labrador is on patrol, hackles up and paws slithering on the edge. As they slide past Martin calls to him. 'Come on good boy, jump in and have a skate,' but he growls and backs away, this water dog who does not trust the ice.

Just before the bend by Hollerton field, they steer towards the bank and climb on to the footpath behind the cottages. The spot where Daphne fell has disappeared, marked only by the blanched tips of reeds spearing through the snow. Suddenly, from around the bend a small figure appears, midstream. A real skater: the swish of blades cutting through the ice; the easy, graceful movement as she swerves the alder branch; the powerful swinging arms. The skater's leather gloves are a flash of scarlet in the monochrome. She does not notice the two of them gawping at her from the footpath, instead her gaze is fixed upon the river-road, alert for sudden hazards.

'Who was that?'

Daphne explains, briefly. She leaves out the encounter on Hangman Lane; boys don't go in for that sort of detail.

'Wish I could skate like her,' he says wistfully, gazing after the retreating figure. 'But I know mum wouldn't let me.'

They walk up the frozen cart track on to Church Street as far as the lychgate and the junction with Church Lane. This is as far as Daphne is prepared to go.

Martin's trying to poke his walking stick into the drift by the lychgate wall, but it's rock-frozen and glittering like Christmas icing.

'I don't get it, Daph, why hasn't the curse gone away now the skull's put back?'

She bites her lip. Martin's voice sounds all croaky and strained, like he's trying not to cry. 'This isn't like normal snow,' he says. 'It's getting worse and worse everywhere. We've unleashed a terrible spirit, that's what we've done.'

She watches him walking slowly up Church Lane, leaning on his stick like an old man. Every now and then he has to stop to catch his breath.

'Mind out for avalanches!' she calls, hoping to lighten the mood, but he doesn't turn round.

On her way home, Martin's words are a dead weight in the pit of her stomach. 'What's done cannot be undone'—Mr Duckford's favourite phrase, applied to maths tests, fibs, playground fights—has a different meaning now. She is passing opposite the row of cottages when the thought strikes. The terrible spirit could be lurking in the place where Miss O'Dowd was murdered. Vita Robinson could be in danger. She should warn her, give her time to leave Glanmorfa before it's too late.

Daphne crosses the road and knocks on the door of No 3. There is no answer. She waits, practising what she will say when Vita opens the door. 'Hello, I need to tell you about the curse. You're probably going to die, just like your friend.' That sounds ridiculous. Vita will laugh and say she's talking nonsense. 'You should have grown out of fairy tales by now, Daphne. Not so clever after all, are you?'

She hears a noise inside the house, someone is walking towards the front door. Daphne backs away and hurries up the street, pulling up the hood of her coat to hide the tell-tale hair.

CHAPTER 26

The sea freezes. Nobody, not even the oldest inhabitants of Glanmorfa can remember such a thing happening. People come out of their houses and shops to stand awestruck on the shoreline. Everywhere, the surface of the sea is ridged and crusted; ripples are caught mid flow, suspended like bubbles in amber. Two herring gulls rise into the air from the prow of a fishing smack frozen fast between the mudbanks, their dismal cries echoing across the tundra. Curlews and sandpipers have all deserted; fish lie belly up below the surface; cockles perish in the bitter sand.

Terry Dunn sticks his head out from the snow tunnel, excavated from the huge snow drift banked against the wall of Lundy House. He waves to Daphne and the others, released from lessons early on account of the phenomenon.

'Come and take a look.'

The interior is surprisingly domestic, a Christmas grotto without the decorations, though someone has strung a line of carnival bunting above the entrance. There are a couple of deckchairs, some upturned crates, an old stool and a wooden plank balanced on two empty oil drums with bottles of pop and bags of crisps. The ice walls and roof are smoothed and rounded. All this wondrous, purposeful activity going on while the chosen six have been stuck indoors doing pointless tests. The girls cluster at one end of the tunnel, the boys at the other, no-one seems very sure what to do next. Terry stands in the middle, arms folded, proprietorial.

'Good job,' says Dilys, approvingly. She settles herself in a deckchair.

'You can have one of these if you like,' smiles Terry, magnanimously waving a crumpled bag of sweets: pear drops, flying saucers, liquorice strings, little squares of pink gum wrapped in shiny paper. He takes the other deckchair and the two of them sit chewing and admiring the architecture.

'You could do with a little heater in here,' says Graham. 'Eskimos have fires in their igloos, it said in *Look and Learn*. You have to make a hole in the roof for the smoke to get out.'

Terry's mouth is working the gum. 'Don't need a fire, stupid. We got this.' He fishes out a motheaten bit of blanket from inside one of the crates and wraps it over his knees. 'See? Warm as toast, we've thought of everything.' He leans over and rummages around in the crate for a bit.

'Want one of these?' He's waving a cigarette at them. They eye each other nervously, who's going to make the first move. In this moment Terry Dunn, king of the ice palace, makes them all feel foolish. Daphne takes a deep breath and holds out her hand. Terry places the cigarette in her palm and one of the older boys, Raymond, comes over with a matchbox. She feels everyone's eyes on her; she knows what to do, she's watched her mother and Mrs Daley light up many times. She holds the cigarette between middle and index fingers, watches Raymond lean towards her and strike the match. She puts the right end between her lips and breathes in, magicking the red glow. Quickly, she puffs out a trail of greyish smoke. She's enjoying this moment: the envy of her friends, the admiration of Terry and his gang. She takes a second drag. The cough is rising, scratching at her throat, her lungs feel like they're bursting. She struggles on for a few seconds more until the coughing lets rip.

Terry snatches back the cigarette and sticks it in the corner of his mouth, like Mrs Daley does. He grins round at his pals.

'Look at her, vicar's daughter! Bet your dad'll go mad when he finds out.' He takes a long drag, purses his lips and exhales three impressive smoke rings, one after the other. He sees her horrified face and starts to laugh.

'S'alright, maid, only jokin', I won't tell on you.'

'What you do that for, Daph?' She and Graham are heading upstreet, walking in the middle of the road between the drifts.

135

'I've done it loads,' she lies. 'My mother smokes all the time.'

'Didn't look like that to me. Stupid habit, my mother says.'

'Well, it's none of your business, I can smoke if I want to so there, stupid yourself.'

When they get to the top of the street, there's a hearse parked outside the house next door to the butcher's. The front room curtains are drawn.

'Somebody must have died,' says Graham, stating the obvious. 'They'll have to store the body until the weather gets warmer, ground's too hard to dig now.'

'They could always burn it.'

'You mean, like in India?'

'Don't be daft, I mean the crem; my dad takes lots of funerals up there.'

'Bet they'll be running out of wood. Maybe they could turn the body into a mummy, like the Egyptians. Take all the guts out and wrap it up in bandages.'

The following morning Dilys does not turn up at Mr Merchant's house for the lesson. The hearse had come for Granny Gloria.

'Took the driver two hours to drive ten miles from the undertakers,' said Mrs Daley who heard it from her daughter. 'And when he got to the mortuary, they had a job finding space for it. She was 92, poor dab, time to go. Like a little bird she was at the end.'

Daphne thinks of the drawerful of dolly mixtures, the lacy bed jacket, Granny Gloria's white braid lying across the dainty coverlet. A flutter of tiny wings and she was gone.

Later that same day, Sylvia finds the heron on the riverbank by the footbridge. Dead, from cold or hunger, or both. She places the stiffened corpse in a carrier bag and takes it down to the frozen foreshore where she leaves it beside a large rock. It's important to return the dead whence they came.

CHAPTER 27

In his Sunday suit and heavy overcoat, his large feet squeezed into old but serviceable walking boots from his student days, Hywel Morgan braves the blizzard wastes to reach Llanmarlais church, two miles up country. By rights this ancient, crumbling building should have shut its doors years ago, but the tiny Welsh-speaking farming congregation are faithful to the old ways and he owes it as their vicar to be faithful too and continue the monthly communion service, come tempest or blizzard. The deep lanes are choked with snow, passable only by walking on top of the frozen hedge line all the way there and back. His very nearly parting shot, as he left the kitchen breakfast table an hour ago, was 'I may be some time,' but that would be tempting fate, or God, to punish flippancy.

There are only four worshippers waiting for him by the gate as he carefully descends the brow of the hill where the small church lies curled like a sea snail in a hollow of oak trees. Someone has cleared a pathway to the porch door; inside, the little stove near the font coughs a smoky welcome. Raised a countryman and a Welsh speaker, Hywel Morgan is more comfortable amongst his own people than some of the tight-lipped gentry of upstreet Glanmorfa. Miss Annie Evans, white hair curled tight as a sheep, treadles the harmonium in her thick-soled boots. The notes of the hymn, 'Mi glywaf dyner lais', soar and fade and soar again according to the pressure of her soles, but the tune is well known and the singers ride the gusts, 'Arglwydd dyma fi / ar dy alwad di / Golch fi'n burlan yn y gwaed / A gaed ar Galfari.' After the service is over, they gather briefly by the dying stove: tired, worn faces with tales of buried sheep and frozen lambs arrived too early; of dwindling fodder for the cattle; the necessary slaughter of the old and barren. 'Erioed yn cofio tywydd mor wael.' No-one can remember worse weather, not even in '47. The despairing litany echoes in the nave's stone arches and the ancient Ogham cross propped against the north wall. Whispers over the medieval effigy of Maud Marlais, whose youthful body was carved in three by her assailants.

Rev Morgan readies his tired legs to pound the hedgerow homewards and Mrs Lewis, Lan Farm, presses into his hand a bacon sandwich wrapped in greaseproof paper. 'bwyta'r cyfan nawr, ficer'. He doesn't need encouragement; at the top of the lane, out of sight of his little flock, he crams the whole sandwich into his mouth and trudges off across the snowfields. Hungry work, this arctic life.

On the final stretch, as the road begins to dip towards the town, he pauses to admire the hedge-top panorama. On his right, the smooth icefield of the Moor shrouds the fertile strips of land, the right of burgage since the middle ages; it entombs the ancient barrows of the Beaker folk and the long-drowned bones of woolly mammoth and hyena. To his left, the gentle inland hillsides have become the landscape of Siberia. Nothing is but what is not, he thinks. Below him the township's snow-lined roofs, the crenellated castle walls, the silent, stilled waters of the estuary, are a Breughel winter from the distant past, beauteous but also terrifying. Farmers, fishermen like the Parry brothers, whole communities will lose their livelihoods if the weather doesn't change soon. And not just here in Glanmorfa; the whole country is suffering. He thinks of the Thomas children, living in a house not much better than a hovel, and their father bringing in barely enough money to feed and clothe them all. People rally round, of course they do, but there's only so much help you can give when so many are in need. When the thaw comes there'll be a reckoning with history and nature.

CHAPTER 28

Daphne is walking down Church Street towards the Stores. It's another brilliant, sparkling day: the sky is an intense, gelid blue and the crusty tops of the snow drifts are aglitter. Like Bavaria, she thinks, remembering a postcard the Merchants sent her parents from their holiday in Oberammergau to see the passion play. Tucked inside the pocket of her duffle coat is her mother's Lion Brand cash book with its shiny red cover. Inside is the week's shopping list, in Enid Morgan's looping schoolteacher handwriting. The inventory never varies:

> *4lbs Sugar; 2 Kraft Cheese; a box of Winalot; 2 tins Lassie; 2 tins Mandarin Oranges; 2 Heinz tom Soup; 3 Cadbury's Choc; Marmite; 1 small tin of salmon; 3 orange jellies; pkt of Oxo; 1 tin Pineapple Slices; 20 Embassy Tipped; ½ Typhoo Tea.*

Gran has pinned a coupon to the page, cut out of yesterday's *Western Mail*. 'Take this to your local shop and save 4 pence on Milkana de Luxe Cheese Spread.' She had been very insistent.

'Show this to Mr Jones. If it's not in stock, mind you tell him to order it.'

'But we're snowed in, Gran, Mr Jones can't order new stuff, we've got to stick with what's in the shop.'

Gran wrinkles her nose in disgust. 'See here, miss know-it-all, I'm not having those Kraft cheese slices, taste of cardboard they do, set my teeth on edge.'

Daphne has to hover by the door while Mr Jones is busy serving a customer. It's cosy inside the shop, warmed by the little paraffin stove propped on a stool below the wooden counter. Ranged around the walls are shelves crammed with tinned foods and cereal boxes, fat glass jars full of pudding rice, dried beans, sweets. Wooden crates of onions and potatoes, sacks of withered carrots, swedes and turnips. Behind the door a wooden rack for shovels and spades, garden forks. The little stove hisses and sputters.

Mr Jones finishes putting the groceries into a cardboard box on the counter. 'Can you manage that on your own, Miss Robinson?'

'It's not that heavy, thank you Mr Jones,' she replies, lifting the box. 'Once more into the frozen wastes!' She turns and sees Daphne.

'Hello again. I didn't know it was you standing behind me, what a nice surprise.'

Despite the tone of voice, Vita Robinson doesn't look particularly pleased. Her face is very pale and tired looking; the blueish skin around her eyes is hatched with tiny thin lines. She's wearing the same fur coat and hat she wore the day of the funeral.

'Thank you for being so patient.' She gives Daphne a brief smile and goes out of the shop, trailing behind her the faint smell of camphor, like the moth balls Gran keeps in her wardrobe. Daphne feels a pang of disappointment, she wishes she had thought of something to say.

'Right Miss Morgan, what's on the list today?'

She fishes in her pocket for the cashbook and hands it across the counter to Mr Jones. He flicks it open to the right page, runs his eye down the list, then takes the pencil from behind his ear and draws lines through some of the items.

'I'm clean out of salmon and tomato soup, sorry. I'll put in sardines instead. And it'll be mandarins not pineapple, tell your mother.'

He unpins the Milkana coupon, shakes his head, drops it into the wastepaper basket. 'Groceries might be late getting to you on Saturday, I'll be waiting for the van from town. They're still having trouble getting through. Weather's worse the further east you go.'

As she leaves the Stores, Daphne sees Vita Robinson standing in front of the cottage. She is waving to her. Daphne hesitates, glances behind her, perhaps it's Mr Jones she wants. But he's still in the shop and there's nobody else about.

'Daphne,' the woman calls. 'Do you have a moment?'

It's the first time she's been inside the cottage since her last piano lesson, the week before the murder. The drab hallway looks and smells just the same: flaky patches of distemper on the walls; the reek of damp. Only the old threadbare rug that used to cover the stone flags has gone.

Vita shuts the front door behind them and stands with her back against it, her arms folded across her chest. She's taken off her fur coat and hat and is wearing a shapeless navy jumper over brown corduroy trousers. Her short dark hair is very thick and wiry, threaded with grey. There's something carefree about the way it springs back from her face, so different from Daphne's mother and her friends, with their perms and sets and smooth coils of hair.

'Seeing you in the shop just now reminded me I had to give you Eleanor's present. She wrote your name on the label, I'm assuming there's only one Daphne in Glanmorfa.' She smiles. 'Actually, I do know you were a pupil of hers. Your father called round when the snow started to ask if I needed anything. He mentioned his girls had music lessons with Eleanor. I remember what he said about you. "Sylvia is musical but lazy, and Daphne should stick to reading books." That made me laugh.' She opens the door of the front room. 'Come on.'

The lid of the grand piano is heaped with papers; there are books and cardboard folders spread across the floor. The room is perishingly cold.

Vita is rummaging amongst the papers on the piano. 'Eleanor never filed a thing. Brilliant pianist, hopeless organiser. Ah, here it is. I think she intended you to have it before Christmas.'

She holds out a small package wrapped in pale green tissue paper tied with a thin purple ribbon. There's a small label tucked inside the ribbon: *Daphne*.

'Aren't you going to open it? I'm dying to know what it is.'

Daphne undoes the ribbon and carefully unfolds the thin paper. The book is bound in scarlet leather with the title in gold embossed

141

lettering: *'Morte D'Arthur' A Poem By Alfred Lord Tennyson*. Daphne opens it and leafs through the pages. They are a wonder. The margins are densely decorated with flowers and leaves and tiny birds; each verse is illustrated in vivid, dazzling pictures. Armoured knights in combat, a jewelled sword caught mid plunge into a lake, a black barge bearing a trio of ghostly-looking women in long veils.

Vita gently takes the book from her and flicks back through the pages.

'Knowing Eleanor, she will have written something for you. Yes, here it is.' As she starts reading her face darkens.

To Daphne Morgan from Eleanor O'Dowd, Christmas 1962.
'The true old times are dead, the old order changeth.'

'God, that's so typical of the woman! The same old harking back to the past, trying to make everybody feel sorry for her. It's meant to be a Christmas present for a child, for goodness sake, not some inscription on a bloody gravestone! You'd think she would have written something more cheerful, wouldn't you?' She thrusts the book back into Daphne's hand.

Daphne is quite bewildered. Why would Miss O'Dowd give her anything? She was hardly her favourite pupil. Silently, she starts reading the opening lines of the poem.

So all day long the noise of battle roll'd
Among the mountains by the winter sea.

It's the kind of language she loves.

'Eleanor never understood young people, she had absolutely no sense of fun. She wanted them to behave like grown-ups, better still to be exactly like her, always so serious about life. She had no experience of joy, you know.'

Daphne drags her gaze from the poem's lovely words, but Vita's not looking at her, she has forgotten she's in the room.

'And if you chose not to be serious, if you just wanted to be yourself and not be controlled, then she'd simply wash her hands of you, rub you out. That's hard to forgive when you're young, don't you think?'

Daphne has no idea what she should think. She closes the book and wraps it in the tissue paper, trying to find an excuse to leave. She is out of her depth. She is starting to back away when Vita suddenly turns and looks at her.

'Eleanor wasn't one for giving presents, she must have seen something special in you. Why is that, I wonder? I would have thought your sister was the chosen one. So you tell me, Daphne Morgan, what is so interesting about you?'

Daphne shrugs. 'I don't know, I'm not very good at anything, except spelling. She ... I mean Miss O'Dowd .... didn't like me very much, she thought I was a bit stupid.' There was more she could mention—the sarcastic comments, the torture of the scalding water—but right now she just wants to go home.

'You have my total sympathy on that score. I've got no musical ability either, can't play a note without someone blocking their ears from the noise. I expect Eleanor gave you the present because, as your father said, you like books. She was always a great fan of the romantic poets, all that business about heroic knights and wilting maidens really appealed to her. Thank God nobody believes in that guff anymore.'

Daphne clears her throat. 'Sorry, Miss Robinson, I've got to go, I have to take the dog for a walk.' The words come out all quavery and she stumbles out of the room, clutching the book to her chest.

At the front door Vita puts a hand on her arm; she's looking a bit sad now.

'Forgive me, Daphne, I didn't mean to sound so flippant just then. It's still the shock of her murder, I think. Goodness knows what motivated that wretched man to kill Eleanor; I just wish they would get on with the trial and hang him.'

Vita lingers at the open door, watching Daphne make her way

up the street, her hair a spurt of flame between the snow drifts. The girl's sharper than she looks; it was stupid of her to let her guard down like that and scare the poor thing off. Tomorrow she will send Daphne a little note of contrition, with an invitation to tea and to choose another book from Eleanor's shelves. That should do the trick.

Vita closes the door and goes back into the cold parlour. She seats herself at the piano, her stern features mirrored in the ebony. The fingers of her left hand are poised, ready. C sharp major. *Tempo agitato.* She takes a deep breath, bends forward, and plunges. The narrow cheerless room swells with the restless, driving urgency of Chopin's *Fantaisie Impromptu.* The stormy triplets, the complex interweaving of rhythms, are like her beloved speed skating— unnerving, desperate and overwhelmingly joyous, over too soon.

CHAPTER 29

Emrys watches his nephew from the kitchen window, a dark figure on the far side of the frozen river. Johnny has been out there since early morning, crossing to Black Scar before he and Ifor realised he was not in the house. But they're not his prison guards; they have stuck to the rules, kept him at home most days or else gone with him to the shops to buy his fags and comics. No more visits to the old ladies, mind, they've been strict about that. No chopping their wood or lighting their fires. The weather's helped; everyone is indoors these days apart from the children, though even the tunnel on the Strand is losing its novelty, chunks of it kicked down and trampled, ice boulders scattered across the road. Everywhere you walk there's a whiff of sewage and blocked drains; the pumps at both ends of the town stopped running weeks ago. And hunger in the air, too. Their own livelihood has died with the weather—fish belly-up under the frozen surface, the ferryboat ice-shackled. They're all making do with eating spam and baked beans, the pickled beetroot and a bit of salted pork Miss Roderick from Beacon House brought them the other day. Worse than rationing, this.

Emrys turns from the window and goes over to the stove to add more fuel. Hopefully, when the thaw comes, they'll be able to get down the Point to forage for coal washed up on the sands. He leans closer to the stove and blows hard on the embers, draws up a thin plume of smoke, a small wavering flame. The kitchen table is littered with papers and pencils, all Johnny's drawings; he's had so much time on his hands these past weeks. Emrys riffles through the sketches: kids on sledges up Hollerton fields, John Edgar driving his cows past the school, a woman in a man's cap and coat, walking on the footpath under the castle—she's in a hurry, Johnny's got the movement just perfect. If only he'd had the right teacher, someone to recognise this gift of his. No good now, the police will be setting a new date for the trial once the courts open again. Snow's done them this favour, at least. Kept the three of them together.

Johnny scans the snow-clad hillside. The scribble of ash trees at the top of the wood, the derelict, ivy smothered buildings of Danyrallt farm. A rusted slice of corrugated iron, torn from the roof by the blizzards, splinters the grey sky. Down the farm track from the brow of the hill a line of sagging electricity poles, their cables sheared off and dangling above the snow drifts. He leaves the Scar behind him and climbs up through the field, boots crunching deep into the snow, leaving prints where none have trod for months. Heavy winter clothes make sweaty work. Halfway up the hill, he sheds his father's old oilskin jacket, then the navy jumper patched with sacking at the elbows. In cap and shirt sleeves he reaches the gate, now only a heap of broken spars shattered by the driving blizzards.

He crosses the yard, noting the signatures left in the snow: fox prints, the soft press of rabbit paws, bird scratchings. His mother's old home regards him through the broken windows, the gaping threshold. He walks inside. Snow has invaded the gaps in the stone walls and carpeted the broken flagstones in the kitchen. A drift of wizened chestnut leaves has blown in from the autumn gales and soot piles clog the blackened hearth. Upstairs, in places where the slates have gone, the rooms are open to the elements. In one of them is an iron bedstead with a rotting mattress, broken floorboards, creeping ivy. He will not find her here; she was never comfortable indoors.

He goes back outside. On one of his visits here in the spring, he rooted out a clutch of pale narcissi from the little garden she had made at the front of the house, overlooking the estuary. They were blooming against the low stone wall that separated the house from the farmyard. He found a lilac tree too, he remembers its fragrance as he passed, and the following year he came back and took a cutting from it; now it's a small tree in a corner of his garden at the Ferry

House. And on that same visit, growing amongst the weeds at the side of the front door, he found some fragile white hyacinths she must have planted all those years ago, before she moved to Glanmorfa. He made a sketch of the scene as he imagined it, his mother kneeling by the door firming in the tender roots, her glowing hair fastened in a knot, soil dusting her aproned lap. Every spring the offspring of these plants appear on the slope above the Ferry House. They are all he has of her, though he can recall still the feel of her arms around him, and imagine he hears her voice singing to him—the faintest of melodies, even back then it was only a whisper in his deafening ears. When she left him, she took away all the sounds.

The piano lady understood, she let him sit next to her on the stool covered with hydrangea flowers so he could follow her leaping fingers up and down the keyboard; he could feel her body next to his, swaying with the music he couldn't hear. She always closed her eyes when she played. She had no need of notes, the music was playing inside her head; he could understand that. When she first saw the drawing he made of her at the piano, her face closed up and her mouth was a frown. But then she smiled and took his hand and held it tight in both of hers and he could feel the tiny pulse beating in her thin wrist. The next time he called at the cottage with her firewood there was a little packet waiting for him on the kitchen table, wrapped in blue paper: a clutch of shortbread biscuits she had made especially for him. Now she, too, has gone away. But not the other one, who watches from the upstairs window. The one whose hands are red.

Johnny's cheeks are warm. He wipes the wetness off with the back of his hand and leaves the empty farmhouse and the broken cattle sheds. Slowly, he picks his way over the snow-filled ridges of the field, down towards the Scar, picks up the oilskin and the navy jumper discarded on a snow drift by the hedge; he has forgotten all about the cold until now. As he pulls on the clothes, he remembers he's not supposed to be away from the Ferry House on his own. The uncles will be mad at him, so will the policeman who gave him the pack of Woodbines to keep after he made his sign at the bottom of that paper full of words. He hurries across Black Scar, eager to get home before there's trouble.

A sudden movement catches his eye, brings him up short by the old ferry hut. A group of waders clustering at the blurred margin between ground and frozen sea, the first marsh birds he has seen in weeks. Stalking this borderland on their stiff pin legs, curved beaks stabbing the ice. A riff on three high notes: bird chat. They know something is up. Johnny takes a deep breath. The air is warming— tang of salt, a whiff of shellfish, reed sap. Beneath his feet the iron ground feels unsteady; it gives as he takes a step forward. Small cracks are opening in front of him, splintering the frozen ice sheet. Trapped bubbles of seawater burst, leak silvery trails across the surface. The weather is changing fast. Testing each step before he moves forward, Johnny walks out into the middle of the estuary, crosses the icebound river, for the moment still a smooth, pristine highway to the interior. Behind him the clap and scrape of melting ice. Johnny Nebo is first witness to the great Unfreezing.

CHAPTER 30

It is March 1st, St David's Day. Mr Merchant has opened the school hall specially for the junior pupils, to celebrate the national day and test the heating system is still working after all these weeks. The roads out of the township are passable now, though snowbanks line the verges and the hinterland beyond is still deep frozen. In The Furthest Room, Gran's mouth is full of pins, making last minute alterations to Sylvia's old costume so Daphne can wear it. Trussed in a scratchy red flannel underskirt, white apron, blouse and paisley shawl, Daphne leaves the vicarage and sets off along George Street towards the school. On her head wobbles the tall black cardboard hat Gran made four years ago for Sylvia's smaller head; the brim is lined with some frilly lace she's glued on as an afterthought.

'Daphne!' She turns to see her mother running towards her. She is clutching a limp daffodil, decapitated from the garden. 'Sorry, completely forgot.' She pins it to Daphne's flannelled chest. 'There you are: a daff for Daphne.'

She feels a bit self-conscious now, walking down the street on her own, all dressed up. Until she sees Janice, clutching the brim of a stiff Welsh hat far too large for her tiny head. When she lets go the hat slips and swallows up her face so she looks like a black and red skittle with legs. They agree a thankful swap. Janice's wrist is almost healed now; her arm is bound in a pink elastic bandage instead of the ugly plaster cast. In the hall most of the girls are wearing Welsh costumes and daffodils. The boys—who are not required to dress up—are nibbling at their leeks and puffing onion breath. Mr Merchant calls them to order and they stand in their class groups and sing the national anthem, then Mrs Ceinwen Griffiths, the peripatetic teacher who comes once a week to give Welsh lessons, bustles them all outside—'Brysiwch blantos! Hurry up!'—for the photographer from the local newspaper. In front of the building, she arranges them in height order, boys one side girls the other, then plonks herself at the back of the group, pompous and bosomy in camel suede and fox fur collar, lipsticked and coiffed for the photo. Janice, standing in the row in front, wrinkles her nose and whispers to Daphne, 'Smell that pong, bet you threepence Mrs Griffiths's been eating leeks.'

That afternoon, Daphne is lying on her bed amongst the prancing horses, the deerhounds and a scatter of books. She's given up on 'Childe Roland to the Dark Tower Came', the poem Vita Robinson selected from Miss O'Dowd's bookcase that time she came for tea—'I thought this sounded like your kind of thing.' The poem isn't her thing at all; apart from a sad section about a poor starving horse and a hateful cripple, she lost interest halfway through. No helpful illustrations to spur her on to find out what happened when Roland finally got to the Dark Tower. She tosses the book aside and goes back to *Morte d'Arthur*. She reads aloud, losing herself in the sounds and rhythms of the verse. She has just got to her favourite bit where Sir Bedivere is rushing back to the dying Arthur.

The bare black cliff clang'd round him, as he based
His feet on juts of slippery crag that rang
Sharp-smitten with the dint of armed heels—

The bedroom door bursts open.

'Help me Daph, I don't know what to do!'

Daphne does not look up. It will have to be silent reading, perforce, but the voice inside her head still sounds magnificent.

And from them rose A cry that shiver'd to the tingling stars.

'Daphne Morgan, put that book down right now.'

'What do you want? Can't you see I'm busy?'

'Not busy enough to get off your bottom and come for a walk, this minute. I've got to get out!'

Daphne infers that Darren Gough has broken up with her sister yet again; Sylvia only calls for her when there's a crisis. Her sister has no moral backbone. If this sort of thing happened to her, she would do the same as fair Elaine, lie down and die on her velvet covered barge, having first arranged her hair in a becoming manner. She turns over the page, listens to her internal, thrilling voice.

Then she that rose the tallest of them all
And fairest, laid his head upon her lap

The book is snatched out of her hands. Sylvia is standing over her, face like a thunderstorm. She's wearing her old black bobble hat pulled low over her forehead, and her eyes are bloodshot.

'Look Sylv, I'm sorry he's dumped you again, but I really don't want to go for a walk, I've been out all morning already.'

'This is not about Darren, stupid, it's about this!' She yanks off the bobble hat. Underneath, her hair has gone a deep shade of plum.

'Oh my God, Sylvia, what have you done?'

Her sister is properly sobbing now. 'It said on the label, 'dark chestnut'. I've tried rinsing it over and over but the dye won't wash out. It's permanent. Mum's going to kill me.'

'Probably. You could try dyeing it again with a different colour. Go to the chemist's tomorrow.'

'Shops aren't open tomorrow, it's Sunday, idiot. How can I go to school on Monday looking like this?'

Daphne sighs. 'You'll just have to pretend you're sick then. Maybe really sick, like consumption. That colour will take weeks to grow out.'

At this point Sylvia's distress overwhelms her; tears are streaming down her face, next thing she'll be howling. They need to get out of the house double quick. Daphne gets off the bed.

'Come on Sylv, it's not that bad, we'll think of a plan. Let's go up the lane to Hollerton, see how much ice is left in the river. There'll be nobody around to see you.'

They climb down the bank beyond the footbridge where the ice looks thinner; in a few places where it has already begun to melt, the water is running smoothly, but midstream the broken bits of branch and plastic are still frozen fast. Sylvia strides ahead along the river margin, ice shards splintering under her boots. Out in the open, her hair looks lighter, more lavender than plum; perhaps she'll grow to like it. All around them now the ice is cracking. Each step makes a satisfying crunch, like breaking glass. On impulse, Daphne has decided to wear her father's wellingtons instead of her own, thinking they'd be better in the deeper water; she hasn't forgotten how quickly her own boots filled up when she fell in the river. Her sweaty feet slip and slide about inside the man-sized wellingtons, making it much harder to wade upstream. Sylvia is now well ahead, already level with the footpath at the back of the cottages. By the time Daphne begins to catch up with her, a blister is burning the sole of her right foot and her calves are aching; it feels like she's walked a hundred miles. She'd rather walk barefoot home by the footpath than endure a return journey in the river. She notices that Sylvia has stopped; she's bending over, looking down into the water. She doesn't even stir when Daphne sloshes up behind her.

'What's the matter, Sylv?'

'There's a body under the ice.'

The dead man stares up at them beneath the glassy surface of the water. He looks a bit surprised, as though he hadn't expected to see two strangers peering down at him. It's a powerful face: a strong nose and chin; curling shoulder length hair brushed back from a smooth, wide forehead; thick knotted eyebrows. He's definitely dead, Daphne concludes—his eyeballs are turned up, the whites marbled and unseeing like the pictures of corpses in Gran's novels.

'Where's the rest of him?' she whispers to Sylvia. It's difficult to see clearly through the ice. The body must be lying on the riverbed, half submerged in silt and weed. The dead man is only visible from the chest up, he seems to be wearing some kind of shirt with a high collar, buttoned under the chin.

'We have to tell the police.' Sylvia straightens up decisively. 'I'll go and fetch dad, you stay here to mark the spot.' She's gone before Daphne can say she'd rather go instead and not be stuck in the river with a dead body and a throbbing blister. And besides, this is unfamiliar territory, she's never waded quite so far before. Like she said to Martin, everything looks different when you see it from the middle of a river, frozen or not. If she were up on Church Street now, which is only a hundred yards or so from here, she would know exactly where she was, but down here, hemmed in by the high banks and the dark clustering trees, she's lost all her bearings. She could be anywhere.

It is very quiet. She listens to the slow drip, drip of snowmelt from leaves and branches and the slide and slump of ice from the shed roofs beyond the trees. The thump of her heart. The current is pulling at her legs; she daren't look down.

All his face was white and colourless, and like the wither'd moon

She closes her eyes and sees the barge, a black-veiled woman at the helm, moving inexorably towards her.

'What's this, what's this?'

Her father is standing on the bank looking down at her; he's surprisingly tall from this angle. He's carrying a garden hoe. She watches him taking in the situation, noting the borrowed wellies— he's probably been looking everywhere for them. He's wearing his old walking boots and one of the laces has come undone, perhaps he forgot to tie them in the hurry to get here. Sylvia is there too— she's taken off the bobble hat, this is more serious than her hair crisis. Her father jumps down off the bank, his boots chomp through the slushy ice towards her.

'Move over a bit, girl, I need to see.'

He bends over, starts scraping at the ice with the hoe. She hears the distant sound of a car, a door slamming, footsteps running along the path, crunching through the thawing snow. Constable Jenkins appears on the bank and slithers down to help. He starts stamping his boots hard on the ice to free the body. Suddenly, it splits open, fractures into jagged pieces. The two men peer into the water, which is now running freely. After a while her father straightens up and tosses the hoe on to the bank.

'Go up and join your sister, quickly now.'

Daphne clambers out of the water and tries to climb the bank, but the wellingtons are heavy and her legs feel stiff from standing still for so long. Sylvia has to grab her by the arms and haul her up. Down in the water, the vicar and the policeman lower their arms into the shattered ice. They raise the body—or what's left of it—from its muddy bed and lay the corpse gently on the verge. Her father is whispering something to Constable Jenkins.

'Is everything alright, dad?' Sylvia calls. The men look up; they are both grinning broadly.

'False alarm, Holmes and Watson,' their father shouts.

He bends down again and lifts whatever it is in both hands. He and Jenkins carry it up the bank and on to the path and place it on the ground. It's a head alright, but not a real one. The pale alabaster is cracked and streaked with mud and river slime, but Daphne recognises it at once. She can tell from her sister's stricken face that Sylvia knows too; in contrast to the purple hair, her complexion is the same colour as the marble.

'You can laugh all you like,' Sylvia says bitterly. 'You weren't the ones who found it.'

She turns on her heel and stalks away.

CHAPTER 31

News travels fast in Glanmorfa. Beyond the Georgian house fronts and the meaner cottages, across shop counters and bars, over hedges and backyards where the snow is fast turning to slush, through barns and slaughterhouses. At the kitchen table, Mrs Daley puts aside the Silvoed candlesticks and takes a long drag of her Woodbine.

'That old marble had a crack from where he bashed her head in. She never stood a chance, Ian Jenkins said. Why the bugger had to stab her too, God only knows.'

'Yes, he does,' says the vicar, passing through the kitchen on his way out to feed his chickens. Enid Morgan folds today's copy of the *Western Mail*—front page headline, 'Murder Weapon found in River'. She takes another sip of her black coffee, taps the ash from her cigarette into the saucer.

'Strange isn't it, how nobody noticed the bust was missing from the front room. Sylvia says it used to give her the creeps, stopped her concentrating on her lessons. I always thought that was just a convenient excuse for giving up the piano, not that she ever practised much.' She frowns at Daphne sitting on the other side of the table. 'And you're just as bad; you never told us you mitched your piano lesson that Friday, did you?'

Mrs Daley pauses mid-drag, her eyes alight; this is a new one on her.

Daphne can feel her face burning. 'I had a bad headache, went for a walk instead. Sorry, mum, I meant to tell you but then I forgot about it ... you know.'

It's the best she can come up with, put on the spot. Her mother's looking unconvinced, she's got that I-am-not-amused teacher look.

'That's a pathetic excuse, Daphne, I wasn't born yesterday. All that money we've wasted on you girls, don't expect me to find you another piano teacher. You'll regret it one day.'

Mrs Daley picks up the polishing cloth, starts pummelling a candlestick.

'Lucky she wasn't there, missus; she could've got her head bashed in as well. There's a few sayin' it wasn't Johnny Nebo did the murder. That Miss Robinson's the one to watch my Elsie says—she been in that cottage a while now, nobody really knows why she come down here. Elsie reckons the old lady wouldn't give her the money so she killed her.'

'You shouldn't spread that kind of gossip, Bessie.' Mrs Morgan stubs out her cigarette, shaking her head. 'Miss Robinson wasn't even here when it happened and in any case those rumours Miss O'Dowd was keeping hundreds of pounds under her bed were all nonsense. The truth was she was very short of cash—she was quick enough when it came to demanding the money for Sylvia's skipped lessons. They won't find any money; you mark my words.'

'Say what you like,' mutters Mrs Daley. 'I still think there's something fishy about that woman.'

'That's not very fair since you've never met her; she's actually very nice.' Daphne keeps her eyes on the collection plate she's polishing, she can feel their eyes on her.

'And where have you met this Miss Robinson?' her mother asks.

'On Hangman Lane, before the snow came. She was asking the way to the cliff path. Me and Dil thought she was really friendly.' She's not going to mention her visits to the cottage; they are her secret.

Her mother glares at her across the table.

'Dil and I,' she says.

The statue's discovery is now the one and only topic of conversation in the town.

'Bloody miracle spotting that, we missed it first time round,' says Ian Jenkins in weekend civvies, downing his second free pint of the evening at the Captain's. 'Had to hack through the ice to get to it. The vicar thought it was a body!'

The customers crowd around him, the man of the moment.

'What's going to happen next, Jenkins?' asks Walter Evans. 'Will they put him away?'

'Not up to me, boy, job for the forensics now, isn't it?' The constable puts his empty glass on the bar, picks up the next pint; at the rate they're lining up, he'll be under the table by closing time.

'In my opinion,' he says, taking a swig of beer, 'the murderer's still out there. If it was up to me,' he says, swivelling his long legs round on the stool so he can better address his audience, 'I'd be wanting somebody else to come crawling out of the woodwork now, get Johnny off the hook, like. He's a good lad, we all know that. Never hurt a fly.'

But, of course, it is not up to him. It is not up to Sergeant Phillips, either, who earlier in the day has taken a call from Scotland Yard. No friendly pint for him this Friday evening: at the police station the lights are burning in the interview room where he sits at the table, checking the case notes are in date order, the buff folder labelled *Parry, John* extracted from the filing cabinet. A new trial date has been set, the original postponed on account of the Big Freeze as all the papers are calling it now. Once the last of the snow is cleared Inspector Blight will be travelling west again.

Lent: CHAPTER 32

Early Saturday morning the adult population of Glanmorfa is already up and about, stretching tired limbs and stiffened shoulders, rubbing eyes that have not seen a wink of sleep all night. The worst of the storm is over, the rainclouds driving eastwards now to swell the Tawe and the Loughor, the lower reaches of the Nedd, the Rhondda and the Taff, the Usk and the Wye, all the thawing rivers of the Isles of Britain. By nine o'clock the children are on the streets in raincoats and wellingtons, converging on the Strand where the spring high tide has joined the swollen Gwennol and the Morlas, and completely engulfed the lower reaches of the township.

'Tell your dad to fetch the ark!' Alun Hughes calls up to Sylvia and Daphne as they come down Perrott Street to find the water already lapping the bottom of the hill. The Strand has become a lake, while out in the estuary it is impossible to tell sea from river. Some of the fishing boats have broken their moorings and are drifting between the houses; the red keel of the *Betsy* is wedged hard against the market cross. The castle looks like a scene from an old painting: an ivied ruin glimpsed through mist, lapped by a rising tide the colour of dishwater. The current moves sluggishly, churning with rubbish and flotsam, empty beer bottles, a child's plastic bucket. A van belonging to one of the shops has tipped onto its side and the water is flowing through the open window. The ice tunnel on the corner has completely dissolved; one of Terry's crates bobs sadly beside the garden wall of Lundy House and shards of deckchair, caught in an eddy round the lamppost, chase after each other like a game of tag.

There are small dogs and children paddling in the shallows at the bottom of Orchard Street. Just when the snow had all melted and school was opening again, nature has conjured up this new adventure playground. The bigger kids are piggybacking through the water; one of the dads is towing a small boy on a blow-up lilo. Jason Dunn, Terry's older brother, sculls past the old cockle factory in a plastic bathtub. He yells across to Sylvia, 'Wanna lift, love?' but she pretends she hasn't heard. Her eyes dart about, looking for Darren. They find him, sitting with his mates on the wall in front of the Anchor Arms, swinging their legs, passing sly cigarettes behind their backs. Without a word to Daphne, she hoists up her blue raincoat and wades across the square to join them. The boys smirk and whistle as Darren hauls her up on to the wall beside him. He drapes an arm around her shoulders and pulls her close, nuzzling her plummy hair. Sylvia doesn't look too happy.

Daphne can see Janice and other kids from their class milling about on the far side of the Strand. The water looks too deep to cross safely, she'll have to go the longer way round, past the row of cottages where the fishermen and cocklers live. These small, low-roofed dwellings have tiny backyards, just enough room for hanging out the washing, with an outside toilet and a communal pump at the corner. Like most upstreet children, Daphne has never been inside any of these houses. It's the unspoken rule: outside the school day, children who live in the lower part of town don't mix with the ones living at the top end—children like Dilys the butchers and the vicarage girls, or the James twins who never venture beyond the castle end of George Street. The downstreet children—small, undernourished and dangerous—run in packs and win all the races on sports day; most of them go to the secondary modern after they leave primary school. Expert skippers and chasers and hulahoopers, they can juggle four balls in the air without dropping any; they are unbeatable at upsies and overs and unders and swearing. They look out for each other in a fight and gang together if there's punishment. Which is more than can be said for upstreeters who know a thing or two about treachery.

On that day of the flood, Daphne, averting her eyes from her sister canoodling on the wall with Darren Gough, sees Mrs Daley come out of the front door of one of the cottages. She had no idea Mrs Daley lived here, no idea she had a baby. The water is almost up to the woman's knees, the bottom of her coat is drenched. In her arms she carries the tiny baby wrapped in a shawl. Behind her is an elderly man with straggling white hair. He's wearing dark glasses, which is odd because there isn't any sun only thick glowering rainclouds. He's got a walking stick in one hand and with his other hand he's feeling his way slowly along the walls of the houses, trying to keep up with Mrs Daley and the baby. And then Daphne notices more people struggling through the floodwater: tired-faced women with crying children; a man in waders pushing a wheelbarrow heaped with bags and bits of furniture; the fish woman with the bristly chin who calls at the vicarage every Friday with a basket of cockles and flatfish. She's wearing her leather cap and apron and her body is almost bent double under the weight of a sack slung across her shoulders.

Someone comes round the corner at the far end of the row of houses. He's wearing a long grey raincoat with a hood that covers most of his face. He strides through the water and catches up with the fish lady. He lifts the heavy sack from off her back and slings it across his shoulders, then he takes her arm and carefully steers her to the end of the lane, past the drowning cottages, to the higher ground where many of the people are now gathering. He puts the woman's belongings safely on the ground and then he turns round and starts going back up the lane. Which is when Daphne recognises her father. She starts to wave—he'll be pleased to see her—but one look at his grim face tells her now is not the time. He's talking to a woman struggling with a large suitcase and a toddler balanced on one hip. The child is barefoot, dressed only in a thin vest and shorts; he clings to his mother and screams when her father tries to carry him.

Hywel Morgan is not the only rescuer that morning. There are many faces she recognises—Manny Edwards, Mr Spiller the bootmaker, Dilys's mum, Mr James Portland House, the scary ferry man Ifor Parry and his brother—they're all busy helping the people and animals from their flooded houses; carrying crates and boxes out of the shops which have been inundated by the water; catching the straying dinghies and roping them to lamp posts and telegraph poles. On the higher ground, out of reach of the floodwater, women are handing out blankets and coats, mugs of tea and sandwiches, tending to the very old and the very young. She can see her mother with Mrs Merchant and Miss Bryer and some of the GFS girls. One of them, Hubert Morris's daughter Jean, has her arms around an elderly woman in a muddy housecoat and sodden stockings. Through all its centuries of seafaring, this town has experienced storms and floods innumerable, but nothing like this.

On the other side of the Strand, Janice cups her hands to her mouth and yells, 'Water's going down, Daph, come over!'

Daphne stands on the rim of the slowly ebbing tide. She shakes her head, no, she won't come over now. Her stomach feels queasy, like she's swallowed a bucket of floodwater. The air is filled with the rank stink of mud and sewage, a miasma of things lost or drowned, the reek of ancient bones. The worst snows and the worst floods in living memory. She looks up at the leaden sky, freighted with another deluge. The curse has infected the whole town; they will never be free.

CHAPTER 33

The deluge does not come after all. The weather changes, the clouds lift, pale sunshine at last. There are signs of real spring, released from ice and tempest into buds and blossom: the cat-pee whiff of flowering redcurrant in garden hedges; early apple blossom; everywhere the greening countryside. The blackened ice lumps in corners of fields are the only reminder of the terrible winter. Sylvia's tortoise Tommy stirs in his bed of shredded newspaper, and old Rusty gives up the ghost.

They bury him in a quiet corner of the garden, at the foot of a damson tree, deep enough so the foxes can't dig him up. Their mother makes a little cross out of some sticks and Daphne drapes it with a necklace she made specially, early daisy heads strung on a cotton thread. It's a grave made with love, she thinks, not like that snow-filled hole they put poor Miss O'Dowd in. Or the bottom of the Irish Sea. Below the little cross Sylvia lays a large pebble she found on the beach last summer. It's a lovely oval shape quartered by a thin seam of quartz which seems appropriate for a vicarage dog. Sylvia's hair is almost back to normal now, the dye only visible at the back of her head as a pale lilac sheen. Their father makes a bonfire at the bottom of the garden and burns the old spaniel's tattered wicker basket and blankets; he sweeps the shed clear of fleas and chewed up tennis balls. Rusty arrived with Sylvia—for a dog, fourteen is a lifetime.

Though the spring tides have long receded and the rivers sunk well below their banks again, the aftermath of the flood takes a long time to clear. 'High time I went home,' grumbles Mrs Daley, leaning out of Daphne's bedroom window and shaking the duster on to the pavement below. She's been camping for weeks in rooms at the back of Elvira House with her father, daughter Elsie and her baby who is called Polly. 'People been very good to us but it don't feel right living upstreet.' She shuts the window and fishes in her apron pocket for another cigarette, talks between puffs.

'Elsie says we should be grateful for a roof over our heads but it's not the same as your own, is it? It'll still take weeks till the place is dry enough.'

Over tea in the kitchen, their mother asks about the baby.

'She's doing well enough, Missus. Bit of croup with the damp 'n' all but Elsie's got her on the bottle. She's a tough little thing, like her granny. There's a lot worse than her, mind. The Thomases got it really bad, half the house washed away and Mrs Thomas only a stick of a thing. Pneumonia, that's what they're saying, she's been in the hospital a week.' She shakes her head. 'I think it's the drains myself, they come into the house, see. Like the bad old days with the typhoid. Some of the other kids is really sick.'

Daphne catches up with Martin and the others on the corner of George Street by the castle gateway. They are heading downstreet to watch the clearing up. From this distance, the Strand looks quite normal. The roads and the pavements have resurfaced, most of the shops have re-opened and the flooded van has been towed away. All the boats are back in their moorings. The tide is far out and the estuary sparkles with silvery light; the air is loud with birds. A fat seagull perches on top of the market cross, preening its feathers in the sun. Yet the signs of the catastrophe are visible everywhere: in the slicks of mud coating the base of every wall, the rotting door frames and windowsills, the empty cottages and the stinking mounds of debris on the street corners. Scraps of sodden carpet are heaped against a lamppost, a child's broken pram lies abandoned, metal drain covers have been lifted and smashed by the weight of water. And everywhere the smell, far stronger than it was that first day.

Dilys holds her nose, making a face. 'God, what a stink! It's worse than the slaughter-yard.'

'Nearly as bad as the girls' toilets,' says Graham.

They wander down to the foreshore, past the bags filled with empty bottles and debris stacked along the wall of Lundy House. Graham finds a plastic football with a dent in its side and the boys have a quick game, sliding around in the mud and gravel deposited in the wake of the tide. Janice and Daphne go to jump the stepping stones over the Morlas; some of them have been washed away and the gaps between the remaining stones are too wide to jump.

'We could put that in the middle.' Janice is pointing to an object lying at the water's edge a few yards away. 'Go and fetch it, Daph.'

It is rounded and smoothed by the water, the colour of rusted metal. A small boulder, she thinks, until she stoops down to lift it up. The Beaker woman's skull has surfaced from the clutch of river mud or whatever has imprisoned it these ice-bound months. Its pate has the greenish tinge of long immersion in the elements but there is no mistaking the savage split from crown to eye socket.

'Hurry up, it can't be that heavy!'

She could let it go, turn away, pretend it wasn't suitable. Nobody would be any the wiser. They all think she put it back in the bone house ages ago.

Cursed be he who moves my body; thereof cometh death, and flood, and pestilence.

She glances back across the Strand at the piles of rubbish, the mud-filled houses. Spring sunshine doesn't make life better for people like Mrs Thomas and her children. Nor Miss O'Dowd and Johnny Nebo.

'C'mon Daph, what you waitin' for?'

She picks up the skull. It is surprisingly light, like one of those green glass buoys marking the fishing nets out in the estuary. No blood or brains to weigh it down; water passes through it smooth as silk. She turns and walks back to Janice. Who stares at the skull, then at her, wide-eyed, mouth open.

164

'It's not ... is it...'
Daphne nods. The boys come over then; Martin looks furious.
'You said...'
'I know I did,' Daphne answers.
And then she tells them.

CHAPTER 34

The key is still in the pocket of his overcoat. A good detective needs a final sniff around the crime scene. Check how the dust has settled. A point he's made a few times in the chapters he's already written; he'll include it in 'Drownings and Depravity', it will probably be the last entry before the trial. He fits the key into the lock and turns it. The sudden light flooding the hallway from the open kitchen door dazzles. A figure stands at the end of the passage. Pull yourself together, man: trick of the light.

They sit at the little scrubbed table in the kitchen and she pours him a cup of tea. 'I knew Eleanor years ago, when she was living in Oxford. She was an old friend of the family, gave me piano lessons for a while until she'd had enough of my terrible playing. We kept in touch down the years, the usual Christmas cards, birthday messages. She had no relatives, you see; I was probably the nearest thing she had to a family. I read about the murder in the papers and came down as soon as I could.'

Miss Robinson is a small thin-faced woman, in her late forties he estimates, scruffily dressed, hair cropped short like a man's. One of those blue-stocking types, definitely not his sort of woman, but pleasant enough once you get beyond the appearance. She wouldn't let him have a smoke though—'Please don't, Inspector, I can't stand the smell of the things.'

They are in the front room. The window's open and the place smells fresh, clean. She's obviously given it a scrub-down since he was last here. Those idiots at the station should have told her to leave things as they were until after the trial. No trace of chalk marks on the floor, cobwebs vanished, fireplace and mantlepiece all swept clean. And the piano's had a good polish, the first thing he noticed when he walked in.

'I've been tidying up. She always was a bit of a hoarder, you see; every room was crammed with her books and papers. I wish now I'd offered to help her, before...' She breaks off, runs a hand through her hair. Something genuine about the way she talks, he can always tell when a person's putting on an act.

'Eleanor always had a soft spot for misfits, you see. She wanted them to know she understood what their life was like. I expect that's how it was with that man, she'd have been kind to him, tried to take him under her wing, given him things perhaps.'

'Such as?' She has his full attention now.

'I know there's talk in the town that Eleanor had money hidden somewhere in this house. I keep wondering whether that's why Parry turned violent, when she wouldn't show him where the money was. I can't think of another reason why he would want to kill her. And to choose that weapon of all things just breaks my heart. Lizst was her favourite composer, you know; his music was her great companion.'

She leads the way to the door, opens it for him. Sunshine fills the narrow hallway. He bends to shake her hand. She really is quite tiny, barely comes up to his chest. More fragile than he thought at first, judging by her anxious expression.

'Inspector, I couldn't bear to think there was no retribution for what that beast did to Eleanor. The court will find him guilty, won't they?'

He smiles to himself. She obviously doesn't know Ronald Blight, the man who always holds the cards. He gives her a grave nod. Of course they will find him guilty.

CHAPTER 35

Graham comes over with an old plastic bag he found snagged on a branch. He shakes the floodwater out of it and turns it inside out. Carefully, Daphne lowers the skull into the bag. It has been agreed: this time she will really, really put it back in the bone house, where it will stay for ever. And then the curse will lift, and everything will be alright. Perhaps.

The bag clunks awkwardly against the side of her leg; she's walking fast, anxious nobody should see what's inside. She's done this before. On the way she rehearses what she will say. What bit of the story will make her father most angry? Fibbing about the reason for mitching her piano lesson, though he won't be too happy about the grave robbing either. She will also have to tell him about the curse.

She closes the front door behind her, puts the bag on the hall floor and pulls off her boots. It's very peaceful just standing here in the hallway in her socks. Fairy dust is dancing in a shaft of sunlight from the long window at the top of the stairs. There are sprigs of yellow forsythia and daffodils in the copper jug on the hall table. The smell of beeswax. From their pegs, all the familiar coats and scarves and hats hang quiet. Except for a man's dark overcoat and, on the chair beside it, a man's brown hat.

It's a courtesy call, to let the vicar know he's back in town, preparing for the trial which starts after the Easter weekend. There'll be no further investigations, the police have all the evidence they require for a conviction. There's still a deal of sympathy for John Parry swirling round the place, Sergeant Phillips said. Nobody likes a local lad convicted, gives the town a bad name, rakes up those old stories about Glanmorfa back in the day—drunkenness, piracy, thieving, incest, the odd murder. Even a spot of witchcraft, so Mrs

Price told him yesterday, no wonder they put that giant cross smack in the centre of town: it's there to fight off the evil spirits.

Blight has decided to put the vicar in the picture. Get him to spread the word, there's no need for alarm. Parry will have a fair trial and once the business is over, everyone can get back to their lives. In a year or so the events of the murder will be old news. In circumstances like these, assurances are best made by a local padre: they know the lingo. In the Hackney Towers trial a few years back, he sent the priest round the flats to calm everyone down, quell any thoughts of riot. 'Leave justice to God' can be a useful blandishment, so long as it doesn't interfere with the business of the courts.

Rev Morgan's nodding away. The chap doesn't say a lot, but he seems to have understood the message, if you can get past the Welsh accent. His wife had to call him up from the bottom of the garden. He'd been busy planting the second earlies while the weather's dry, he explained when he eventually turned up. Still in his gardening clothes, with his shirt sleeves rolled up, bits of earth in his trouser bottoms. These country padres have a good life. While he was waiting, he'd had a nose around the study. Papers all over the show, tatty old books and pamphlets, everything falling out of the shelves. There's no room to swing a cat in here. If he were Rev Morgan, Blight thinks, folding his long frame into one of the shabby armchairs with sagging springs, he'd get rid of those po-faced clergymen on the walls and put up a photo of the cricket team or the darts club. Chuck out half the stuff on the shelves, smarten up the place. Make it more like the front room in Palmers Green, neat as a pin; a place for everything with everything in its place, that's how everyone should live.

He hears the front door open. Nice timing: he and the padre have run out of things to say. He gets up to leave. Mrs Price'll have his afternoon tea ready; he's quite missed this little ritual and Madras House has warmed up since that cold December week. He drove down in the Hillman this time—too many train delays and track repairs after the floods. Thank the good lord he got away before the

Freeze. Hell on earth to be stuck down here for weeks with only Constable Jenkins for company. He's a bit leaky that young man, enjoys the sound of his own voice too much. You can't carry on like you're one of the lads if you're serious about the job.

The ginger-haired daughter's standing in the hallway, looks like she's seen a ghost. Back in December he'd had a question for her, no need to bother with that now, the case is finally open and shut. Parry probably thought he'd got away with it, chucking the bust in the river, but the Robinson woman knew exactly where it came from when the police showed it to her. To be fair he always thought that old stand in the corner of the room was missing something. No fingerprints on the bust, on account of the water, but he's convicted others before on far shakier evidence. Especially now he's got something more than a Woodbine and some drawings to nail the charge.

Inspector Blight reaches past the girl for his coat and hat. She leaps back like a scalded cat. Those parents should have a serious word with her about being polite to visitors. He puts on his coat, fastens up the buttons and takes his fedora from the chair.

'Been missing any more piano lessons?'

It's meant to be a joke, but she's off up the stairs like a bat out of hell. Time to get out of here, can't stand bawling kids. And there's a nasty smell, like she's wet herself. On his way out he almost trips over a plastic bag lying by the door. Blimey, if they're having that for their supper, he's bloody glad he ordered lamb cutlets at Madras. That fish is well past its sell-by date.

CHAPTER 36

Hywel Morgan is struggling to turn the key in the padlock, which has rusted during the savage winter. The metal screeches against the catch, setting Daphne's teeth on edge, and there is a sudden scuttering noise as a blackbird, disturbed from its nest deep in the ivy above the door, flees into the darkness of the yew trees. The afternoon sunlight, filtered through the pale leaves of a sycamore, makes a shadow play across the mottled surface of the gravestone commemorating Sarah Elizabeth, relict of Benjamin Elias of this parish, laid to rest March 1773. The tombs in this part of the churchyard are very ancient; many of the inscriptions have worn away, leaving no record of the names. Some of the headstones have cracked or capsized into the earth; others lean at angles, choked with bramble and strange plants with hairy stalks and leaves the size of dinner plates. Daphne's stomach is rumbling—'No time for food,' her father said, as they left the house. 'Let's get this business done before your mother comes home, better she doesn't know.'

The key turns and the padlock opens. The door jamb is swollen and her father has to lean all his weight against it until it gives. Inside, the bone house is like a cave, with a low, rounded ceiling and walls lined with stone shelves. Beyond, a deeper darkness, a shaft leading down to the heart of a pyramid. Hywel Morgan picks up the basket where he has left it on the path and carries it inside the vault. He takes out the skull, holding it reverently in both hands, like he does when he raises the silver chalice in front of the altar at communion time. He places it gently on the shelf in front of him. Watching this from the threshold, Daphne thinks of the last time she was here. She remembers the careless way Martin shovelled the skull into the cardboard box, how clever they all felt when they pulled off their plan. Tomb robbers. And then she let the river seize it, bury it in mud and ruin.

Her father beckons her inside, his face is solemn. She steps over the lintel and enters the vault, leaving the door ajar to allow a sliver of sunlight into the darkness. In the left pocket of her duffle coat is a small candle and a box of matches. She fishes them out and with trembling fingers strikes a match then lights the wick. He has explained what they will do. The flickering candlelight plays across the stone wall and the niche carved with little angel figures; it pools on the shelf where the skull is sitting. Earlier that day, her father filled the washing bowl from the kitchen with water and took it into the garden and she helped him carefully wash off the mud and river slime. Afterwards, they wrapped the skull in a white linen cloth from the cupboard in the study. In this soft candlelight the smooth cranium shimmers with a colour deeper than bronze, older than iron. It is the first time she has really looked at it, face to face, bone to bone.

There are other dead people gathered in this vault, her father has told her. A family of many generations, brought together in one resting place. The mortal remains of some of them lie still intact inside their coffins somewhere in the darkness; others have separated, severed by time, the weather, vandalism, who knows. Outside the candlelight's narrow circle, they are invisible, and she wonders whether they can hear the words of the Lord's Prayer her father speaks so quietly, first in Welsh and then in English. In the deep silence that falls, the air seems full of the gathering dead. Her father gently nudges her arm. She stoops down and takes from the basket the little bunch of spring flowers she has collected from the garden—late snowdrops, primroses, tiny narcissi, a forsythia sprig. The air is scented with their presence as she lays them on the shelf next to the candle.

'Lord, we entrust again your servant Martha to your merciful keeping,' her father says, and Daphne whispers the words he told her. 'May she rest in eternal peace.' 'Everything will be alright now,' he whispers, and blows out the candle. She picks up the basket and steps into the sunshine of the late afternoon. The churchyard is full of birdsong. Behind her she hears the heavy door swing shut and the sound of the key turning easily in the lock.

'How do you know everything will be alright?'

'Because it's Easter,' Hywel Morgan says.

They've only been inside the vault a few minutes, but she feels as though a burden has been lifted. Not a Beaker skull, but certainly a woman. Martha Eliza Rees, youngest daughter of Captain Henry Rees and his wife, also Eliza, was only eleven when she died of smallpox in December 1794 and her parents placed her body in the family vault. Her life had been cruelly short. She left parents, grandparents, a brother, Lieutenant Edward Rees, and a younger sister Jane. They are all together here, their names recorded in the parish record book her father brought out of the safe in his study to show her, after she had told him everything.

As I am now so shall you be/ cut off by Death and follow me.

They walk back to the vicarage in silence; they have said all there is to say, and the vicar's mind has turned to other things. Tomorrow is Good Friday, the start of Easter, and the church has already been stripped of its fine purple altar cloth, the colour of Holy Week. The silver candlesticks and collection plates, the tall brass flower vases, have been removed. The altar is a plain wooden table again. In the painted windows, the blue and silver angels, the disciples in their gaudy cloaks, the lush green valley, seem out of joint. Resurrection hasn't happened yet. Tomorrow, for three hours starting at midday, Rev Morgan and the faithful few of Glanmorfa will mark the Crucifixion; they will read from the scriptures and pray and sing hymns like 'There is a green hill far away without a city wall' and 'O sacred head sore wounded' and after that they will all go home for tea. There are Good Friday rituals at the vicarage too: no flowers, dark clothes, plain fish for supper. Not even hot cross buns.

'Here we go,' says Gran at breakfast next morning. 'Another day of sackcloth and ashes.'

'Why do you always have to be so dramatic, Mam?' Enid comes into the room from the scullery, carrying a basket. She looks at Daphne. 'Tell your father I'm taking some food over to the Ferry House. Mrs Daley says they're having a hard time selling their fish. That poor young man's already been convicted in some quarters before the trial starts. It's high time people showed some faith in John Parry: he and his family need our prayers not our criticism. That's what we should be thinking about on Good Friday of all days.'

The front door slams behind her. Gran shakes her head, 'Someone's got out of bed on the wrong side.' She levers herself up from the table.

'You and your sister picking flowers this afternoon?' Daphne nods. It's a Good Friday ritual. 'Excellent,' says Gran. 'Best to keep in your mother's good books.' She goes back to her room.

Daphne sits and thinks about Johnny Nebo and how she has failed him. She should have spoken up when she had that opportunity, standing outside the kitchen door just before Christmas. To save her own skin she chose not to tell what happened on the riverbank; now, nobody will believe her.

Easter: CHAPTER 37

Sylvia's sitting on a patch of bracken. It's starting to mizzle. Fine waterdrops cling to her hair, restored now to its normal light brown. She pulls up the hood of her raincoat and takes a KitKat bar out of her pocket, waves it in the air.

'Want some?'

Daphne is on her knees higher up the hillside, her hands full of primroses. The girls are always let off the last two hours of the Good Friday service, to forage on the Moor for primroses to decorate the church. The basket is almost full. The recent days of sunshine have produced a bumper crop of flowers, perfectly timed for Easter. Daphne plonks herself next to her sister and accepts a stick of chocolate. Forbidden treats always taste better. Sylvia produces a ball of string from her other pocket and a pair of scissors. They start making up the little bunches of primroses and leaves, looping string around each one, tying them off. It's one of the few things they do together these days.

'That's odd.' Sylvia is inspecting the hem of her raincoat. 'I don't remember this getting torn, looks like it's been mended. You haven't been wearing it have you?'

Daphne is suddenly very busy with the string, all thumbs, primroses spilling from her fingers.

'Give them here, I'll do it.' Sylvia swiftly gathers up the fallen flowers, ties them together and crams the bunch into the basket with the others. She gets to her feet and brushes off bits of earth and bracken from her coat.

'I think we've got enough now, let's do the moss on the way home.' They slither down the hillside back to the gate which opens on to a farm track, with a narrow stream on one side and a high bank on the other, carpeted with thick moss and ivy. The moss is cool and spongy beneath their fingers and comes away easily, exposing bare patches of earth and startled woodlice.

Sylvia leans against the bank, picking the dirt out of her nails with a hairgrip. 'Funny to think you'll be doing the eleven-plus soon, Daph. I can't believe you've nearly finished in primary. Are you scared?'

Daphne pauses from stuffing the heaped moss into the other bucket. So much has happened in the last days but she's not forgotten about the exam—it's next month, less than six weeks away.

'Haven't thought about it,' she lies. She peers at the clump of moss she's holding, watching the tiny insects scurrying amongst the fronds.

'You'll have no trouble, you're bound to pass,' Sylvia says, airily. 'The stuff they ask is easy-peasy.'

Daphne thrusts the moss into the basket. Her hands are clammy and streaked with earth; she wipes them on her trouser leg.

'Don't tease, you know I hate those stupid questions. You're the one who's good at maths.'

Sylvia sticks the hairgrip back in her fringe. She picks up the primrose basket. 'I could give you some practice if you like. Honestly, Daph, once you get the hang of it, the questions are a doddle.'

As she is setting off along the track, she calls over her shoulder, 'If your brain's foggy, try communion wine. It works like magic.'

The following morning, Daphne and her mother are standing on the long pew at the back of the nave with the primrose basket, the moss which has been soaking in the bucket overnight, a roll of netting, two large flat stones, wire cutters and an old towel. The pew is a bit wobbly; someone's propped it up at one end with a pile of old hymn books because the timber is rotting. Enid Morgan is no flower arranger, she made that clear when they arrived in Glanmorfa. Shocked that a vicar's wife should be so lacking in this department, Flora Lloyd and Miss Bryer, keepers of the Easter flower-arranging list, allocated her the ledge above the huge west

176

window at the bottom of the nave—a long, wide slope of dusty, cracked stone. Spider heaven. Perilous booby trap for any flower container. Every year the ladies watch to see how Mrs Morgan will avert catastrophe.

Enid Morgan does not give a toss what they think. Expediency, ingenuity, a neat solution, are the hallmarks of a classical mind. Daphne stands tiptoe on the rickety pew as instructed. She reaches up and spreads a carpet of dripping moss all along the window ledge. Spiders scuttle into cracks in the masonry, leg it across the walls. Her mother stands beside her and uncoils the roll of netting wire, drapes it tight over the moss to secure it, and fixes the whole lot in place at either end with a small flat stone. They work fast, plugging in the primrose bunches in a zigzag pattern across the window ledge. A mopping up of drips with the towel and the job is done.

Up at the altar end of the church, Flora Lloyd and her team trim and tweak and prink. The Easter lilies in their silver vases (buffed to perfection by Mrs Daley); the yellow tulip-and-carnation extravaganzas on the pulpit steps; the pots of greenery along the choir stalls; the artful trailing ivy round the eagle's gleaming brass claws. Then it's out with the beeswax polish and the floor cleaner and the Ewbank until the place is full of dust and sunbeams and the sappy smells of Easter. Tomorrow, the vicar and his choir will be busy: the dawn vigil, two morning services, the choral evensong. New Sunday coats and hats, roast lamb and chocolate eggs. Halleluiah.

Relieved from her tasks, Daphne sets off for home. Her mother has to stay behind to admire through gritted teeth the superior arrangements on the altar. She walks slowly along the path through the old graveyard, pale spring sunshine dappling the tombstones, the fluttering of wings in the ivy. The sound of footsteps crossing the bridge from the new graveyard. Vita Robinson's wearing a vivid green jumper over a pair of brown slacks; she's carrying a small canvas shopping bag.

'Hello!'

She comes up close, peers into Daphne's face. 'Gosh, you look very pale, you haven't been ill, have you?'

Daphne's a bit surprised by this concern; she's feeling fine, better than she's felt in ages.

'Sorry,' Vita draws back. 'I didn't mean to startle you. I've been shut away these past weeks, mopping up after the floods. Now I understand why there's a wall at the end of the garden, though this time it didn't deter the river. The ground floor was inundated.' She waves an arm at the sky, the budding spring. 'Isn't it grand to be in the sunshine again! I've just been putting flowers on Eleanor's grave. I gather this is what people do at Easter. The whole churchyard's looking very cheerful.'

They walk together down the path.

'How've you been getting on with King Arthur and Childe Roland? Have you had enough yet of knights and damsels in distress?'

'I've been too busy to read much poetry, actually,' Daphne answers.

That's not strictly true, but she has had enough of Tennyson. Drowning yourself for love or dying over your sword isn't real life. Real life is animals frozen to death, people losing all their possessions, Mrs Thomas dying of the pneumonia. At the lychgate Vita pauses to let Daphne open the gate.

'You and your friends must be sorry the excitement is over. No more weather catastrophes to give you time off school.'

'Not really, we had to do extra lessons to prepare for the exams.'

'Ah,' says Vita Robinson, looking at her quizzically. 'In that case I think you deserve a reward.' She fishes in her shopping bag and brings out her purse. 'Here, buy yourself something special. Or add it to whatever you're saving for. I don't know what young people like these days.'

Daphne stares at the note in her hand. Ten shillings is a lot, at least twenty weeks-worth of Sunday washing up.

'It's very generous of...' she's starting to say, when Vita interrupts.

'Please don't thank me, Daphne, it's my pleasure. I've enjoyed our few conversations. Without those I'd have felt quite lonely shut up in that morbid place with no other company but my sad self. I'll be glad to say goodbye to it.' She indicates the straggle of houses along Church Road. 'Not exactly the centre of civilisation, is it?'

Daphne's heart is beating fast. 'Are you really leaving?'

'Yes, I am, but not until the trial's over. I want to be sure that man Parry is convicted, I owe it to Eleanor. Besides, I have to find someone to rent the cottage before I go; I can't leave the place fall to pieces.'

They walk along Church Street as far as the Stores. She has to ask the question before they part. 'Will you come back to Glanmorfa?'

'I doubt it; it's not a place I'd choose to revisit. Though I wish I'd got to know you better in the time I've been here. You're an interesting person, Daphne, I'm beginning to understand what Eleanor saw in you. She wasn't so discerning about me unfortunately; she often said I was ungovernable. You've got a mind of your own, as I have, but the difference is you know when to keep your counsel. That's an enviable skill.' She pauses and looks directly at Daphne. Her face is stern. 'As I think I said to you once, Daphne's the wrong name for you.' She leans forward and plants a sudden kiss on Daphne's forehead. 'I hereby name you wise Athena, keeper of secrets; you are hereby transformed.'

Daphne walks slowly home along Church Street, pondering this strange, unsettling conversation. What secrets? She can't have known about the business with the skull, the woman wasn't even in Glanmorfa when they stole it. Daphne's forehead is burning. Athena? Such a ridiculous name. Vita Robinson has been laughing at her all along; she won't be sorry if they never meet again.

179

CHAPTER 38

The Parry brothers are waiting in the kitchen, spring sea-light spilling across the windowsill where the little jug of white hyacinths and purple scilla is still blooming four days after Easter. None of the family are churchgoers but they like to mark the occasion. There's always an Easter egg for Johnny, who loves his chocolate. This morning, the brothers are awkward with each other, trussed in their best and only suits, boots brushed clean of mud, hair combed and stiff with Brylcreem. Ifor fiddles with his shirt cuffs, pulls at a fraying thread. Emrys is facing the window, screwing up his eyes against the light. The tide is far out, a solitary heron stalking the shallows. Hearing the heavy, lopsided footsteps on the stairs, he turns away from the window as Johnny enters the room. In his father's old suit, his likeness to Jack is unmistakeable: the strong shoulders, boxer's nose, hair the colour of sand. That open gap-toothed smile. Jack always had plenty to say for himself, his hearing keen as a bird's. Whenever he was home on leave, the house was full of noise and laughter. Always after the women he was—until he met Mari Beynon Danyrallt. At least he never lived to see his son on trial for murder.

A knock at the door. Ivor goes to open it and Jenkins and Sergeant Phillips step into the kitchen, uniformed and helmeted, their faces serious. Two policemen this time—as if, now Johnny is on trial, they need a show of force.

'You coming too?' Phillips asks.

Ivor nods. 'We borrowed a van.' He looks across the room at Johnny, who is smiling at him. 'You'll be fine,' he gestures, 'Go with the men, they'll look after you.' Ian Jenkins's face flushes bright red. He pulls a pair of handcuffs out of his pocket—'Sorry about this, Ifor, it's the law, see'—takes Johnny's hand as if to shake it and

180

attaches one cuff to his wrist, the other to his own. Puzzled, Johnny looks down at his manacled hand, then at his uncles. Emrys forces a smile, gives a thumbs up. Ifor's face is impassive, only the muscles in his jaw working. Meekly, Johnny turns and lets the policeman lead him out of the front door, up the steep path through his lovely garden full of the flowers of springtime, and into the waiting car.

The Crown Court trial lasts three days. During this time Parry is held in a cell below the courtroom, well fed and warm. There is a bed, white walls, no windows. These are the sounds of jail he does not hear: the crisp ring of heels on stone, the jangle of important keys, the duty sergeant's hacking cough, an alarm going off somewhere on the floors above. Johnny Nebo hears the ebbtide's roar, the cockles whispering beneath the mud, the cormorant's plunge. At night when the lights are dimmed his mother comes. She winds him in her long fair hair and rocks him back to sleep. There is a small table in his room with paper and a clutch of pencils. Inspector Blight's idea, this waiting time often makes a criminal cough up that last bit of evidence; it's always worth a try. Johnny draws the same face, over and over; he scrunches the paper into a tight fist and hurls it at the wall. Each evening when he is brought back from court the drawings have gone and there's a new pad on the table. He wishes someone would give him a fag instead of paper.

Whenever he is in the court room, the lady with the cat-eye glasses is there. She sits on the chair beside him and tries to explain what the tall man is saying, the one who gave him the fags he likes, but he can't understand her hands or her mouth which flaps and flutters like a gasping fish. One time she showed him the folder with all the writing, and he smiled when he saw the little picture of the lilac tree he drew at the bottom of the last page.

Every morning of the trial, Ifor and Emrys leave the house at 6.30 for the long drive to court. Always the first to enter the visitors' gallery and the last to leave, they want him to know they are there with him. It is a deep hurt to see their nephew limping up the stairs into the court room, handcuffed to two officers. On the last day, as they are parking outside the court, the old Bedford bus from Ainsworth's garage draws in beside the van. Looks like half the town has come to hear the verdict; there's been a whip round at the Captain's for the hire, pop and sandwiches for breakfast, chips on the way home.

At noon, the judge, an elderly man with an Irish surname and a whiskered look of David Lloyd George, addresses the jury. Since there is no forensic evidence linking Parry to the crime, if the only material they can consider is a statement by a man with whom communication is almost impossible, then the case for the prosecution is hardly worth considering. The law requires that a man should plead by his own voice and if this man is mute by the visitation of God, then he cannot plead by his own voice. It is important that the liberties we all cherish must not be infringed.

The jury is out for an hour and a half, just time enough for the bus travellers to have a look round the shops and a swift half at the Arcade. John Parry is found not guilty of the murder of Eleanor O'Dowd. Inspector Blight, collecting together the files and folders to put in his briefcase, glances up at the gallery where the Glanmorfa lot are cheering and pummelling shoulders. A small woman in a dark fur coat and hat is seated alone at the end of the bench. She looks down at the well of the court room to where he is standing and raises both hands, palms outwards. A gesture of despair or interrogation? He responds with an almost imperceptible shake of his head; no point in contesting this, Miss Robinson, the jury have delivered their verdict. She's not smiling. Not the outcome she wanted, the inspector thinks; she was so sure the mute was guilty. And for all he knows, Parry may well be the murderer, but nobody will ever know that for certain. What is certain is that the future Detective Superintendent Blight won't be getting himself tangled up in any tricksy civil rights contest, not now his promotion's in the bag.

He snaps the locks of his briefcase, collects his overcoat from the bench beside him, looks up at the gallery. It is empty. Odd woman, difficult to read. And that accent of hers wasn't properly English. Not one of us. He smiles to himself. Tomorrow afternoon he'll be driving west to Tenby for a few days, testing the Hillman on those narrow Pembrokeshire lanes. Spending a few days in a nice guest house overlooking North Beach with a view of Caldey Island, like the one in Mabel's postcard. He might even find time to revise his chapter on the O'Dowd case. Give it a new title. Getting Away With It.

Pentecost: CHAPTER 39

Dawn on Whit Monday. The air is sharp and clear, with a promise of fine weather, at least for the next couple of hours. People are gathering on the pavement in front of the Town Hall, eyes glued to the stone staircase leading to the Court Room on the first floor. A gaggle of excited children, housewives, cocklers, teachers, farmers, churchwardens. All the Morgans from the vicarage are there for the fun of it, even Gran, trussed in her winter coat and hat, though neither she nor Enid will be walking the boundaries of Glanmorfa today. Twenty miles through bog and briar, over streams and moorland, are for the foolhardy not the fainthearted.

Different season, different kind of courtroom. The terminology is much the same—there are constables, attorneys, a jury and a foreman—but no-one's on trial and there's free tea and buns if you get there early enough. And beer in the pubs which opened their doors with the birds. The Parry brothers have tied up the ferry and hung a 'Closed' notice on the gate. Ifor has different responsibilities this morning and both of them are in need of a day off. In the rejoicing following the trial they had felt a weight lifted off, the freedom to get on with their lives again. But the stigma has not entirely gone away; the odd whispered conversation in pub or back garden, the shaking of heads continued. 'He might have been innocent this time round, but what if there's another murder?' They've felt the atmosphere in some of the shops, the sudden silence when one of them walks in. Emrys is also aware of a change in Johnny these past weeks: he's become more subdued, keeps away from the town, sticks to the garden and the fishing. He seems to understand he's a free man, Emrys hopes, waiting in the crowd in the chill morning air. Yesterday his nephew drew a picture of a man, standing in the prow of a boat, his arms raised to the sky in celebration.

The crowd stirs. Mervyn Jones the Stores and Constable Ian Jenkins, who is another kind of constable today, have appeared at the bottom of the Town Hall steps. Each carries a fearsome wooden truncheon and the watchers obediently part to let them through. Voices fall silent, even the children. Down come the halberdiers with their flags and pikes, the mattock men, the foreman and the chaplain, the portreeve, followed by the burgesses of the town. The crowd line up behind them, the clock strikes the half-hour and the Walk begins. Three times round the Town Hall, three times round the market cross. A medieval ritual nobody wants to change.

It will take most of the day to walk the bounds and people are wearing their old clothes, stout footwear and hats in case it rains. A handful of visitors, misjudging the weather and the distance, have turned up in shorts and skimpy tops because it's the end of May; two girls are wearing skirts and flip flops like they're heading for the beach. The locals wink to each other: you wait till they meet the mud. Daphne finds Janice and the others in the midst of the procession. It's the first time any of them have been allowed to join the Walk, the privilege of being in their final year of school. Her sister has already disappeared to join a noisy group of teenagers at the rear. As the procession completes its final lap around the cross, Martin's mother pushes her way through the crowd and thrusts the fox-head walking stick into his hand.

'She's scared you'll fall in the bog, Marty,' Terry sniggers.

The procession crosses the foreshore along a muddy path strewn with seaweed and the flotsam brought in on last night's tide. At the end of the path just before the pumping station they turn sharp right and scramble up a steep path through the wooded hillside, a tripwire of tangled roots and broken branches. Over a stile, through fields, across a main road, and up again, until they reach the Moor where the burgesses admire their ancient strips of land, whose tussocky fingers reach past them to the distant world of Norman knights and ruthless bribery. Now and again the procession halts—at a track, a gate, a crossroads—and someone is hoisted above the crowd to name the place, jeered if they get it wrong. You are expected to know your boundaries.

It is only 7 am. The leaders call a halt, a necessary breather, a chance to catch up for the stragglers and the early beer drinkers who have stopped for a piss in the woods. Hywel Morgan breaks off from a conversation with the warden of Llanmarlais church and comes to check on Daphne and her friends. He's wearing his old gardening jacket over the clerical shirt and dog collar; mud spatters the bottoms of his trousers.

'You lot bearing up?'

The boys stare at the ground, embarrassed by the vicar's attention.

'Just look at that,' he exclaims, gazing down over the sunlit estuary and the sparkling roofs of the town. 'Like a slice of heaven.'

And later, when they have come down off the Moor and marched along the lane below the primrose slopes and crossed the brook and climbed up through Mrs Humphrey's orchard and stopped for another breather, Daphne understands what her father means. It is heavenly, on this early May morning, in the sunshine and apple blossom and bluebells and singing birds. She wishes this moment could last for ever, that she would be always this age.

By nine o'clock. the walkers are massing at the gates of Penlan Farm, the breakfast stop. Hubert Morris has parked his van in the lane with a load of bacon sandwiches, crisps and buttered bara brith; lined up on a makeshift table are kegs of home-made beer and bottles of lemonade. Mr Merchant, this year's portreeve, thanks the ladies of Glanmorfa for preparing the food for the day and tells everyone to tuck in. Daphne is sitting on the road verge, her mouth full of sandwich when Mr Duckford suddenly looms.

'Didn't I tell you not to write a novel; you know you ran out of time on the maths questions.'

He's wearing a shabby green jumper with leather patches on the elbows and there's a big tear in his trouser leg.

'Too late for tears now, Miss Morgan.' He winks and walks away.

'Bloody cheek!' says Dilys. 'He's not supposed to look at our exam papers. You should tell your mother what he just said, she'd give him what for.'

Daphne's not really listening because she's watching Sylvia and Darren over by one of the farm sheds; their backs are turned but it's pretty obvious what they're doing. Sylvia tosses her head back and downs her beer, takes another swig from Darren's glass; she turns round and sees Daphne looking. Puts a finger to her mouth, no telling. A burst of laughter from the rowdy group over by the beer table. Walter Evans has his arm tight round the waist of one of the blonde flip-flop girls; she's trying to pull his hand away but he's not letting go.

'If I were her, I'd keep my distance from him,' says Dilys. 'He's got a filthy temper, my dad says, she should watch her step.'

'Perhaps you should tell her he's the real murderer,' whispers Graham. Dilys rolls her eyes.

But Graham is serious. 'Look, nobody knows for sure it was Johnny Nebo; the judge let him off, didn't he? So don't look so smug, Dilys Hughes. The murderer could still be lurking somewhere.'

'You'd better keep an eye out then,' Dilys retorts, 'case he creeps up and stabs you. Walter's the devil with a knife, dad says.'

Janice, walking behind them, taps Graham on the shoulder and he jumps.

'Hey Graham, don't look so worried, only jokin'. Nobody's going to kill you. Don't you remember? That old Beaker woman's back where she belongs, we're all safe as houses.'

The walkers set off again, just as the sun disappears behind the clouds and the morning darkens. By the time the halberdiers and their flags arrive at the top of Beggar's Lane, a sunken farm track bounded by a steep field, the rain is sheeting down and the lane is turning into a river. But nobody cares. The home brew is working its magic and down they plunge, into the mud and the stony ruts and the mounds of watery cow shit. A group of young bullocks, attracted by all the shouting and screaming, comes thundering down the field. They jostle against the sagging barbed wire between the field and the walkers, pawing the ground and snorting. By the time Daphne and the others catch up with the rest of the group near the gate, Beggar's Lane is a quagmire.

'See, mum was right,' says Martin smugly, passing Terry Dunn and Harry Boyce struggling in the mud. 'Handy to have a walking stick.'

Ian Jenkins, truncheon in hand and looking remarkably clean considering what they've come through, counts the walkers and stragglers through the gate on to a narrow, tarred road. The rain has ceased, the clouds are lifting. The younger men shed their jumpers and vests, let the sunshine invade their wintry skins. Soon they are shouting and shoving at each other; somebody punches Jason Dunn and then there's a bit of a fight. Nobody intervenes, there's a long way to go. Daphne and her friends overtake Sylvia walking slowly and leaning against Darren. Her face has a greenish tinge and there's a line of spittle dangling from her mouth. Darren sees them looking, whispers something to her and she wipes it away with the back of her hand. Serves you right, thinks Daphne.

Lunch stop is a field off the main road two miles out of Glanmorfa, laid out by the women on trestle tables brought up from the Memorial Hall on a farm trailer: sausage rolls, cheese and tomato sandwiches, tea, cake, more beer and lemonade. The walkers lie on the grass or lean against the field fence, batting away the flies from their sweating faces. This is the finishing line for the younger ones; the last stage of the walk can be treacherous. Some of the older adults decide to call it a day too and limp back into town to wash off the mud or sleep off the beer—which is also what Mrs Morgan, having been informed of the puking by Miss Bryer, decides Sylvia must do. Bryn Watkins, Pentre, gives her a lift home to the vicarage in the back of the trailer with the folded tables and empty crates and Darren, freed of this burden, slinks off, laughing, to join his mates.

The portreeve and his chaplain, the constables and halberdiers, aldermen and burgesses, shake off the crumbs of sausage roll and chocolate cake, gird their aching legs, and lead the rump of walkers across the field and down towards the Gwennol, the swallow river: crossing route for pilgrims and palmers; provisioner for Cromwell and his armies; carrier of lime and coal to inland settlements. On this sultry afternoon, two miles inland from the estuary, the Gwennol moves sluggishly between its banks, through fields lush with early summer grass and grazing cattle. The tide is out, the mud flats sleek and glinting in the sunshine. The walkers clamber over a stile and move in single file along a grassy track between high gorse bushes. There's not much talking now, the air is heavy, headache-making.

Emrys Parry and Ian Jenkins hang back to chivvy the stragglers— 'Keep up, you lot, no slacking now.' The track ends abruptly at a padlocked gate. There is much debate at the front—'Bugger's got no right to lock up town land'—but nobody's thought to bring wire cutters. The halberdiers point their flags and down everyone slithers towards the shoreline, through the bramble and spiky gorse, the pesky, biting flies. In front of them, the oily gleam of estuary and the green bulk of Cowyn Head.

From now on, the going will be hard because everyone is exhausted. Boots sink in the gummy mud, get tangled up in thick skeins of seaweed.

'Worse than the bloody Somme,' grumbles Manny Edwards. His face is bleeding from gorse scratches and smeared white with river clay, a soldier returning from battle. Walter Evans grins and hoists the blonde girl on to his back. Her head lolls against his shoulder, her feet are bare, mudcaked, the flipflops long abandoned. The hill above the Strand comes into sight, climbed with such ease nearly eight hours ago, and then a line of boats, among them *Betsy*'s scarlet keel, anchored in the narrow pill below the castle. They are in sight of home. Soon they'll be up on the cliff path and into town for that celebration drink.

Shouts up ahead. The flags stop moving. The walkers stumble to a halt, peer over each other's shoulders, what's going on? Emrys Parry, bringing up the rear, hears his brother shout his name. He shoulders his way through the straggling line to where Ifor, with Mr Merchant and the vicar beside him, is talking to a figure in a peaked cap, Harry Darke, garage apprentice and part-time fisherman, who has run all the way from town to tell them.

'Are you sure it's the boat?' Ifor is asking. Darke is nodding, 'Course I'm sure, I saw him take it out this morning.'

'What's this about?'

The men turn and see Emrys. Ifor, grim faced, gives him the news. Late that morning, on his way back from fishing, Harry Darke spotted Johnny's boat drifting in the middle of the river out by Black Scar. When he caught up with it, Darke said, the oars were lying in the stern alongside the rope and the anchor—'All neat like, as if he'd never been there.' No sign of Johnny. Darke towed the boat back to the Ferry House and then rowed out again to search for him, but the tide was on the turn by then and he had to row for shore. He'd searched the Ferry House, the fish shed, the garden, called at the houses where he thought Johnny could have gone.

'Honest to God, I been looking everywhere, boys, he's just vanished.'

'What time was it you saw him take the boat out?' Emrys says.

Darke wipes the sweat off his forehead. 'Must have been, I don' know, about half past nine maybe. I was getting ready to go, had all the tackle in the dinghy. Looked up, and there was Johnny way out in the river, heading to Cefn y Morfil. I'd know his boat anywhere.'

The brothers exchange a look.

'Right,' says Ifor, 'we'd better go and find him.'

CHAPTER 40

He stops rowing, lets the oars go limp in the rowlocks, rests his bare elbows lightly on the wooden gunwale. The boat rocks gently beneath his feet and his body sways with the rhythm, lifting, settling, lifting. When he closes his eyes, motes of sunlight dance inside the lids and the skin of his face feels warmed and stretched. The smell of a spring tide and the lilac sprig pinned to his shirt, plucked this morning from the garden.

A shadow passes across his eyes. He opens them and sees a small dipper has alighted on the prow of the boat; it balances tiptoe right on the edge, white bib bobbing, cheeky wren's tail thumbing the sky. Suddenly it takes off, skimming low across the water to land on the scree at the edge of the Scar. Beak down, busy with the day.

Other shadows move across the sun and a breeze gets up. The oars are restless in his hands, water slaps the sides of the boat. Out on the horizon, waves are clamouring to mount Cefn y Morfil's flanks. He tightens his grip and leans forward into the stroke. The jetty, the Ferry House, cliff and castle, strand and shoreline, vanish into the soft spring light of another life. He's feeling hot now, even though it's easy work rowing with the current. He holds the oars in one hand and lifts off his old cap, tosses it into the water, runs a hand through his damp hair the colour of old sand. Feels the breeze cool on his scalp. He can see the roofline of Danyrallt in its cradle of ash trees; swiftly it recedes, disappears. He looks over his shoulder at the advancing line of tide, bends again to the oars.

The squall sweeps in, funnelling from the west, and swells the incoming sea and the river racing towards it. On his right, the cliffs below Cowyn Head loom closer, no more than half a mile away now. Once more, he downs his oars and fumbles at his shirt, tearing buttonholes and seams, shrugging it free of his body and casting it upon the water. The other clothes follow, there were never any boots. For a little while, as the boat comes level with the Head, these cast-offs keep pace, propelled onwards by the chasing current, until the rain slowly beats them down beneath the water. Lilac blossom floats upon the surface.

Now sea is river and river sea and the little boat halts, uncertain; it swings around, trying to turn for home, veers seaward once again. He lifts the oars out of the rowlocks and places them side by side in the stern. Coils the rope neatly beside the anchor. Then he stands up midships, raises his naked arms towards the sky, the boat swaying and bucking under his feet. A hundred yards out from the Head, at the point where the currents collide, Johnny Nebo spots the swirl of darker water, with the blackness at its centre. The voice in his head is louder now, it is fathoms deep. She's calling to him.

'Dere, cariad bach, don't be afraid, I'll catch you.'

And he jumps.

Ifor and Emrys Parry linger at the end of the jetty, looking out over the water. The afternoon is waning, the rain has ceased, watery sunlight glinting off rock pools and sand banks. The brothers don't say much. The sea has retreated behind Cefn y Morfil and Johnny's boat lies beached at the end of its long rope some yards from the shrunken Gwennol. Ifor and Emrys are in no hurry to board it, though each understands he must be seen to search. They know where Johnny went, knew it long before Harry Darke showed up.

A heron hunts low across the mud banks below them, loose-winged and snake-necked, like some ancient pterodactyl lost out of time. This, too, was only a matter of time. Johnny was never going to come out of this experience unscathed. Lack of evidence and unfitness to plead do not remove the possibility of guilt, the whispers in doorways. Guilty or not guilty: everyone prefers a clear verdict. At least their consciences are clear; for eighteen years they stood by him for his father's sake, gave him the home his mother never could provide, kept a roof over his head, taught him useful skills so he could earn a bit of money. Loved him, mostly. Too much Beynon blood in him, they hope people will say; no surprise he went the same way as Mari Danyrallt in the end. Though Ifor and Emrys would never confess this to each other, a cloud has lifted with Johnny's passing. The trial was always going to be a problem for their business, the way gossip gets around, how the word 'murderer' sticks to a family. They can get on with their own lives now.

The Sunday after the body was found washed up on the rocks by Cowyn Head, Rev Morgan led the prayers in church for the family and commended the soul of John Parry to God's grace. It was all in the papers for a while but now nobody talks much about the court case. It's one more story in Glanmorfa's history of violent deeds: unsolved murders, brawls to the death between rivals, bodies buried in fields, washed up with the tide. Magistrates had to read the Riot Act to stop the fighting, back in the day.

Trinity: CHAPTER 41

The flowers have been in water longer than a fortnight. Daphne averts her face and yanks the withered bunch from the jam jar, holds it at arm's length.

'Why do they stink so much?'

'Cos that's what happens when you die, dumbo—your body just rots. Remember how that old skull ponged. Give 'em here.'

Daphne hands over the reeking flowers and Janice carries them down to the fence at the bottom of the graveyard, chucks them over into the field. When she comes back, Daphne is pouring fresh water into the jar from the can. The new flowers—clumps of sweet William, some orange marigolds, a bit of fern—are lying on the path by the side of the grave, rolled in a torn page from yesterday's *Western Mail*.

'Funny to think Terry passed,' Janice says sniffily, plonking herself down on a patch of grass beside the grave. 'Bet he cheated.'

'P'raps he's brighter than he looks, he was always better at sums than me.' Daphne arranges the individual flowers in the jar, the tufty heads of sweet William first, the drooping marigolds: clashing pinks and orange, offset by a green plume of fern. Only a fortnight left of summer, of the old life. She and Janice, Dilys, the boys, Terry Dunn, a couple of others from downtown, all going to the grammar. The old order changing. She picks up the brimming jar in both hands and places it carefully at the foot of the simple slate headstone, wedging it tightly between two large stones. She steps back and examines her handiwork.

'Looks a bit of a mess, doesn't it?'

Janice is looking at the scrap of paper they found sticking out of an empty bottle of Guinness propped against the headstone. She looks up, casts a quick eye over Daphne's arrangement.

'It'll do. He was an artist; he'd be pleased with your colourful creation. He wouldn't be with this rubbish.'

She tosses the paper scrap on to the grass—a swirl of lurid colour, another attempt to copy the famous *Sensations of Sunrise*. They were always finding this kind of thing, like votary gifts at a shrine. 'Whoever drew that had drunk more than one bottle of Guinness. I don't know why they bother. Just because he died young doesn't make him a saint.'

It's that time of year when the fans arrive. Scores of them, from all over the world, America especially, wandering the paths and lanes of Glanmorfa, taking photographs of the artist's old studio and the estuary, queueing awestruck for a seat in his favourite pub, leaving their pathetic drawings at his graveside. Daphne and Janice get five bob between them from the parish council for tidying the grave once a fortnight: refreshing the flowers, collecting the jetsam of beer and whisky bottles, cigarette packets, soggy messages and prayers left out in the rain.

Janice sticks the note back inside the bottle and rolls it up in the newspaper. She sings, 'If there's anything that you want, if there's anything I can do...' Daphne shakes out the last drops of water from the can and joins in, '...with love from me to you.' Below them, the first acolytes of the morning are making their way slowly up the churchyard path towards the new graveyard, solemn-looking hippy types in jeans and flowery shirts and sunglasses, hungover from last night's pub crawl. Sunshine lights up the grassy folds and hedgerows of Hollerton fields on the opposite hillside, some leaves are already turning with the thought of autumn.

'I'm getting my new uniform in town on Saturday,' Janice announces. 'Plus a new satchel and a geometry set.'

Janice is the first in her family to go to grammar school: it's a big thing for them.

'Have you got yours yet?'

Daphne shakes her head. 'My gran's altering Sylvia's old tunic, it's

195

a bit tight, you know ... round here.' She waves a hand in the general direction of her chest—growing breasts, not a thing to talk about. The tunic is long on her, old fashioned looking; in form one you get detention if your knees are showing, Sylvia says. The older girls are allowed to wear skirts; they bunch them up under their jumpers to look like minis. Most of the teachers aren't bothered, they're too busy getting them ready for O Levels.

'I'm also getting a new satchel and a geometry set and a Parker pen,' says Janice, smugly. 'What you getting, Daph?'

Daphne has to make do with Sylvia's old leather satchel. Mrs Morgan pronounces it 'perfectly serviceable' after hours of scrubbing off the worst of the ink stains and the gobs of chewing gum stuck to the inside lining. Some of the stitching at the bottom has snapped, a job for the bootmaker. Mr Spiller's workshop is opposite the post office on George Street, at the end of a narrow passageway at the side of his house. It's a damp cavern, the walls painted in green distemper like most of the houses and lit by a single bulb dangling from the roof above the workbench. The whole place smells of sweaty feet and old leather, and every inch of wall is crammed with wooden crates of shoes and boots waiting to be mended, shelves of wooden lasts of different sizes, boxes of nails, wrenches, small hammers, knives. Mr Spiller is a large man, moonfaced and wispy haired; he wears a long leather apron over his work clothes and lives with his ancient mother and his aunt who hardly ever come out of the house. Some people call them the two witches.

'Nice bit of leather,' Mr Spiller says, putting on his spectacles to examine the stitching, running his broad hands over the satchel. 'Could do with a good polish.' He smacks his wet lips and reaches past her to the shelf where he keeps the boxes of cobblers' needles and waxed thread. 'Mind you look after it, maid, don't go throwing it after the boys now.' He giggles and takes down a glass jar full of liquorice allsorts. 'Here,' he says, 'have one of these.' She hesitates, the taste makes her stomach turn. 'Come on girl, hurry up.' She sticks her hand inside and selects the smallest, keeps it in her fist.

196

'Tell Mrs Vicar I'll have it ready for tomorrow afternoon.'

Grateful to be released, she steps out of the gloomy passage on to the street, screwing up her eyes against the strong August sunshine, and blunders into someone walking past on the pavement.

'Look where you're going!'

She recognises the voice but there are sunspots inside her eyelids and the street is only a shimmer.

'Oh, it's you,' says Vita Robinson. In her summery clothes—wide-legged navy cotton trousers and white blouse, her hair swathed in a brightly coloured scarf—she looks younger than when they last met.

'I was rather hoping I'd see you again before I left. How are you getting on with Tennyson and those dreary knights?'

Daphne is startled by the question. The noble Arthur and Sir Bedivere are long gone. She's become a lover of darker deeds: 'The Red-headed League', 'The Speckled Band', Edgar Allen Poe. Murder is much more interesting than chivalry. The wallpaper knights with their falcons and hounds are only faint ghosts beneath the new paint, Gentian, that she chose for her birthday, to go with the posters of the Fab Four cut out of magazines. She is in her twelfth year and *The Piper of Dreams* has stayed put on the wall of Sylvia's attic bedroom. Daphne is preparing for her new life.

Vita Robinson, waiting on the pavement in the sunshine, answers her own question. 'Sorry, I expect you're far too busy for poetry, especially when the weather's so wonderful. You and your friends must be off to the beach most days I imagine.' She smiles. 'I'm off too, back to England at last. The removal men are coming tomorrow to take the piano and a few bits and pieces I want to keep.'

Daphne fidgets on the pavement, wanting to escape this conversation of adults, the way they talk for hours about nothing very important. She's supposed to be meeting Graham and the others on the cliff path.

'Come with me for a short walk?'

It's not really a question, she knows, and it would be rude to refuse. As they make their way along George Street Vita chats away.

'I was planning to have a last look at the estuary, it would be nice to have some company. I think the local people are still a bit wary of me, you know, staying on in this place after all that's happened. They'll probably be glad to see the back of me.'

The street is busy, people going in and out of the shops, gossiping on corners, enjoying the weather. Hetty Lewis passing with a pram full of shopping; Mr Ainsworth standing outside his bus garage in his boots and breeches and porkpie hat talking to Dilys's mum; Billy Two Gates pedalling fast; the usual dogs and children. Sitting on the pavement outside the Captain's are a couple of visitors—a bearded man in shorts and sandals, and a woman with braided hair and a long skirt with a pattern of yellow and orange swirls.

'Odd isn't it,' says Vita, 'all these people travel across the world to visit the home of a dead artist, just because he lived a glamorous, rackety life and died young. His paintings aren't anything special, I'm told.' She gives a short laugh. 'Oh well, I expect the locals make a good living out of the tourists in the summer. It's the same in Oxford, only we have more dead people and buildings to make money from.'

They turn up Hangman Lane, past Lucknow House, and on to the cliff path. It's so hot. Daphne takes off her cardigan and ties it round her waist, perspiration prickling the back of her knees. Behind them the town clock strikes two. The tide is full, an expanse of sultry greyness, Cowyn Head a pale shimmering above the water. Vita Robinson halts at the stile above a narrow stony path leading down to the shore. She's staring out to sea, the white curl of waves beyond Cefn y Morfil.

'So beautiful,' she murmurs, 'you'd never guess the treachery.'

The iron railings on this side of the path are submerged in dogrose and clouds of old man's beard, thick bramble and frothy nettle heads clamouring for space. Daphne wonders where the others have got to; there's nobody else about.

'Come on,' says Vita, turning round at last. 'Let's go down to the shore.'

She clambers over the stile and scrambles down the path between the nettles and roses. Reluctantly, politely, Daphne follows. They come out on to a spill of red rocks above the foreshore, the seaweed crisp under their sandalled feet, the darker rockpools dried out below the waterline. The tide laps blue-grey and listless around the rocks; everywhere there's the mud-salty smell of late summer. Vita settles herself on a flat slope of rock and pats the space next to her.

'Sit here, we shall admire the view.'

Reluctantly, Daphne kneels down, trying to keep a distance without offending, wondering how long this ordeal will last, when she will be set free. She can see the ferryboat making its way sluggishly across the estuary from the other side, Ifor Parry pulling at the oars, his brother sitting in the stern. There are three passengers in the boat, an elderly man wearing a straw hat, and two children, one of whom is trailing his hand in the water. There's a small dog too, a terrier of some sort, standing on the edge of the boat, yapping. The old man's voice carries across the water, trying to shut it up—'Taw sŵn, 'achan, taw!'

'That poor man,' says Vita, watching the ferry's progress, shading her eyes from the glare. 'I wonder whether he meant to drown himself.'

Startled, Daphne glances at the ferry, then colours at her own mistake. Of course, the woman's talking about Johnny Nebo, not the man with the dog. Dilys said it was an accident, Johnny must have slipped off the boat and drowned because he couldn't swim. But then Graham said, surely Johnny of all people would know about the whirlpool, he wouldn't have taken his boat anywhere near it. A whirlpool can suck a body down to the bottom, it said so in *Look and Learn*. Maybe you'd never find it, said Martin, or maybe it'd be washed up on the rocks weeks later. Remember what happened to those choirboys.

Vita Robinson picks up a seaweed frond, scrunches it her hand. 'I used to think they should hang him, but I'm not so sure now; it's a brutal thing to do to another human being, we should be better than that. Your father certainly thought so...' She breaks off, seeing Daphne's look of surprise. 'He called round, just before the trial, and we had a brief chat about forgiveness. He's a wise man, even if I don't believe in his religion.'

The sounds of the ferry boat docking carry across the water: the clank and thud of chains and rope, the voices of the passengers, footsteps crossing the wooden slats of the jetty. A noisy family of ducks bobs up and down on the water, idle chatter on a hot afternoon, waiting for the tide to turn. Daphne steals a look at her watch, a present from Gran for passing the exam. A quarter past three, where are they?

'Eleanor would forgive Parry, I think. She was quite fond of him, you know. She believed he wasn't just a poor deaf and dumb man trying to earn a couple of bob here and there. She mentioned him once, in one of her letters, said he seemed to like her playing the piano even though he couldn't hear the music. A sensitive soul, she called him. I keep wondering what she might have said or done that made him kill her.'

'But he didn't, did he?'

Vita Robinson spins round. In the sun's glare her face is hard, drained of colour despite the vivid headscarf. 'What the hell are you talking about?'

'Kill her, I mean. It wasn't Johnny.'

'Of course it was, you stupid girl. It was that Scotland Yard chap's fault, for not making the case properly; he had enough evidence, despite what the judge said.'

She is not a stupid girl. How could she have forgotten that face, even if she only saw it for an instant? That figure leaping the wall, the flapping raincoat rising like wings. Those cold, hard eyes meeting hers in the moment before she fell into the river. How could she have forgotten?

A stone lands a few feet away from her, bounces off and splashes into the water. The ducks ruffle their feathers in alarm. Another, heavier stone crashes on the rocks behind them, and then a third which skims the top of her head. Vita Robinson starts; she stares wildly up the cliff. A low whistle from the bushes up on the top path. Graham's voice.

'Daaaaphneee!!'

The woman scrambles to her feet. 'Bloody snooping kids.' She glares down at Daphne. 'Are they friends of yours?'

'Maybe'. She will be loyal.

'Well, if they are, tell them to behave better. Look, I can't stay any longer, there's still so much to do at the house before tomorrow.'

Already Vita is at the foot of the path, climbing rapidly, small stones skittering from under her sandals.

Daphne stares numbly across the water towards the wooded slopes of Cowyn Head. If he had asked her, would she have told the policeman what happened that winter's afternoon? Probably not, she concludes, not then. Poor Johnny Nebo.

'Blimey, that Miss Robinson was in a hurry!'

Dilys flops down on the rock beside her. 'I think we scared her off, the way she belted past us down the road. What were you two talking about?'

'Nothing much,' Daphne answers. 'I'm glad you lot arrived, couldn't think how to get rid of her.' She unties her cardigan and puts it on, buttons it with trembly fingers.

'You ok, Daph? You look a bit weird.'

Graham comes over, has a look at her. 'Could be heatstroke,' he pronounces, importantly. 'Have a paddle off them rocks, cool you down. You better go with her, Dil.'

The mud is soft, it squishes between her toes, she feels the sharp edge of a cockle shell, something alive and squirming. Dilys squeals, 'It's a jelly fish, I'm getting out!' and turns back. Daphne walks on, until the water is nearly up to the edge of her shorts.

'Don't go so far, Daph,' shouts Graham from the safety of the rocks. 'Tide's on the turn.'

Her head is so hot. The sun's blistering her pale skin, she should be wearing a hat like her mother always insists. She bends over and swishes her arms through the water, white flesh like the underside of a fish. She peers into her wobbling reflection, raggedy hair coming undone from its plait. Her floating dead face looks up at her and the sky darkens, all the sound fades away. She's swaying, losing her footing. The water closes over her head; its touch is cool, tender.

'Bloody hell, Daph, you nearly drowned!'

She's lying on the sandy shale below the rocks and Janice and the others are standing round her with worried faces.

'Lucky we pulled you out, you could have been washed away,' Dilys says.

Daphne drags herself up to sitting position. Her shorts are soaked and clinging to her legs and she's shivering despite the heat. 'I just slipped,' she says, her voice coming out strange and quavery. 'It was the mud.'

'You'd better get home and change,' says Graham, 'before your mum sees you and gives you what for. Go the long lanes, just in case.'

The long lanes skirt the edge of town, they are very ancient and deeply hollowed, their crumbling banks held together by the gnarled roots of oak trees and bramble. In summer the lanes are choked with rough grasses and nettles. Few people pass this way, except Mr Ainsworth who grazes his coloured horses, Bess and her daughter Christmas, up in the top field. Elsewhere, the afternoon buzzes in the heat but in the depths of the lane it is very quiet, only distant bird calls and the odd rustle of some small animal in the dappled undergrowth. Overhead, the clustering branches of a line of sycamores temper the brightness.

Daphne pushes her way through the tangle of vegetation, seeds and grass stalks clogging in her sandals. In one place she has to find a stick and beat a pathway through thick shoulder-high fronds of fern and cow parsley, a thicket of brambles which snag her clothes and hair. At last, she reaches the gate above Pantglas Farm. Her legs are all scratched and nettle stung and she is sweating from the effort. The gate is padlocked so she has to clamber up and over the hot metal bars and drop down into the tussocky meadow which slopes towards the farm buildings and the boundary wall above George Street. There are cows grazing on the far side of the field and she keeps to the left, along the hedge line. One of them lifts its head to watch, but the others pay no attention, it's too hot for curiosity. The sheds are deserted, the grey stone farmhouse silent in the afternoon heat. By the kitchen door, Bob the old sheepdog is snoring at the end of his long chain. He doesn't sense someone creeping past him to the side gate, does not hear the lifting of the latch.

From across the road she can hear music. Her sister is sitting on the bench in the vicarage porch with Tyrone beside her. He's playing his guitar and she's singing along in a slow dreamy voice. 'For the times they are a changin'.' Sylvia is wearing a short cotton dress with navy polka dots and a matching hairband. She's dyed her hair black for the summer. Tyrone lives in California, he arrived in Glanmorfa only a week ago with his rucksack, guitar and battered sketchbook. He's tall, with thick shoulder length blonde hair and a little goatee beard and Sylvia is in love.

'God, you look a fright,' she says as Daphne hurries past them. 'You haven't been swimming, have you? You know what mum will say if she sees you.'

'Sh, babe,' he mutters, 'you're breaking the mood.'

Perhaps it was his bottle of Guinness they found, thinks Daphne; Sylvia should have stuck with Darren. She's about to open the front door when her sister calls out, 'Hey, this is for you.' She's waving a small envelope. 'The lady said she couldn't wait.'

Daphne takes the envelope and goes up to her room, leaves it on the bed while she changes out of her wet things. She undoes the straps of her sandals and shakes the grass seeds and dirt out of the window. Then she goes back to the bed and picks up the letter. Her heart is beating fast.

Dear Daphne

Forgive me for rushing away like that, it must have seemed very rude after we'd had such a lovely chat. I didn't even wish you good luck in your new school. I'm sure you will be very successful, perhaps you'll live up to the name I gave you and study Classics. Learn more about Athena.

I shall take with me many memories of my stay in Wales—not all of them sad. It was fun to be a castaway for a while, marooned in the snow. Did you know I skated down your little river once, wearing an old pair of Eleanor's skates I found in a cupboard? But then those terrible floods—a biblical punishment for our sins, as your father might say.

I'd like to ask a favour. Would you every now and then put a little bunch of flowers on Eleanor's grave? And perhaps tidy it once in a while? I don't want people to think she's been forgotten. I would do this myself, of course, but I shan't make another visit to Glanmorfa.

I enclose a cheque towards the cost of flowers and a little gift for you, in thanks.

Yours

Vita Robinson

PS Our memories are strange, shifting things, Daphne. Don't let them trick you into believing what isn't true.

The cheque for £5 is made out to Rev H Morgan. Daphne takes out the pound note and puts it in the pineapple tin under the bed. It won't be going into the kitty for the pony with the ridiculous name. She's got enough money now to buy the *Please Please Me* album.

And sucks to you, Vita Robinson, she thinks, turning to chapter three of *The Hound of the Baskervilles*. What she saw that December afternoon was true.

June 1938: CHAPTER 42

The photographer is late. There's no guarantee the rain will keep off, the sky's already clouding over. And where in God's name is that wretched girl? Be here at a quarter to three, no later. In the garden, by the rose arbour. Wear something pretty.

Eleanor O'Dowd stands by the open French window, appraising the scene she has so perfectly arranged: the elegant cast iron bench placed at just the right angle for the afternoon light and draped with the fringed Kashmiri shawl—worn at her own christening, a nice touch that, for this occasion. And then the background, the blossoms of the Cécile Brünner—so often at its climbing best in early July—framing the picture. Such a pity the Stuarts next door took down the old beech tree, that outhouse of theirs does spoil the camera view. But the garden is looking lovely, perhaps she will persuade the photographer to take a few extra photographs. Free of charge, of course, the penalty for poor timekeeping.

The doorbell rings and she waits at the window for someone to respond. Muttered apologies in the hallway, footsteps crossing the parquet. Mary ushers in a short, stooping man with a greying moustache carrying all the paraphernalia. 'Mr Miller for you, miss.'

He follows her down the garden steps, across the lawn, past the shrubbery—'keep to the paths please'—to the bench. 'I shall sit here; my companion—when she finally turns up—there…'

He starts to set up his equipment. Tripod, box camera, large black umbrella, the necessary bits and bobs. His fingers are stained with nicotine, she notes. Dreadful habit. Great Tom peals three o'clock, further away the distant chimes of the other city bells. One year on, the girl still persists in showing scant regard for English custom, plain good manners. She sighs and straightens her shoulders, walks over to the bench and arranges her tall, thin body against the cashmere shawl in the elegant posture she has already pictured: legs neatly crossed at the ankle, the grey silk dress smoothed beneath the long matching cardigan, rope of pearls arranged just so. A cloud passes over the sun and the garden suddenly darkens. Her fingers clench. He might as well get on with it.

A frenzied yapping, heels clattering down the steps, 'Hansi, komm her!' A grubby wire-haired terrier hurtles across the grass towards the bench, lead trailing; he spots the photographer and lunges straight at him, growling and snapping at his heels.

'Dummkopf, lass ihn in Ruhe!!' The girl seizes the lead and tugs the dog away from the poor man who is looking quite terrified. 'Tut mir leid, sorry, he's not usually so naughty.'

She comes over to the bench, yanks at the dog's collar—'sitz du!' and wipes a hand across her sweaty forehead. 'We were down in Port Meadow. I forgot about the time.' That dazzling, false smile. The cloud passes on, sunlight glisters the laurel leaves.

At least the girl has listened to one instruction; she's wearing the dress Eleanor bought her to celebrate her first concert in the Orangery— pleated silk organza, a deep apricot, so suited to her pale complexion, those brilliant dark eyes. But then she's gone and tied her hair up in that dreadful yellow scarf, too flamboyant, too ... other.

'Sit here, Vita. Take that scarf off, dear, your hair's so pretty without it. Do we have to have that dog in the photograph?'

'I know it is your birthday, Eleanor, but I want Papa and Mutti to see what he looks like, my letters don't describe him so well.' She pulls the straining terrier to her side, makes him sit again. Ah those dear hands, she must not strain them today of all days.

'How long is this going to take? I am so hot!'

The photographer man is waiting, tripod steady, camera poised.

Something is not quite right about the scene, it must appear happier, more relaxed. Perhaps if she were holding something, a flower?

'One minute, please.' She gets up from the bench and goes to the roses, plucks a long stem, returns to her seat, adjusts her posture.

'Now, try leaning into me a little more, yes, that's it.' She extends her left arm across the back of the bench behind the girl, that touch of damp warm skin so close to hers. The rose droops becomingly from her fingers.

'I think we're ready now.'

A figure appears round the corner of the shrubbery. She feels the girl's body stiffen, she is about to leap from the bench and ruin the moment. Even the dog is suddenly attentive, ears pricked, tail a-quiver.

'Watch the birdie please, ladies.' Light bursts upon them.

'Such a lovely picture you make, the two of you, like a scene from Chekhov!'

He's certainly personable, this Henry Stuart, in that careless, tousled manner young men assume these days; they all think they are entitled to the good things of life. And he's charmed the girl, she's practically on the edge of her seat, the little fool. Even his voice is musical, she notes irritably. Later this evening, seated at the Steinway in her candle-lit music room—the heavy damask curtains, patterned with white hydrangeas, tied back and the windows open to let in the fragrance of her roses—the two of them will play the *Hungarian Rhapsody no 2,* the perfect showcase for this pair of shining young spirits with the world before them. His fair English head, her dark glory. And then he will leave as Eleanor has instructed him—a train to catch, the regiment is mustering at Dover. After the brief interval—a light Muscovy, canapes of salmon mousse, quails' eggs—Avital Rosenberg, whom she has renamed, transformed into Vita Robinson, will seat herself once more at the piano, this time alone: vivid, transcendent. The programme they have worked on for so many months: Liszt's *Années de Pelerinage,* the *Spanish Rhapsody,* and finally the Chopin *Fantaisie Impromptu.* The small audience—carefully chosen, the kind of people who have influence—will be enraptured. All those hours of practice, often late into the night, the two of them wrapped in blankets in the chilly winter evenings, Eleanor ignoring her own suffering—the stiffening fingers, the ache in the joints that will not go away. If Simon and Hannah were still alive—already, she hears, Berlin is ridding itself of Jews—they would be so proud of what she has achieved for their daughter. How faithful she has been after she agreed to be the girl's guarantor, to give her a home in the same house where nearly thirty years ago, Vita's father, then a student, came for one year to be tutored by her own father. Eleanor was a child then, not much younger than Vita. She hopes someone this evening will remember it is also her birthday, her triumph too. Her applause.

She watches the young couple crossing the lawn, hand in hand, towards the house, the little dog dancing at their heels. Don't spoil this moment, she wants to call out, please Vita, remember who you are. Don't let him entice you with his false words, with that vigorous, unsubtle body. Don't let him persuade you he has only these few precious hours before the concert, before he leaves for France. Who knows when, if, he will return. The dreadful seduction of loss.

The photographer coughs, discreetly. She has forgotten he is waiting, his tripod folded, the camera already packed away. She gets up stiffly, wrapping the long, fringed shawl around her shoulders. The rose lies discarded in the grass.

'The maid will show you out. Do take a piece of birthday cake with you, there's some on the drawing room table. I don't expect the young people will have noticed it.'

He will need paying too. How much longer will she be able to live like this, pretend a fortune that she does not have? She goes up the steps, into the drawing room, past the statue on its polished plinth. Her fingers lightly caress the cool alabaster head of Franz Liszt, whose memory they will honour this evening—for it is his anniversary too, albeit death not birth.

She has saved a life, honoured her promise, opened the way for a dazzling musical career. Avital Rosenberg has a heavy debt to pay.

June 1974: CHAPTER 43

'Don't get in a fluster, read the questions through twice, decide which fits best, make a five-minute plan... oh God, I'm sorry, darling, I sound like you're still doing your O Levels! Of course you know what to do.'

Through the misted glass she can see Morag still hovering outside the phone booth, both of them doing the regular Sunday phone routine before heading to the pub, though this time a phone call home is something, anything to keep the nerves at bay. Better stick to just one pint tonight, need a clear head for the morning: two three-hour papers with an hour's desperate revision in-between.

'Remind me again what you've got tomorrow.' Mum's not doing a good job—her voice sounds more anxious than her own.

'Beowulf to Chaucer in the morning, 19th century poetry after lunch.'

'Well, make sure you have an early night, have a cup of Horlicks before bed. You were a fan of the Romantics weren't you, Tennyson and that lot? Remember the book that poor Miss O'Dowd gave you when you were about ten? You used to read it aloud in your bedroom, it sounded very dramatic.'

She really doesn't want to talk about exams just now, her stomach is churning. Sylvia's sent a good luck postcard from some French beach, post-marked Biarritz. Lucky devil, the French schools closing so early for the long summer holiday. Perhaps she and Paul will hitchhike over there, celebrate the end of finals, stay a few weeks with Sylvia, if she can save enough money from her summer job at the milk factory. Boring though it is, the pay's not bad.

'Oh, that reminds me there was something I wanted to tell you,' says her mother. Morag's fingers are tapping at the windowpane. 'Be quick, mum, someone else needs the phone.'

'Your father had a call from the undertakers the other day. Would he give permission for them to open up Miss O'Dowd's grave, they want to bury another body in there. That friend of hers, distant relative whatever she was, remember she was holed up in the old cottage through the Big Freeze of '63? Vita something or other? Died of breast cancer last month, she was only 55, same age as me. Apparently, she stated in her will she wanted to be buried in Glanmorfa, in the same grave, which is a bit peculiar. Janice Shaw told me in the post office the other day that this woman was quite friendly with you, is that true? I don't remember it. Anyway, you can imagine the gossip, but you know your father, always seeing the other side, wanting to be helpful. He's got the archdeacon's blessing, so he's given the go ahead for the grave to be opened. Coffin's coming down end of next week. Are you still there, Daphne?'

It was a long time ago, she thinks, twisting her tangled hair into a rough knot as she leaves the flat and heads towards the city centre. I was only a child, what did I know about anything? At the corner of South Bridge, she turns left on to Princes Street, threading her way through the jostle of early summer tourists. Paul and the others would already be at the Abbotsford downing their pre-exam pints. She turns up Hanover Street and a cold northern breeze catches at her thin cotton skirt. Winter's threads still clinging on. Icy fingertips from a room without windows; the chill reek of the burial chamber. Maybe I should have told someone.

CHAPTER 44

He hadn't reckoned on rain. Flaming June, ha bloody ha. 'Like the bloody Somme'—always a favourite saying with his dad. Dougie Edwards places his boot on the spade, feels the blade slice through the clay. Rain trickles down the back of his neck. Step by step he cuts a neat square in the centre of the grave, three feet diameter, three feet deep. It isn't a coffin, the vicar said, she was cremated back in England, easy job for you, Dougie. Not if it rains it bloody isn't: clay sticks to your boots like glue. Different story this time last year when they buried Manny—nice dry day, earth soft to the blade, coffin slipped in smooth. He can see the grave from here, up in the corner plot with mum, the headstone keeping nice and sheltered under the fir trees.

He lowers the measuring stick to check he's got the depth right. Thank God it isn't another coffin he's burying on top, could have broken into the first one by mistake, it's happened before. Wouldn't want to see that woman's skull grinning up at you, give you the bloody willies that would. Across the fields he can hear the town clock striking. They'll be here soon, sometime after eleven Mr Morris said. They've gone to town to collect the urn from the guard's van off the ten-thirty from Paddington.

Dougie reaches for the pile of sacking to keep off the rain until it's time. Some friend or other she was, not even a relative, can't understand why the vicar allowed it. He bends over the hole, starts to pull the sacking across. Something is sticking out of the clay, a foot or two down. He leans in and prises it out with his fingers. Scrapes off the gouts of dirt and gravel. Some kind of ancient weapon maybe; you never know, there's lots of old stuff buried in the soil of Glanmorfa. He turns the little knife over in his hand, runs his thumb along the narrow blade, drawing tiny beads of blood.

211

Duw, that's sharp. He pulls out a handkerchief and wraps the knife in it, stows it away in his tool bag. Might be worth a bob or two; if not he'll hold on to it, sharp enough for gutting fish.

They are coming over the footbridge now. Dougie removes the sacking and steps back from the grave side, stands at a respectful distance. He takes off his cap and bows his head to the small group of mourners: Rev Morgan in his cassock, Mr Morris under a black umbrella, Peter Evans the undertaker carrying the little casket, and Mervyn Jones the Stores bringing up the rear. The men line up around the graveside. Footsteps clatter across the bridge. Mrs Morgan, out of breath, in a green coat smudged with rain and no hat, comes over to join them.

The interment is brief. No eulogy, no flowers. Thou knowest, Lord, the secrets of our hearts; shut not thy merciful ears to our prayer.

Rev Morgan leans over the grave and takes a little box from his pocket. He opens it and sprinkles the dry earth over the casket of ashes. And he says, in the Hebrew he has practised, for he and his wife now know something of her story, the Jewish refugee from Berlin, gifted pianist and protegee of Eleanor O'Dowd, whose terrible breakdown in 1946 destroyed her brilliant career.

Adonai natan, Adonai lakach. Yehi shem Adonai m'vorach.

Thus Vita Robinson, born Avital Rosenberg, enters the quiet earth of St Mary's, Glanmorfa. Sanctuary for its citizens and burgesses, for emigrees and outcasts, pilgrims and men of war, drowned mariners, murderers, famous artists—people of interest to local historians, lovers of stories, biographers. There is also another grave, perhaps less interesting to the visitor. It's right up in the top corner near the little gate which leads to the long lanes. The inscription on the low grey slate is too weathered to read the name, but the lilac bush somebody has planted in the hedge behind it is blooming now and the air is filled with its fragrance.

Acknowledgements

Thanks to my family for their boundless encouragement, and to my writer friends for their experienced and helpful insights. My gratitude, too, to those who commented so helpfully on the early drafts – Bruce, Kate, Matt, Kath, Claire, Lynne, Monica, Betsan. I am also grateful to Monica and John for lending me a quiet warm space to write in the midst of a rare snowfall. I am indebted to the team at Honno for taking me on and feel especially fortunate to have had the enthusiasm and perceptive supervision of my editor and friend, Rebecca F. John. The events and the people described in the novel are fictional, but they have their roots in a particular place and time.

 Born in St David's, Pembrokeshire, and raised in Carmarthenshire, Siân has lived much of her life outside Wales. An Edinburgh University graduate, she has taught Anglo Saxon and Medieval Literature to university students in South Africa, worked as an assistant editor on the medical journal The Lancet, and ran English and Drama departments in several well-known London secondary schools. In 2007 she returned to Wales to teach and write in the Tywi valley. Her first novel *Unleaving*, set in Wales and South Africa, was published in 2019.

ABOUT HONNO

Honno Welsh Women's Press was set up in 1986 by a group of women who felt strongly that women in Wales needed wider opportunities to see their writing in print and to become involved in the publishing process. Our aim is to develop the writing talents of women in Wales, give them new and exciting opportunities to see their work published and often to give them their first 'break' as a writer.

Honno is registered as a community co-operative. Any profit that Honno makes is invested in the publishing programme. Women from Wales and around the world have expressed their support for Honno. Each supporter has a vote at the Annual General Meeting. For more information and to buy our publications, please visit our website www.honno.co.uk or email us on post@honno.co.uk.

Honno
D41, Hugh Owen Building,
Aberystwyth University,
Aberystwyth,
Ceredigion,
SY23 3DY.

We are very grateful for the support of all our Honno Friends.